Rum River

BOOKS BY RAYMOND FRASER

Fiction
Seasons of Discontent
Bliss
The Madness Of Youth
Repentance Vale
The Trials Of Brother Bell
In Another Life
The Grumpy Man
In A Cloud Of Dust And Smoke
Costa Blanca
Rum River
The Bannonbridge Musicians
The Struggle Outside
The Black Horse Tavern

Memoirs, Essays & Stories
When The Earth Was Flat

Biographies
Todd Matchett: Confessions of a Young Criminal
The Fighting Fisherman: The Life Of Yvon Durelle

Poetry
Before You're A Stranger
The More I Live
I've Laughed And Sung
Waiting For God's Angel

Rum River

Raymond Fraser

Definitive edition, revised and
corrected by the author

Lion's Head Press

Author's Note

Parts of this book appeared previously in the following periodicals: *Antigonish Review, Canadian Forum, Fiddlehead, Matrix, New Brunswick Reader, Pottersfield Portfolio,* and *Rubicon*. All have since been revised. "Caught" was included in the anthology, *Shout And Speak Out Loud*.

For this edition I've removed "Man With A Flair" (now in the 2014 revised edition of *The Black Horse Tavern*) and replaced it with the chapter/story "Uncle Vic". I've also moved "A Case of Identity" so that it now follows "Carnival". Other changes are chiefly to the beginnings and endings of chapters – some considerable, as with "Caught" and the opening pages of "Lady Luck". Finally, I've divided the book into three Parts, and appended a brief Epilogue.

I would like to thank the Arts Branch of the New Brunswick Department of Municipalities, Culture & Housing for grant assistance during the final phases of the writing and preparation of the original edition of this book. And a more current thanks to Christian LeBlanc who did such a masterful job proofreading this edition.

Cover painting by Manuel Ocaranza (1841-1882)

Library and Archives Canada Cataloguing in Publication

Fraser, Raymond, 1941-, author
     Rum River / Raymond Fraser. -- Definitive edition, revised and corrected by the author.

ISBN 978-1-928020-10-3 (paperback)

     I. Title.

PS8561.R3R86 2016   C813'.54   C2015-908051-7

Lion's Head Press
Toronto • Canada

Rum River

CONTENTS

What It Was Like

Earlier Times

Up The Road

Epilogue

WHAT IT WAS LIKE

"Well, we're supposed to tell what it was like, what happened, and what it's like now . . ."

THE BLACK NORTH

April 27, 1973. We're home from Spain and into our old house in Rum River.

It was hard to leave Spain, with the palm trees and orange groves and our villa by the sea. Cigarettes ten cents a pack and gin seventy-five cents a litre.

There are some striking differences between the two countries, Spain and Rum River, most notably the four feet of snow I had to shovel through to get into the house.

When I went out to check the mail I couldn't find the mailbox. I thought it was just buried, and shovelled all around where it was supposed to be, but there wasn't a trace. It must have got knocked over and carried away by the snowplow.

I got around to replacing it a few days later. With the ground frozen I couldn't dig a hole to put a new post in, so I made a stand out of two fish boxes roped together, and then nailed an old tin breadbox on top for a mailbox.

It looks a little unusual but I kind of like it. Anyway, it does the job. There was a downpour of freezing rain the day I went out and set it up.

While we were in Spain two of the tires on the truck went flat, and when I tried to change them the jack broke. I had to borrow a jack from George Carmarthen, the farmer up the road, and get him to drive me and the tires to a garage in Baie-Sainte-Lucille and have them patched.

When I got back and put them on and tried the ignition nothing happened. I cleaned the battery posts and tugged on wires and beat on different parts with a wrench but to no avail. In the end I had to get the truck towed to a garage. Gas tank cleaned, new plugs, anti-freeze, new starter. A hundred and seven dollars.

A few days later the water pump went. Off to the garage again. The replacement cost me twenty-five bucks.

Before the week was out I noticed gas leaking where the gas line enters the carburetor, and in trying to tighten the nut I stripped the threads on the carburetor — which meant I had to get a new carburetor. This time I hitchhiked fifteen miles into Bannonbridge to get one at Canadian Tire where parts are cheaper.

Yesterday my chamber pot started leaking like a sieve, and we can't use the outhouse because it's full of snow inside and the door won't open.

This morning the handle on the kitchen pump snapped off. Now we have to melt snow on the stove for water.

Another thing that happened while we were away was most of my quart bottles of homemade beer broke because the beer froze and expanded.

Early this afternoon it began to snow, tiny flakes flying by the window on an east wind.

Later those tiny flakes turned into big ones and it stormed all day. Now it's night and it's still storming. The date is April 27! There are five foot drifts in the yard and the driveway is completely buried.

I recall that our first storm of the winter came last fall, in mid-October. That makes over six months of winter and we're liable to have a few weeks more, with this latest lot on the ground. Seven months of snow. This country is not fit for habitation.

May 3. The weather has been mild the past few days. A fine mist this morning. Flocks of geese going over, and a few ducks bobbing on the river in a pool where a section of ice has gone out. The geese were very close yesterday, right down in front of the house. Every so often they made a terrific racket, all honking at once. I started the truck up to drive to town but it didn't scare them.

Yesterday my electric heater caught on fire at the plug, where I'd connected it to an extension cord. White and blue flame came shooting out and there was a buzzing sound like a large fly caught in a spider web. I pulled the plug out and saved the day. It could have been disastrous. The floor was charred and one prong of the plug had burnt clean off and part of the extension cord was melted and blackened. If it had happened while I was downstairs the whole place would have gone, a dried-up old house like this.

I'll be glad when I get my boat in the water. I don't like owning a house. I never wanted this one – it was Eva's idea. She got tired of always moving from place to place.

July 30. We've been living aboard our boat for the past month and a half. It's quite a big boat, 38 feet long and 10 feet wide, and at one time belonged to a lobster fisherman down in Baie-Sainte-Lucille. When age overtook it the fisherman hauled it up on the shore to rot and it lay there until a guy from the Air Force Base in Bannonbridge saw it and bought it off the fisherman for a couple of hundred dollars and fixed it up.

He was quite a handyman and turned it into a regular yacht, to all appearances, from a certain distance.

He put in an old secondhand car engine and added a cabin and built some bunks and painted the hull and the cabin white with blue trim. After a couple of years he decided to sell it and buy a sailboat.

When I saw the *For Sale* sign in the cabin window I couldn't believe my eyes. Seven hundred and fifty dollars! I thought there was a zero missing, or maybe two. I almost didn't call I was so sure. But then I called anyway and the man said yes, that's what he was asking, and I said, well, uh, I might be able to give you six hundred and fifty. And he took it.

So all of a sudden I was the captain of a ship.

A few weeks later, while drinking rum and staggering about the deck, I drove a ten-inch splinter into my foot; and when I went to the hospital the nurse told me I had to apply for a Medicare Card. On the form they wanted to know if I had a title (like Doctor, Professor, Captain, etc.), so I put down Captain. And that's what my Medicare Card reads, Captain Walt Macbride. Which makes it official.

I decided to call my vessel *Black North*, after the ship my ancestors came over from Scotland on, as family tradition has it. It was a toss-up between that and *Rum Runner*. There was a case for the latter, since the boat lived in Rum River, and was always running upriver to stock up on rum. But good sense got the better of me. I christened her *Black North* with a pint of Schooner beer across her prow; and as a proper captain would, commenced to take my duties seriously and keep a log. Which I did as follows:

The Log of the Black North

June 23. *It's nine in the morning and we're anchored in the shelter of Parsnip Island and a light rain is falling and we're besieged by mosquitoes. It's impossible to go out on the deck for more than a second. We've killed hundreds that came in through the cracks but they keep coming and we've been bitten many times.*

Yesterday we anchored offshore from our house in Rum River (near the mouth where it flows into Wilawac Inner Bay) and rowed ashore and finished planting the garden. We've planted corn and beets and carrots and cabbage and spinach and beans and cucumbers and tomatoes and lettuce. Then we sailed for the island again and I dug a half bucket of clams which we had for supper.

June 26. We're anchored again in Rum River after being driven by the mosquitoes from Parsnip Island. We tried Leper's Island but there was no shelter there.

I rowed to shore yesterday and dropped in on old Tommy Waggoner. Hubert MacLannigan was with him and we all did quite a bit of drinking. Hubert has cirrhosis and heart trouble but he doesn't let that stop him. Old Tommy's not in much better shape.

Tommy told us about a fellow up the far end of Rum River who hung himself with rabbit wire a few years back. His name was Jago, and according to Tommy he'd been a mean and hateful man all his life.

He was found hanging in the barn, and a Mountie was sent for, and as the Mountie was untying the wire and taking the body down, Ashley's John came along.

"John's a real quiet little man," said Tommy, "hardly ever opens his mouth. He was watching the Mountie undo the fellow, and when the Mountie finished John looked at the rabbit wire and said, 'Why don't you set 'er again.'

"He says, 'Why don't you set 'er again. You might catch another one.'"

And there it is, the log of the *Black North*. As logs go it's not much, but then there's no money in writing logs. Chopping and selling them for firewood, maybe, but not writing them. In any case I don't have the time. I'm already keeping this journal and working on the book I started in Spain.

What I'm doing now, I'm sitting here with my feet up on the gunnel waiting. When the tide changes we're going to weigh anchor and sail for Bannonbridge to replenish our supplies. We're down to our last quart of rum and case of beer.

§

We spent the night tied up at Morgan's Wharf. Next afternoon Eva went ashore to visit her sister. I'd been out to the tavern the night before and was having a few beers to come around, just sitting on a deck chair and relaxing in the sun, when a car drove onto the wharf and a man got out with a large paper bag under his arm. It was Ozzie.

I hadn't seen him in ten years and almost didn't recognize him. He was as bald as an egg and had a full beard and he was a lot bigger than before. He was still short — that couldn't change — but he'd grown very burly.

"I heard you were down here." He ran his eyes over the *Black North*. "Quite a ship you got there!"

"C'mon aboard. Let me take that bag."

"No, it's okay."

Using one hand he climbed down the wharf ladder and stood on the deck. "Jeez, I don't want to get seasick. I better have a drink."

"I'll get you a beer."

"No, don't bother." He opened the bag and drew out a quart of rye and a quart of scotch and a quart of rum.

"Is that all you got?" I said. "Where's the vodka?"

"Take your pick. I didn't know what you drank. I didn't want to bring the wrong stuff."

I unfolded another lawn chair and fetched a couple of mugs from the cabin and we opened the scotch, one of my favourites among the hard liquors, along with the other kinds.

"So what've you been doing all these years?" I asked.

"Oh, this and that." He was doing pretty well, he said, working out of Toronto driving tractor-trailers for a transport company. He'd been all over Canada and the States more times than he could count. He was home for a couple of weeks vacation, the first time in three years.

"Well, you look like a truck driver. You must weigh two hundred pounds. I can hardly believe it."

He laughed, pleased with the compliment. "I drink a little beer on the side."

"Just a little, eh?"

"A few dozen a day. Not too much. It builds up the body."

I gave him a brief rundown on my own past wanderings: the years in Montreal as a tabloid journalist and little magazine editor; fighting and scratching to get a few books published; some travels in Europe; leaving Montreal and landing back east — the usual story, off to see the world and home again, a chip on the tide of life.

He told me of the rigs he'd rolled and the jails he'd been in, and how some of our other classmates were doing. Quite a few of them had gone to Toronto.

"That's where Hog ended up," he said. "He was doing great there for a while, flashy clothes and lots of girls and a new sports car. He was involved with the drug crowd pretty heavy."

"I think I heard something about him. Someone said he'd been found floating in the river."

"Yeah, the Don River, with a bullet in the back of the head."

Then there was Wiener Robinson... Mousie Burns... Herbie Beek... Names from way back, all doing one thing and another in Toronto.

Bird was still around, he'd got married and was working at the pulp mill. Not everyone had left.

As names came to mind I'd ask him, what about this one or what about that, but all the while I was thinking of someone else, biding my time and waiting for the right moment to bring her up.

After all these years, even with a few good tots of scotch in me, it was still hard to inquire about Angela. It wasn't a case of painful regrets or anything like that, just the old childhood inhibition. As if he might start razzing me: "You still like her, eh, Macbride? Ha ha ha!" Straight back to the schoolyard.

I had to remind myself I was a man of the world.

She was about the last one left we both knew before I finally slipped it in, like an off-the-cuff remark.

"By the way.... Do you ever run into your cousin, you know, Angela? How's she making out these days?"

He had the mug of scotch halfway to his lips and it stopped there. Then he shrugged and went on with his drink. Like he wasn't sure whether to answer or not.

I waited and he just sort of laughed.

I said, "Well?"

"I don't think I'm supposed to say anything," he said at last.

"Why not?"

Another shrug.

"C'mon, Ozzie, what's the secret?"

"Oh, nothing. You know. One of those things."

"One of what things?"

He had my curiosity aroused, which he was well aware of. He had a secret and had me hanging. But on the other hand it's almost impossible to keep a secret and drink at the same time, not to mention he was a guest on my yacht. At any rate it only took another tip of the mug before he let it out.

"What the hell... It's not like you're gonna blab it around. I saw her this morning. She's up at Eddie's."

"She's in town *now*? She's here in Bannonbridge?"

"Yeah. In fact we were talking about you. She wanted to know if I'd ever run into you."

I was all attention. "No kidding? And that's the big secret?"

"Well, not exactly."

"Her husband's with her."

"No, he's in Brockton."

"Why don't we go see her? It's been quite a while."

"I'm not sure that's a good idea," he said.

"Why not?"

"She's not in very good shape. She's on her way to the nuthouse."

"What!"

"Yeah. She's kind of fucked up. I don't know..."

"What's wrong?"

"Don't ask me. Bad nerves... Her prick of a husband... She goes into these depressions. Drinking and everything."

"She's not crazy, though? Is she?"

"I don't think so. I wouldn't call her crazy, exactly. Just kinda fucked up."

I shook my head. "That's terrible. I mean, if they're gonna throw her in the bin. I don't like the sound of it. I've heard about those places. They stuff you full of pills, turn you into a zombie."

"She's already on pills. They're trying to get her to stop drinking. They say she's an alcoholic. Eddie's in AA now... He says there's no detoxes in these parts so the only place she can go is the nuthouse. Get her off the booze."

"Bullshit! If she goes in there she'll really be in trouble. She'll end up nuts whether she is or not. That's what happens."

You can imagine, here I was drinking myself, with life feeling better by the minute, and they'd commit someone to the insane asylum for doing what I was doing!

And a beautiful girl like Angela. That I was just in the mood to go see.

I thought I'd better try and do something about it. I ought to warn her, let her know what she was getting into. She couldn't possibly be insane — she'd never shown any signs of it. What could have happened?

There wasn't much escaped my suspicious mind. Who had the motive — who was the moving

21

force behind this monstrous deed? There could only be one answer. Her jealous husband! She'd fought his restrictions, and like a medieval lord he was going to lock her in a cell, so she couldn't be unfaithful. That was his way of fixing her.

"I'd like to see her," I said. "She probably has no idea what she's letting herself in for."

A few more drinks and away we went.

Over the past years I'd done some serious thinking about life. It was no highway of roses, and you had to do what you could to get by. You fought and scratched and – if you had any sense – you drank. I'd found that out for myself. It was an important part of survival. Booze eased the pain, kept hope alive, brought some light into every day. It helped you love your friends and forget your enemies. The only mystery was why so few people had caught onto this.

Not that I wasn't sensible of a certain risk for some people, if they drank too much. But these were the alcoholic types, the guys who'd end up hanging around the liquor store bumming dimes. Obviously they'd be better off not drinking. But for people who were steady on their feet a drop now and then could do nothing but good.

§

Angela's parents were living in a three-room shack in the South End, which was the hard up end of town.

It was still afternoon and Eddie was away at work. Apparently he had a steady job now. So there was only Angela and her mother in the house.

Her mother let us in, a woman I remembered as having been fairly attractive in her day, but then that was quite a few years ago. Time and the trials of life had left her looking wrung-out and haggard.

"Angela's in the bedroom," she said. I could hear music coming through the open door.

"Can we go in and see her?" I asked.

She looked at Ozzie.

"He's okay," said Ozzie. "He's an old friend of Angela's."

"She's not feeling very well. Does he know that?"

"Yeah, he knows."

"I'd just like to say hello," I said.

She looked at Ozzie again.

"It might cheer her up," Ozzie said.

"We'll only stay a minute," I said.

"It's okay," said Ozzie.

"Well, I suppose it wouldn't hurt... I'll see what she says."

She opened a door off the kitchen and stuck her head in. "Angela, you've got some visitors."

I heard Angela's voice. "Visitors? What kind of visitors?"

"It's Ozzie and a friend. They want to see you. Can we come in?"

"Sure. I don't care."

I followed her mother and Ozzie into the bedroom and saw Angela sitting on an unmade bed. It was my first sight of her in ten years, and it gave me a start. It wasn't only her mother who'd aged. Angela was only thirty-two, like me, but she looked closer to fifty. Her skin was coarse and dry and yellow, with an

23

unnatural tautness to it. Her hair was a mess and she was wearing old crumpled pyjamas. She sat smiling at nothing, listening to the music, humming along with it.

"You remember this guy?" said Ozzie. "Walt Macbride?"

She seemed to take a while to focus on me. Then she laughed. "Sure, I remember you. Sit down. Make yourself comfortable."

I sat on the bed beside her.

"Would you like a drink?" I said. We'd brought the full quart of rye along and I pulled it out from under my jacket.

Her mother shook her head. "No, no," she said. "We're not drinking. We're both off it. If Eddie caught us he'd throw a fit."

"I'm not supposed to drink," said Angela. She smiled, as if that was amusing.

She was obviously on drugs of some sort. Her remote and strange air, and her skin... I'd seen heavy prescription drug takers with skin like that, half-mummified.

"You don't mind if we have one, do you?"

"Go right ahead. Don't let us stop you."

I took a snort from the bottle and passed it to Ozzie.

"So what've you been doing with yourself?" said Angela.

"Oh, one thing and another."

"He's living on a big yacht," said Ozzie.

"Really? It must be great to be rich."

"Oh, I don't know. I'm not exactly rich."

"It must be fifty feet long," said Ozzie. "He's like that Greek guy. The one that married Jackie Kennedy. Cruising around counting his money."

We got gabbing on, and on the next round I noticed her mother eyeing the bottle with more than casual interest.

"Come on, have one," I said.

"Don't say that. Don't tempt me."

"As my late Aunt Rose used to say, bless her soul, this is a special occasion. I haven't seen Angela in I don't know how many years. Not since... when, nineteen sixty-three?"

"Ages ago," said Angela.

I could see she was gazing at the bottle, too.

I took another belt and held the bottle out to her. "Here, why don't you have one."

She put her hand around the bottle. "I don't know. I'm not supposed to."

"Who said?"

"Eddie. And the doctor."

"Don't listen to them. The music's playing, the sun's shining. A drink'll brighten you up. You should enjoy life."

She gave a little shrug. "Oh, what's the difference. I can't get any worse." And she took the bottle and upended it, and then her mother grabbed it and poured down a stiff one herself.

"That's better," I said.

I felt a rush of affection and put my arm around her and kissed her on the mouth. She didn't move one way or the other, just accepted it passively.

"You shouldn't let them do this to you," I said. "You get up in that place you'll be in real trouble."

"What else can I do?"

"Do you want to go?"

A lift of the shoulders. "It's all the same to me. I don't have anything now. I don't care about my husband, but they took my kids from me. What difference does it make?"

"C'mon, it's not that bad. You can't let life get you down. It's not like everybody's against you. I'm here."

That's what I thought. I'm here so now there's nothing to worry about. I could help her, give her the inspiration she needed. All she had to do was listen to me. She was depressed and feeling defeated, but she didn't have to be. Look at me – wasn't I in good shape?

It was simple really. We had everything right here to lift a person out of a slump. She was a woman and I was a man – we could have a drink and hold each other. When you got down to basics that's all it took. Did there have to be anything else?

She was looking better to me already. Nothing like what she used to be, but I was adjusting, and I had warm loving feelings in me. She was a damsel in distress, after all.

The bottle went around some more, and while Ozzie and the mother gossiped I whispered words in Angela's ear, uplifting words, letting her know I understood and cared. I kissed her, smoothed her hair, caressed her, told her I found her attractive. She seemed to enjoy my attentions; she was certainly absorbed by them, listening with a half-smile on her face.

It was inevitable these intimacies would have an effect on me. I couldn't help it. I won't say I got horny, that wouldn't be proper, but I felt a powerful desire along those lines.

There was such a closeness between us I was sure she felt the same.

"You know what I'd like?" I whispered.

"What?"

"To make love to you."

"Would you?"

"Yes. How about you?"

She laughed. "I haven't had sex for a long time. Maybe that's what I need."

Her mother and Ozzie were tossing back the rye and paid us no mind, nattering on about something. It was turning into a nice little party – in the bedroom, the bottle going around, Angela feeling better with each drink, snuggling up to me in her pyjamas with the top buttons undone. She was a little thin but she still had a good figure. The music played and the sun streamed through the window...

"Do you think we could manage it?"

"I don't know how."

But my inventive mind was already gearing up. There was always a way if you looked for it.

"Couldn't I meet you tonight?"

She shook her head. "Daddy'll be home and he won't let me out. I haven't left the house since I got here. He's afraid I'll find something to drink." We both laughed at that. It was a reminder to take the bottle from Ozzie and have a swig.

"What time does he go to bed?"

"About eleven."

"And you sleep in here alone? All right... What about leaving the window open and I'll come around after everyone's asleep. What do you think?"

She laughed. "If you like."

"You'll remember?"

"I'll try."

"I'm serious."

"Okay. I'll leave the window open for you and you can climb in. Don't make too much noise!"

She laughed again, so that I didn't know if she really meant it. But she kept agreeing. We were in the middle of a long kiss when I heard a door shut. I broke away and got to my feet.

It was Eddie. He came into the room, took in the scene, and said:

"What the hell's going on here?"

"Hi, Eddie," I said, as if we were old friends. He gave me a quick glance and turned to Ozzie.

"For Christsake, Ozzie..."

"Now, look here, Eddie," I said, "you're not going to send her to the nuthouse, are you? I don't think that's a good idea — "

"What do you know about it?" His eyes flashed at me. He looked really angry, and then seemed to catch himself. More calmly he said:

"You'd better leave, the two of you. You shouldn't have come around here. And take that bottle with you."

Ozzie never said a word. With a sheepish expression he headed for the door, and I followed him. Eddie came after us and caught us on the back step. I could see it was all he could do to restrain himself. But he did.

He ignored me, talking straight at Ozzie.

"Have you no sense at all, bringing booze here?"

"Yeah, but this idea of locking her up in the bin," I began. "You know – "

"You don't know nothing about it. She's sick – can't you see that? Giving her liquor for Godsake. I spent the past three days getting her off the stuff and now you guys come along..." He shook his head. He gave us a look that made me turn my eyes away. He wasn't angry – that had passed. It was more like pained exasperation.

"I'm trying to help her, but she needs to stop drinking. She's an alcoholic."

Despite myself I felt slightly chastened, like I hadn't been entirely in the right, to some degree. I don't know why I felt this way, perhaps something in Eddie's face. Or the fact he was her father and I'd been caught red-handed. Whatever the case I decided not to push my point.

Ozzie didn't say a word. He was like a dog with its tail between its legs. We got in the car and didn't talk much on the drive back to the boat. What was there to say? It was like a rainstorm had come down on our picnic. He dropped me off at the wharf and said he'd see me again but he never did. He went back to Toronto and to this day I've never again run into him.

I went into the cabin and lay down on my bunk. In no time a drowsiness came over me. I often dozed off in the late afternoon. I knew there was a chance I'd forget some things, and before drifting away I drilled myself to remember. Angela... Midnight tryst. Eleven was a little early so I'd better make it more like midnight... that ought to be safe enough... The household would be asleep but probably not Angela... She didn't sleep much... she said she hadn't slept in a week. Don't forget... important rendezvous...

When I awoke I automatically reached for a pint of beer under the bunk.

I hadn't forgotten. But I was rested up enough to reassess the situation and have some misgivings.

Eva was back and making supper in the galley. I said "Hi," and took my pint out onto the deck to think things over. I wanted to go, at least part of me did. But was it such a great idea?

The house was very small and sure as hell we'd wake Eddie, bedsprings being what they are...

And did Angela really mean it? The way she kept laughing... She didn't seem altogether with it. There was no predicting what she might do if I started climbing in the window.

I'd got thrown in jail once before when a father heard me climbing in his daughter's window, even though she was helping me in. Cop cars screaming up with lights flashing. All I got was a night in the cells and a drunk charge, but still it was not a pleasant way to wake up in the morning.

And there was another consideration. I'd already had a lot to drink, especially all that hard stuff, and as sure as the minutes ticked by on the clock I'd be drinking beer the rest of the evening. A long evening of waiting for the hours to go by, drinking one beer after another. I'd have to scotch-tape my eyes open. I was almost sure to be asleep by the time midnight rolled around – or so groggy I wouldn't be able to get up the ladder onto the wharf. And what kind of story would I give Eva when I left? I couldn't leave early and go sit in the tavern and wait. I'd get wiped out even quicker there, with everyone buying rounds the way they do. Besides, I'd been to the tavern the night before and I just didn't do that, go two nights in a row. She'd be suspicious for sure.

Okay, I could come up with some kind of a story, but...

But the truth was, I felt fatigued, like I didn't have the energy. I was listless in body and spirit. My heart wasn't in it.

It was too much work and too risky and a crazy idea to begin with. That's what it was.

I wasn't aware of too much else about it that bothered me. Perhaps a vague little gnaw somewhere, but nothing worth taking into account.

I decided to postpone the decision and carry on as usual and see how I felt as the night went on. And at ten o'clock I climbed into my bunk and passed out.

MONTREAL REVISITED

Three calendar years later. It's January and four-thirty in the morning and I sit up and swing my legs out of bed. My entire body is vibrating; I have trouble getting my breath; I don't know where the hell I am.

There's a woman beside me. In the dark I can't make out who she is. Ah yes. It comes back. I'm in Montreal and the woman's name is Janet.

I lie down again. I don't have the strength, there's nothing left of me. I ought to go back to sleep.

I try but my heart's banging like mad and the shaking only gets worse. Panic sets in. I'm starting to think. The whole load of rotten reality is about to come down on me.

I pull on some clothes and make for the bathroom, and falling to my knees stick two fingers down my throat. I do this every morning; I like to get it over and done with. I haven't eaten for days – I don't know how many – and all that comes up is sulphurous bile, bright yellow and bitter.

Wiping my mouth with a handful of toilet paper I get to my feet and grope along the hall to the living room and find the light switch. Then I find a bottle of scotch. I swallow a mouthful and begin pacing.

It's my morning routine, wherever I happen to be.

Another couple of drinks and the shakes subside. But there's no lift. I'm getting heavier rather than lighter. I feel groggy, stunned. I try another drink but I can't seem to get myself going.

I remember my new cavalry boots in the bedroom and go in and put them on. I like my boots. They ought to brighten me up some. Shuffling around in my sock-feet I feel like an old man.

Moreover it's time to get civilized. I pour the next drink into a glass before downing it.

I try to picture myself as a dashing figure in my smart new boots.

Up and at the day.

Every organ in my body feels bruised and battered, as if I'd been worked over with a crowbar the night before.

I resume my restless march. Back and forth across the carpeted living room, up and down the hall outside the bedroom, boots striking on the hardwood floor. The bedroom door slams and I jump a foot in the air. It takes me a minute to comprehend... I'm in no condition to be defiant or self-assertive, not this early. I slip the boots off.

I can't seem to get in gear. My head is getting worse, my mind clouding. I catch myself lurching as I walk.

I know what it is. I got up too soon. Too quick off the mark. I need more sleep.

I return to the bedroom and strip off and climb in beside Janet, snuggling against her. She starts away with the same pointedness as she slammed the door. Rolling over I plummet into sleep.

I'm startled awake by the toilet flushing. I have to move quickly. I can be very quick in the morning. Before she's out of the bathroom I'm dressed and sitting at the kitchen table with a half-empty beer in front of me.

She looks older today, pale, frowzy, her skin not so clear. Evidently she's not a cheerful riser. She shoots a sharp glance my way.

"You're up again, I see."

"Yep. And you're up too. Looks like we're both up. How do you feel this morning?"

"Tired. And you?"

"Okay. Not too bad."

My head is ringing, my scalp crawling, my eyes sore, my guts a mass of pain. I can't imagine I've ever been in worse shape. But then, it isn't the first time I've thought that.

I was just fine the night before. It took a full day's drinking to get that way, but when I arrived at Janet's I was in top form. Except I wasn't able to touch the dinner she took such pains to prepare. The wine, yes — I drank all she had — but I had to apologize for a touch of the stomach flu I'd picked up. It plays hell with the appetite.

After she cleared the table we went into the living room and sat on the sofa and I got into her scotch. I talked non-stop for hours. I'm a terrific talker when the mood is on me, a brilliant monologuist. The words flowed effortlessly and with a richness and precision that absolutely delighted me. I could have gone all night. But I hadn't forgotten why I was there. And it was true, she had to get up next morning and go to work. I caught her suppressing a yawn and stealing a look at the clock on the mantlepiece.

I was in good humour. I wasn't offended. Without missing a beat I rounded off a particularly choice phrase and pulled her to me. When our lips parted she said:

"I was wondering what you were waiting for. I thought you'd never get around to it."

She's a woman of forty or so. She seemed very attractive and desirable – though in my condition I would have thought the same of any woman. I've never seen her when I was sober. I haven't seen anyone when sober in over a year, not even Eva, since I'm always out of bed well before her.

We were soon in the bedroom and when she took off her clothes I saw that for a slender woman she had exceptionally large full breasts. I hadn't been able to tell because of the loose blouses she wore. I was as pleased as a baby.

"I was hoping you'd have those!"

"Really? You like them?"

"Oh yeah."

I made love to her twice before I let her go to sleep, and it took some while, because with all the drink in me my end was as numb as a nightstick. And later, waking and feeling the warm body beside me, I climbed aboard again. She was not a great deal in the mood by this time. I heard sleepy mumblings of protest, she had to get up for work, then lying limp as if trying to sleep through it, and finally some excited activity.

When all was said and done it meant nothing to me that she had to get up early for work. The work would always be with her but I wouldn't. And what was her work, anyway? The work other people did was of little consequence. Though in her case it was convenient for me.

She happens to be an editor on a magazine. That's why I came to Montreal, because of her, supposedly to research a story for *This Week* magazine, about my days as a tabloid journalist. She got me the assignment. It's the way these things go, you have to know somebody. We met when she was with the publishing house that did a travel book I wrote about Europe. We hadn't managed a moment alone at that time, however, because Eva was always with me.

On this trip I made sure I came unaccompanied.

Not that I've done much researching. I talked to a few people and got some quotes. I'm going to write it out of my head anyway.

She's banging pots and pans around the kitchen, slamming cupboard doors, muttering under her breath: obviously the grumpy type in the morning. A perfunctory inquiry if I want breakfast. I reply that I'm not in the habit of eating breakfast.

I gulp the rest of my beer down. It doesn't taste like beer. It tastes like ice-cold sewer water. I get another one from the fridge, ignoring the look she gives me.

Bacon and eggs. I avoid watching her eat. I finish the second pint and open another one.

Clattering the dishes into the sink she says, "I'm late already. I'm going to have to leave now."

"No problem. I'll just polish this off."

"I won't have time to drive you back to your friend's place."

"That's okay. I can take a bus."

Maybe it's the food in her belly, but she seems to soften somewhat. At the door she says:

"I'm sorry. I'm not always like this. But I hate being rushed. And I didn't get much sleep..."

"I understand."

"I'll drive you part way, all right?"

"You don't have to. I don't mind, really."

She's quite civil in the car, I might even say apologetic, as if an attack of conscience has come over her. She asks me to give her a call in the afternoon.

§

Next morning, quite early. Rasmin is up and trotting around the apartment naked. He goes by my door grinning. "Good morning, Macbride!" A flush of the toilet, the shower running, and in a few minutes there he is again, standing in the doorway without a stitch on.

I've been awake for some time, watching the expanse of each long minute, staring at the wall across the room: bookshelves, a filing cabinet, prints of Renoir, Utrillo, Picasso. It's Rasmin's study, I'm on the couch. I don't care much for the way he's grinning at me. I've got a terrible case of the shakes, all of the

37

nerves under my skin doing a frantic dance. Yet I'm not up and having my medicine. A massive lethargy is on me, like I'm lying under thousands of feet of water, on the ocean floor. I haven't eaten in four or five days.

"Not a lot of... luck last night..." My words choke and stumble out unsteadily, off-balance, not in the flippant style I wanted, as a shield against Rasmin. I have a foggy recollection of his going on the night before about the advantages of being homosexual, but grinning all the while, being polemical, as he might take the side of murder for the sake of argument. We spent most of the evening phoning women, but they were either not at home or not interested — as so often happens. So we just kept on drinking, and somewhere the night dissolved out of memory.

"Women are a pain in the ass, Macbride. They're more trouble than they're worth. You should be picking up guys instead." Laughing. "You ever consider that?"

He's back at it again this morning, and more direct than last night, from what I can recall.

"Not really."

"Try the gay bars. You'd have no problem. You could pick up a different stud every night. It's a hell of a lot easier than chasing after broads."

"Is that what you're into these days?"

He laughs floridly, his heavy lips folding back over perfect white teeth, meanwhile scratching and fondling his gear. With Rasmin it wouldn't surprise me, after the frustrations he's had himself with women. Maybe he's not joking. He likes to be in the vanguard, and maybe homosexuality is the latest rage.

I have the uneasy feeling he's about to charge in and jump into bed with me. And me with no more strength than a new-born kitten.

"Rasmin, I feel like shit... Go away and leave me in peace."

Another laugh. "Okay, Macbride. You want some breakfast?"

"Not likely."

The very mention of it makes my stomach heave.

Some time later he's back at the door in his lawyer's outfit: ash-gray suit, vest, dark tie, a briefcase in his hand. He looks the picture of a lawyer, but that's about as far as it goes. He has no clients to speak of. He goes to his office on Mansfield Street every morning and sits with his feet up on the desk. He keeps a bottle in the drawer to nip on. In the afternoon it's off to a tavern – the Peel Pub, no doubt – now that I think of it – with its British decor and queer clientele.

He was called to the bar a year ago (the forensic one), fourteen years after graduating from McGill with his B.A. It took him that long to become a lawyer, even though he did nothing else in the interim apart from work elections for the NDP and the Parti Quebecois.

He was a man about town, a *flaneur*, a poet. He published the one thin little book of poems. I think his poetry was an excuse more than anything to avoid the legal profession, which was his father's idea, not his.

His father came to this country an immigrant without money or education and worked hard and ended up owning several factories. Rasmin while "studying to be a lawyer" held the titular position of vice-president of the company on a comfortable salary.

He went to school off and on, a credit here, a credit there, a full year, a partial year, a few years leave, and so forth – however you become a lawyer in fourteen years. When he finally got his degree he flunked his bar exams, then took a year or so off to regroup before going back to his studies and trying again and passing.

He *had* to make it some time, unless he wanted to lose his vice-president's salary. His old man's patience couldn't last forever. And now that he was a lawyer he had to remain one, for the same reason: what his father paid him was still the only income he had. And his father wanted his son to be a lawyer.

He did the odd bit of work for the family business but nothing important. His old man might be pig-headed but he wasn't stupid. He employed a good solid law firm to handle his affairs.

Rasmin's fellow poets, artists and the like, his old circle, brought what legal problems they had to him; but he tried to discourage this, once he found out they wouldn't pay him. He said trying to get his money out of them was costing him all his friends.

It wasn't that he wanted or needed their money, but his self-esteem demanded he make some show, at least, of taking his profession seriously, after all the struggle he'd had in getting there. And there was the secretary he'd hired. She must have wondered what she was supposed to be doing. It helped to have her send out a bill from time to time.

For a while he didn't mind going to his office every day. It got him up in the mornings and out of his apartment before dark. He had a sense of occupying a place in the real world. But this spurt of enthusiasm was soon spent. He didn't quite know what to do with himself, which was no new story with him.

That's Rasmin, at whose apartment I'm staying for a few days while in Montreal.

§

Before long I'm kneeling over the toilet bowl, my stomach rising and jolting and some acrid bile coming up. Shuddering, groaning. In the living room I pour myself a brandy from Rasmin's bar and commence to pace the floor.

I'm restless, I've been restless for days, but with no energy or resolve. It was all I could manage to get my clothes on. Even the smallest task is a supreme test of will.

I put some classical music on the stereo. A few spastic moves and I get the record slammed down on the turntable. I'm like a mechanical man, an automated toy — jerk — jerk — jerk. Lurching arms, no fluidity of movement. I break into a sweat. A quick snort from the bottle.

Around 10:30 I put on my coat and go out for a walk, before I wear a path in Rasmin's carpet. For a half hour or so I drift along the streets following my feet, going west along Roy, then up St. Lawrence, the one-way traffic charging off the lights like a demoniacal herd, the noise running up the nerves of my arms and down to the pit of my stomach. A street of small shops, delicatessens, bargain clothing, bakeries, groceries, fish marts, travel agencies (flights home to Greece, Portugal, Spain).

Rasmin's family lives in a big house in Westmount, while his apartment is in the middle of the immigrant community east of St. Lawrence. He has the whole upstairs of a row house with a view of Mount Royal to the west and rooftops and church spires to the east.

At the Pussycat Cinema I glance over the glass-encased stills of the films showing. It's too early to go in. It might have taken my mind off my misery, about the only thing that could do it – women, sex. You forget about yourself for a while. The sun is shining and the sky is cloudless but it's blustery and cold. It's January, it *should* be cold. I turn right at Duluth and go into Sam's Tavern for a beer. It tastes like liquid gunpowder. I have another anyway and leave, continuing on down Duluth.

Bernard Lawlor lives on Chateaubriand. I know he's moved from his old apartment, but in a letter he mentioned taking over a shed nearby, on the same street. Chateaubriand is further east of Rasmin's (whose place is on Drolet). It's a narrow street, no more than an alley, actually. If you didn't know it was there you'd walk right past it, thinking it was just another of the numerous back lanes that bisect all the blocks of Montreal. There's no traffic, there's hardly room for a car to come down it. The buildings are old and would normally be rundown and seedy, but because of the street's picturesque narrowness and seclusion a number of artists have moved in at cheap rents and fixed the places up, painting them in quite extravagant ways. Not every building but a good many of them. So what you have is a curious blend of rough old bricks and psychedelic murals.

I open a small door in a gray wooden wall and go up a little alley into the backyards, out of sight of the street, and come face to face with a panorama of brilliantly coloured designs covering the full sides and backs of buildings, the balconies and gables, from basement to roof. It's like a fairyland hidden from the street in front, enormous murals, all the colours of the rainbow.

But no sign of Bernard's shed. His old apartment is locked up and unoccupied, the windows vacant, dusty. I stroll up and down the street searching for the shed, but there's nothing that looks like a shed to me. A fellow with a beard and a long muffler steps out of a door. I ask him if he knows where Bernard lives.

"*Non, non.*" He has no time for a question in English. Hostile eyes.

For a minute I stand in the middle of the street pondering where to turn next. The street runs northward and the wind comes channelling down piercing through my coat. I decide to go about my business. As I'm passing Bernard's old address two guys come out a door, both of them wearing army greatcoats.

"You know where Bernard Lawlor lives?"

"Bernard? In there." Pointing to a small door. It's like the door in the wall I went through earlier, but this one is in a wooden adjunct to one of the buildings, a kind of enclosed two-storey porch for storing rubbish and the like, painted gray. It's not surprising I didn't notice it. Shed was too magnificent a word for it.

He must have heard me, for the door opens and Bernard pokes his head out. "Well! Come on in." Chuckling to himself at my sudden appearance. He had no idea I was going to be in Montreal.

He's looking thinner than usual, which is going some. Just a tall frame with a minimum of flesh. He was always thin but now it looks as though he's been on a hunger strike.

It's an odd looking habitation inside. He shows me around; it doesn't take long. Two floors, one room on each floor, connected by a stair-ladder through a hole in the ceiling. On the second floor a high ceiling with a broad bunk at eye level. I've never seen anything like it for a place to live. The dimensions of the rooms are about eight feet by ten — it's much taller than broad, like a square silo.

There are no windows, and a dim rosy glow from a globed candle lights the lower room; and when we climb the stairs he carries another candle in a holder, shadows following him up the almost vertical steps.

"It looks like an opium den."

"I suppose it is, in a way," he says.

The walls as well as the floors are covered with carpets he's scavenged from alleys on garbage collection days. He's even installed some heavy beams to reinforce the roof. He had to put new roofing on because it leaked when he moved in; and he added inner walls for insulation — all from materials he scrounged out of refuse from back alleys and from buildings being demolished. A space heater is burning, it's turned down to its lowest but the place is so confined I find it almost too warm.

"The heater is the only thing I had to buy," he tells me. "And I got that from a junk dealer for next to nothing. It just needed a little fixing up."

Downstairs he shows me his sink. "I've even got running water." He says he climbed into the basement of the house next door through a window in the back and tapped their water line, running a pipe into his shed.

He pays no rent, no electricity, no water or property taxes, no telephone. In other words, his only expense apart from food is oil in the winter, and with such a small house that cost is kept to a minimum.

He doesn't know who owns the shed, it was just there not being used and he moved in, and nobody's bothered him.

He asks me what brings me to Montreal, and I tell him I'm writing a magazine story, and that yesterday I finished my interviews, or the day before – I'm not sure which. It's all down in my notebook anyway, thank God, or I'd never remember any of it. I need a few authentic quotes to justify my expenses-paid trip to Montreal.

"You wouldn't have a beer in the house? I'm not too steady right now."

"Well, come to think of it..." He goes upstairs and comes down the ladder with a pint. "I was keeping this aside. I thought you'd show up one of these days."

"I don't want to take your only beer," I said, opening it. I always keep an opener on my key chain.

"No, no, that's all right. I don't want it. It's for you."

The beer is warm and tasteless, but that's beside the point. I guzzle it down.

"I manage to keep occupied," he tells me. "I get away on weekends and stay with friends in the country. And I have my own summer home I built. I don't stay in the city in the summer. Here, I'll show you a picture of it."

It turns out he made the camera that took the picture too, a pinhole box camera.

His country home is constructed between two large elm trees, like a tree house, elevated off the ground a few feet, and with the whole front open to the air. Beneath the roof there's a roll of canvas like a stage curtain that he can lower to keep out the rain and cold. There's only the one room but it's larger than this shed, and certainly brighter.

"What do you do for money? You don't look like you're eating an awful lot but you must have to eat something."

"I do a bit of this and a bit of that. In the summer I build houses for friends, summer places. And I built a barn last year. I made the house where I go on weekends to visit. And then there are these little things..."

He produces a display of bracelets and rings. They're delicate ornaments made from woven silver wire. "I make and sell these. I don't need much to get along on."

"Very nice. What are you charging for this bracelet?"

"Ten dollars."

"I'll take it. I'm fresh out of bracelets. By the way, do you want to come to a party tonight, I was told I could ask a few friends. You can come over to Rasmin's first and have dinner there."

When I leave he comes with me. He doesn't lock his door — probably the only person in Montreal who doesn't. He has to call in at a community craft school to get more silver wire for some work he wants to do this afternoon.

I follow him down Chateaubriand and we turn right onto Mount Royal Boulevard, his long-legged strides taking him about a half block ahead of me. I've been away from the city for several years and fallen into the habit of ambling leisurely along, like a bumpkin, and besides I'm still sluggish from the previous night's drink. But I begin to feel the cold, the biting wind, and I step up my pace, and before long I'm plunging ahead and dodging traffic and pedestrians like old times. I catch up with Bernard by the time we reach St. Urbain where the school is.

The people in the shop are all friendly, but they're more than a little strange, most of them. I gather they're a group of mental patients involved in occupational therapy — hugging, pouting, sudden exclamations, peels of incongruous laughter, weird-looking eyes. But they're working away like elves and the crafts they turn out seem quite professional to me.

Bernard himself (shades of Angela) was once locked in the bin by his family who thought he had to be cracked, living the way he did; but he got out after a month, thanks to some journalist friends who threatened an exposé.

By ordinary standards he might appear a little nuts but as far as I can tell he's happy with his life. Come to think of it, all these other supposed loonies look like they're doing okay, too. A lot better than me, for one thing. Maybe I'm sane after all.

I watch the work going on for a while, everyone busy cutting and stitching leather and weaving wire and so forth, but I'm too restless to stick around long. Bernard is in no hurry; he takes his time selecting his silver wire and talking shop with the others, ever patient and deliberate, browsing through odds and ends. A giant taut rubber band is drawing me towards the door, the other end fastened to a tavern. I tell Bernard I'll see him at Rasmin's and leave.

§

With a shot of rum and a glass of wine beside my plate I look on as the two of them eat. Bernard, as thin as the silver wire he weaves, effortlessly puts away three big heaping plates of spaghetti with meat and mushroom sauce, half a dozen slices of rye bread, and a couple of large helpings of salad.

Rasmin complains about the weight he's put on, swelling out his pot belly to show us, like a massive stomach tumour. "I'm drinking too much beer," he says. "I'm in the taverns every day. I'm going to have to stop."

"The way you eat might have something to do with it, too," I say. Yesterday he took on enough for two or three people at dinner. And tonight he's only a little behind Bernard.

"Maybe you're right. But I think it's the beer."

"Look, I drink about twenty beers a day and I'm the same weight as always, pretty much."

"But you don't eat."

"That's the point. If beer makes you fat I'd be fat, wouldn't I?" It's a screwy argument, but I don't want anyone to get a prejudice against beer, and maybe quit drinking. I don't want to be any further alone in this than I already am.

Rasmin says: "You should eat more than you do."

"I'm not that interested in food." The most I can handle is a few mouthfuls of spaghetti, and I have to force-feed it into me, like ramrodding it down the mouth of a cannon. I observe them with envy. They actually enjoy the stuff. It all looks so healthy and natural. The thought impels me to pour another glass of wine and toss it down. My rum tumbler is already empty.

"I tried to quit drinking by smoking grass," Rasmin says, "but you know that can become a habit, too. You get a lift so you want it all the time. I had to start drinking again. I was going around stoned the whole time. I still smoke every day but not the way I used to, I don't chain smoke the stuff anymore."

After dinner I telephoned Donnie DeGrace. He picks up his phone but doesn't say anything as usual, waiting for me to identify myself – an idiosyncrasy of his. In case it's Big Brother, possibly. He's a grade school principal with a mind as cryptic as Zelda Fitzgerald's. There's a kind of brilliance to his conversation but for some reason I can never recall anything he's said, or invent something similar. It's not illogical, it's just non-sequential; he leaves out parts. Rather like trying to make sense out of a book when you can only read every fourth sentence.

Like Rasmin and so many others I know, Donnie was once a poet, in the last half of the sixties, during the time I had my little literary magazine,

Fahrt[1]. We all helped put it out, and then we all lost our muses, without exception, a casualty of I'm not sure what.

Donnie says if I have no objection he'll bring a friend along, another teacher. His name is Mel and he has a car and he can give us a lift to the party. The party is being put on by Janet. For some perverse female reason she wants me to meet her boyfriend. Naturally I'm to be discreet. I can appreciate that. And it would be okay, she said, if I brought a friend or two along. She'd like to meet my interesting friends.

§

Matthew is already at Janet's when we get there. He answers the door, six-feet-ten in his sock feet, his head bending to clear the lintel. I've invited Matthew as well. He lives in her neighbourhood. He says he's been there for over an hour with Janet and her boyfriend waiting for me.

The five of us storm in, Donnie carrying a twenty-four of beer. We get out of our heavy coats, our boots – and after that the memory is vague indeed.

Booze everywhere, darkish room, one heavily shaded lamp with an orange bulb, very little furniture. Everyone sitting on the floor on cushions. Records playing, marijuana smoke in the air, voices all going at once. Janet is the only woman, she and seven males.

---

[1]*From the German fahrt*, meaning passage, trip, tour, as in *fahrt ins blaue*, mystery tour; related to *fährte*, track, scent – *falschen fährte sein*, false scent, be on the wrong track.

All day I've been aware of a giddy sensual feeling deep in my guts, like an internal itch, an excruciating horniness. I've never felt anything quite like it before. I tell her there should be more women on hand. She doesn't think so, but finally she agrees to call a friend who arrives an hour or so later, auburn-haired, about thirty, attractive. Her name is Francine.

Everyone wants attention, to say his piece, be centre stage. Mel tries to corner me to talk about a book of my stories he's read, wants to talk at length about them. He's secretly a writer himself. He seems simple and modest and sane, the antithesis of Donnie. He's looking for advice, a few tips. I cut him short; I don't have time for conversation, I've got a plane to catch in the morning. I want a woman. Words between men don't interest me, not now... I settle myself on the floor beside Francine and hope the others will be content to entertain each other and leave us in peace... but no such luck. Donnie hovers nearby, interrupting us, inserting his mysterious comments... I try to slip a few soft words in her ear but when I do the whole room hushes, they turn off the music, everyone's listening, they can hear even when I whisper. There's something comical about it, I can't help laughing myself. It's ludicrous, futile... It keeps up this way and I get more and more drunk, I don't know what I'm saying... Donnie becomes belligerent towards everyone... Nobody will take proper notice of him... Rasmin rambling philosophical gibberish... Matthew sitting back observing us all in wonderment... Bernard smiling to himself, rolling one joint after another...

The girl gets up and moves away. She's talking to Mel, she's relieved to find someone who appears half-sensible... Through the smoke I see Janet and Francine and the boyfriend huddled amongst themselves... He's an arrogant looking character, a PR man... You can see he's not pleased with the level of the company... Donnie stumbles over, needling them, I catch the glances exchanged between Janet's boyfriend and Francine... They've got something going on the sly, you can't mistake it, I'm watching them closely... I shout over at them, insist they reveal what's going on with the three of them, what sort of triangle it is... Donnie abetting me, the remarks he makes really bizarre... He's got them confused, and a little frightened, I think... Bad feeling erupts... Accusations... Retaliations... Malicious insults... Hatred for the bourgeoisie coming out...

At last we're asked to leave...

Janet stands at the door, holding it open, a grim expression on her face...

It all seems to have happened very fast. I know I had nothing to do with it... I'm not mad at anyone. Still, I can't blame her for wanting to clear the place out... It's not a bad idea...

I whisper in her ear: "Can I stay the night?"

She gives me a look of astonishment.

"They're a pretty rowdy bunch," I say. "You're right to send them home. Why don't you get rid of your boyfriend, too? I'll just kind of hang around..."

She hands me my coat.

"Can't I stay?"

"No!"

"But..."

She ushers me into the hall.

"Just get your friends out of here."

"They're not bad guys. What are you so upset about? It's that boyfriend of yours, he's a jerk. You should get rid of him..."

She won't listen to reason. Donnie is pointing his finger at the PR guy and screaming, "Cack! Cack! Cack!"

Oh well. I'm a bit disappointed. I was counting on spending another night with her. But there's always something gets in the way.

In the car Rasmin produces a quart of vodka that he's carried away with him under his coat. I grab it from his mouth. It's the night air, I think. A thick sleepiness rolls over me. I need a good drink to brighten me up.

The next thing I know it's morning.

RUM RIVER

As the plane took off and bumped and shook in the air I sat like a wounded animal patiently waiting to die. Normally flying scared me but not today. I didn't really care. The stewardess leaned over, smiling.

"Would you like something to drink, sir?"

I hadn't had a drink since getting up. I'd poured myself one back at Rasmin's but never touched it. It had stared back at me like a glass of hemlock. I shook my head and in a strangled, barely audible voice said: "Do you have anything to eat?"

I was far from hungry. But some deep-rooted instinct for survival told me I'd better start pulling myself together. To eat something would be at least a first step, a gesture in the right direction. Even if I only nibbled the corner off a cracker.

"I'm sorry, but there's no food on this flight, sir. You're sure you wouldn't like a drink?'

She looked concerned. I was trembling and no doubt white as a sheet.

"No, thanks."

I saw the irony, even if I didn't appreciate it. An airplane with booze and no food. What could be more civilized? Any other time if it had been the other way around — food and no booze — I'd have blown my top.

Not surprisingly Eva wasn't at the airport in Bannonbridge to meet me, since I hadn't called to let her know when I'd be back. In fact I hadn't called her since I'd left a week before.

I took a taxi to Rum River. I was thankful I didn't know the driver, didn't have to talk to him. I sat slumped in the front seat, no longer restless, my eyes dead as marbles, like staring out through the sockets of a corpse.

§

I hardly more than nodded to Eva and went straight to bed and passed out. An hour later I was on my feet, fatigued, devitalized, and yet under my skin there was a frantic activity – a terrific agitation of the nervous system. I got a beer from the fridge and pumped half it down and automatically began pacing the kitchen floor.

Eva was sitting against the blazing wood stove in her woolly housecoat. It was thirty below outside. The old house shook and creaked in the wind. The windows were covered with frost.

She was telling me about the events of the week, all the little things that had transpired while I was away. I scarcely listened. I was thinking I had to do something about myself – get off this deadly carousel of rising sick in the morning and then drinking to cure the sickness, and so getting up sick again. I had to pull myself together, start eating and get down to work. I was okay when I was working. The solid routine, that was the thing. Lock the door and see no one, no socializing; work all morning and have a bite to eat, then out for a stroll and back for a beer. And go easy, not more than a dozen a day, just something at hand to sip on.

But I didn't know how I was going to be able to do it. It was close to a year since I'd done any work, and even that had been when half-pissed.

"So how was your trip?"

"My trip? Well, my trip... I'll tell you later. I'm beat. Those people up there don't give you a moment's rest..."

What I needed was peace and quiet. The dullest life possible.

"By the way, Bill and Leona called and they're coming up from Halifax..."

"What?"

Bill the poet. Another damned poet and drunk. Everyone I knew was a drunk, at least they were always drunk when I saw them. That's what happened, they turned up and drank like there was no tomorrow and then left — and probably didn't drink again until the next time.

But Macbride was the constant, a jolly fellow, taking on all comers, one shift after another. And they'd be all there to drink at my funeral. Another great party thanks to Macbride.

"I know you don't feel much like seeing anyone when you're like this..."

"No, I don't."

"But I didn't know when you'd be home. I thought you might stay another week. And I haven't seen Leona for a while." Without looking up she said, "You could have called."

I didn't bother trying to explain. She wouldn't understand. There just hadn't been the opportunity. I'd been very busy up there.

"Haven't they got anywhere else to go? Do they always have to come here?"

"We haven't seen them in six months. And you like them, don't you? You've always liked Bill."

"It's not that. It's just that I've seen enough people..."

The effort of carrying on this conversation was tearing me apart. I was shaking all over. I fumbled another beer open.

"It's just for one night."

I looked at her helplessly. Couldn't she tell I didn't have one more night in me?

"I'm sorry. Maybe you'll feel better later on. Why don't you go and sleep some more."

"I already slept."

"Anyway, it's only Bill and Leona... You won't have to put yourself out. We can have a quiet evening. I bought a nice ham for dinner and you and Bill can play darts or backgammon or something. You don't have to drink too much."

After all these years she could still say that.

"Couldn't you call and tell them to make it another time?"

"They've probably already left."

I was still pacing about the kitchen. I stopped and she looked up at me. The expression on my face must have got something across to her.

"Well, I can *try*. What will I tell them?"

"Anything. The truth, that I'm not feeling well. I picked up the flu. There's an epidemic in Montreal...

They're all going around with the flu up there... The Mongolian flu..."

She went into the other room and dialled and I waited and nothing happened. She came back looking apologetic.

"No luck. I'm sorry."

"Fuck!" Like everything else it was beyond my control. You want things one way and you get them the other. The same old story.

"What do we have to drink?"

"I went up this morning and got a couple of dozen beer and two bottles of red wine."

"We'll need more than that. Four people... and tomorrow's Sunday."

Eight beers later I climbed into the old half-ton, and with an open pint between my legs and a few on the seat beside me backed out of the yard, wheels spinning on the ice. It was a nerve-wracking drive, but being a man and very tough I couldn't ask Eva to go to town twice in one day. If she did she wouldn't get enough of a supply anyway. She didn't know how to gauge these things, and I made a practice of never telling her how much was enough. She wouldn't understand. Better just to turn up with it.

I drove thirty all the way, holding the wheel in a death grip. When I had to brake my foot shot out like I was having a fit. It was hard to control my separate parts. They wanted to fly off in all directions.

It took a couple of trips into the liquor store, and then I climbed into the cab and scanned the parking lot to see no one was looking, and then − as if checking in the glove compartment − bent down and got a slug from a quart of rum into me. There was no perceptible effect, but I needed it to prepare myself for the drive through town. Once out on the highway I could stop any time for a bracer.

I still felt like death warmed over.

§

The visitors came, stayed the night, and left. I wasn't a very good host. While everyone else ate, drank and was merry, I fasted, drank, and was morose. I drank as much as the rest of them put together but I couldn't get feeling good.

While they feasted at the dinner table I didn't even have a plate in front of me, just my wine glass. You don't have much of an appetite when you've got the Mongolian flu. Leona thought that was a pity. It was such a beautiful dinner. When the table was cleared away I had to play games with Bill. This was our usual practice whenever Bill and I got together, and the show had to go on. Table hockey, backgammon, poker dice, darts...

I was so inept it was pathetic. My coordination was all shot and so was my brain. I could hardly remember the rules of the games. It was bad enough but in the flush of his victories Bill couldn't resist crowing and sticking the needle in.

I came very close to telling him to fuck off and get the hell out of my house.

It was while we were throwing darts that I became disturbingly aware of something. There was no bathroom in the house; we had an outhouse for the warmer weather and a couple of plastic pails upstairs for the winter. But the simplest thing for a man to do was go outdoors and piss in a snowbank. And every so often Bill would set down his darts and do that.

But I didn't.

I suddenly realized I hadn't stepped outside since... Since when? We were drinking an awful lot of beer. Yet I hadn't left the house since I'd come back from town. I thought about it, tried to remember the last time I'd had a leak... It wasn't something you paid all that much attention to... Still, I knew I hadn't budged on the airplane, and I'd gone directly to bed when I got home, and had only gone out to drive to town... I must have put away gallons of beer...

For the past few days I'd had a severe ache in my lower back. I'd mentioned it to Eva earlier, quickly suggesting it must be from the high heels on my boots, to see if that sounded okay to her. "It could be," she'd said.

"Yes, that must be it."

It wasn't the only thing. I kept rubbing my eyes; the left eye especially was dry, sore, dim. And my insides, my bowels, there was a strange sensation down there, a hot and oddly horny feeling. I could feel it in my balls, all through my loins, and it felt unnatural; not entirely unpleasant, but unnatural, like something sickeningly sweet; like a part of me voluptuously burning away.

I gave up trying to remember when I'd had a piss. It would have been sometime in Montreal, but just when I'd never know.

I was afraid Bill was going to notice. The next time he came in from outdoors I made a point of saying, "That's not a bad idea. I'll be right back."

"I was beginning to wonder. You must be about ready to float away."

There was a fierce east wind blowing in from the bay. I stood with it whistling around my ears, staring down at the drifting snow, waiting. Nothing came. I tried to force it, contracting my belly muscles, straining until my ears popped. Not a drop. I was completely jammed up.

When I went back in Bill made a comment about pissing icicles and I laughed and picked up my beer.

I was scared. There had to be something not quite right when you couldn't piss.

It was no fun throwing darts. I couldn't get the board into focus, and when I threw the darts they went nowhere near where I aimed them. I'd never lost to Bill before and he had to keep rubbing it in, how he'd got my number now, making a clean sweep of every kind of game we played. His superiority of technique. Quality coming to the top.

It's the way we'd both have gone on normally, but I wasn't my normal self, and he couldn't seem to see it. It was as if he was maliciously tormenting me.

He was in a good mood, Bill. They all were, all three of them. The more they drank the happier they got. They kept saying things they thought were funny, and laughing themselves into hysterics. But they weren't funny. I didn't find them funny.

I got sick of it after a while. All I wanted to do was go to bed. So I did. I went and climbed into bed by myself. But I couldn't sleep.

We were only using two rooms for the winter, the kitchen and the living room where the bed was set up. With just a door between us I could hear all their ridiculous carrying on. It didn't matter to them if they kept me awake.

"Pipe down, will you!"

A hush. And then within minutes the voices rising. And pandemonium all over again.

Eventually they spun themselves out and came to bed. We had to sleep in close quarters, Bill and Leona wedged together on a small couch at the foot of the bed. Bill's stupid jokes and the sniggering and chortling went on until the last delayed explosion of laughter died out and they fell asleep.

They fell asleep. But I stayed awake... or semi-awake. I had strange dreams running through my head but I was still conscious. Burning hot one minute, freezing cold the next. Writhing, shuddering. I would seem to drift off and then – wham! – a vicious kick in the arse! Square in the pelvis. It happened several times. What was Eva trying to do? Enough was enough. I kicked her back – and a good one, too.

A yelp came out of her. "Why are you kicking me?"

"You're kicking *me*."

"I'm not."

She moved to the far side of the bed, her back to me. And it happened again. I couldn't catch her at it because it only happened when I lost consciousness.

A horrible night. When I wasn't being kicked I was getting up and puking. We'd brought the pails down from upstairs and again and again I lurched out to the kitchen and dropped to my knees and retched until I thought my guts were going to rip apart.

When morning came and the others got up I fully intended to stay in bed all day, maybe for the rest of my life. This was no mere question of a hangover. I was sick, really sick, like I'd never been sick before.

I hadn't been bedridden since I was a kid, but maybe a couple of days in bed was what I needed. Retire completely from the world. Eva was a nurse. She could take care of me.

I lasted until eleven-thirty and then I couldn't stick it any longer. I wasn't getting better fast enough. It wasn't the physical agony so much — it was my thoughts. I was feverishly restless, every thought a torment of remorse and self-hatred; they came at me in waves until finally I sprang from the bed and pulled on some clothes and staggered out to the kitchen.

The three faces turned towards me. I was ready with my statement. Screwing my mouth into what was meant for a wry grin, I said: "That doesn't seem to be working. I guess I'd better try the only cure I know."

I got a beer from the fridge.

I stayed out in the kitchen, shuffling from one corner to the other, paying no further attention to them. They knew by now I had some kind of genuine illness so appearances didn't matter. They'd all heard me vomiting in the night.

They let me be, talking among themselves. From time to time I sighed heavily, involuntarily, and took another swig of beer.

I had to be careful I didn't bump into something or fall over, the way my balance was off.

The windows were still frosted over. Through a triangular corner I could see fields of snow and the old gray shingled house across the river, and beyond that the black tree line.

Our guests left around one in the afternoon after having something to eat. I hadn't said a single word to them since my initial remark. They departed in a flurry of farewells, kissing and hugging and talking all at once while I maintained my patrol of the kitchen. I had to warn Bill off from giving me the traditional bear hug.

"If you do I'm a dead man. It'll finish me."

"Okay, old man. I'll just shake your paw. Can you handle that?"

The car starting, the chattering voices, the inevitable laughter. A blast of cold air and Eva was back in the kitchen. The sound of the car fading up the road.

"Is there anything I can do?"

"No."

"Do you think you could eat a little?"

"No."

I drank beer all day, only beer, and slowly, because I had to prepare myself to give up heavy drinking the next day, on Monday. It had reached that point. My mind was made up.

All through the day I kept waiting to piss. It was crazy, not being able to piss, because if anything made you piss it was beer.

The gnawing ache in my lower back wouldn't go away. In the end I couldn't avoid putting two and two together. That's where my kidneys were. The truth had to be faced. I was having a problem with my kidneys. How serious it was I didn't know, but it was probably not a laughing matter.

I'd been expecting *something*. I'd even said to myself one morning, bottle of rum in hand, that the only way I was ever going to break the cycle I was caught in was to get good and sick and have to stop, whether I liked it or not. And when that happened I could only hope I hadn't gone too far. Something bad but not *too* bad.

Well, here it was. If this wasn't sick the word had no meaning.

I made an effort to look at it positively. At least the crisis was reached at last, after hanging over me for many months. I could now apply myself to taking the necessary measures to recover.

Drinking wasn't fun any longer, anyway. The suffering far outweighed the few lighthearted moments I got from it. I almost never felt well. I'd become a human sponge, existing from one day to the next in a semicomatose state.

The idea was to get myself back into shape. Once I had my health back I'd never again fall into this kind of insanity.

For starters I wouldn't touch a drop tomorrow. I'd take a few days off and establish a sensible regime, and stick to it. No drinks before five-thirty in the evening. No hard liquor. A limit of three beers a day. And a glass of wine with dinner... A glass or two. But that was it. Absolutely.

Meanwhile it was still today, and since I was already underway I had to keep going. It wasn't something you could just cut off in the middle. The way to go about it was to start off fresh in the morning.

§

By nine that evening I was ready to collapse into an everlasting sleep. I hauled myself into bed. A thick bank of fog rolled over my mind. The next thing I knew I was hit by a tremendous shock, a bone-shaking jolt that lifted me a foot off the mattress – far worse than the kicks I'd accused Eva of giving me.

That's how my night began, possibly a worse night than the one before.

It wasn't only the electric shocks that awoke me – and these came on all through the night – but the nightmares. In particular, the black spectre lurking in the shadows, suddenly looming over the foot of the bed, cape outspread, descending on me as I cried out in terror...

It's a wonder I didn't have a heart attack. There was almost no space between the beats. Pounding like a rapid-fire sledgehammer in my chest.

Cringing, shaking, and then very suddenly, like a heavy curtain going down, sleep. And then wham! a thousand volts. Lifted like a rag doll, flung into the air.

And another thing. I began levitating, rising slowly off the bed, and softly subsiding.

Hot all over. Cold all over. Restless and agitated, tossing from side to side.

Eva had to get up and go sleep on the couch.

§

The following day, Monday, I didn't have a drink, not one, and it was the longest day of my life. I'd known years to pass faster than that day.

It wasn't just the pain of all types, but there was nothing I could do with myself to make the time go by. I couldn't read, I couldn't talk, I couldn't listen. I couldn't eat, I couldn't sleep. I couldn't sit still, not even for a minute.

All that was left was an endless pacing. Up and down the kitchen, and later, too sorry a being to be in the same room with Eva, with her health, her soundness, her blissfully happy life, I went upstairs to my summer study and walked the floor in my old army greatcoat. The cold didn't affect me. Cold just wasn't in the same league as the hell I was going through.

It was possible I'd have to go to the hospital — it might come to that. I dreaded the thought. I had a profound fear of hospitals and doctors. I didn't want to find out I had something seriously wrong with me. But I might have no choice.

Only how could I get there? One of the back tires on the truck was flat. I'd seen it earlier out the kitchen window. For no reason it had gone flat during the night. There was always something wrong with that truck.

Somehow I got myself outside and the truck door open and found the tire iron behind the seat. I was shaking so bad it was like picking up a red hot poker. I stared helplessly at the back wheel. I'd have quit right there if the farmer's son from up the road hadn't happened along. He was as big as a bear, Harold. He sized the situation up at once. A neighbour in distress. He came in the yard and took the wrench and loosened the rusted nuts with a few flicks of the wrist.

"They get on there pretty tight sometimes," he said.

I had no choice but to climb onto the back of the truck and throw the spare down to him. I'd have had to do that if it cost me my last breath.

He jacked the truck up and changed the tire. I saw him looking at me, eyes taking in my face then darting away. He was too polite to say anything, like ask me if I was dying or something. I was twitching and trembling and gasping.

"I'm not feeling too spry today... A touch of the flu, I think..."

He nodded vigorously. "Yes, the flu, oh yes, it's going around."

"Thanks for the hand."

"It's nothing. Don't mention it."

§

Though at the time the day seemed to last forever, I later had very little memory of it. I was able to recall changing the tire, and two other things I knew for sure: I hadn't had a drink, and I hadn't had a piss.

The night that followed was a repeat of the one before.

Tuesday came and despite having a full day without booze behind me I felt no better. In the years past I'd slowed down my drinking from time to time, and always after a day of near abstinence had felt vastly improved. But that had been some years ago. And I had an older body now, almost thirty-five. It stood to reason I couldn't recuperate quite so quickly.

In any case, I tried to convince myself I was coming around, since it was only logical, having put the bottle down. A little discomfort was natural. What I used to do at this stage was get back to work. There was nothing like work to lift the morale.

I decided to make a start on the story for Janet. I sat at my desk beside the bed and had Eva bring me a cup of coffee. I took a few sips and an uncontrollable shaking came over me. Coffee was a mistake. I'd forgotten that it was notoriously bad for the nerves. I didn't care much for the stuff anyway, could never understand what people saw in it.

It was all I could do to get a sheet of paper into the typewriter. I was jittering all over the place.

I couldn't get into it. My mind wasn't right. When I tried to get some words down I discovered I didn't know what the words meant, why one might be preferable to another.

And to make matters worse I couldn't type. I hit all the wrong keys.

It was too much of a strain. I got up from the chair and lurched into the wall. After all this sobriety I still hadn't got my balance back, the deck kept rolling from under me.

If I couldn't work I had to find something else to occupy myself with.

I went out to the kitchen and threw darts. I could throw darts for an hour or so. But I didn't last five minutes. I tried hard, I took careful aim. And the darts went straight, as if following my aim. But they landed in the wall a good six feet from the board.

For some reason this affected me more than anything else, or perhaps on top of everything else. I felt an immense surge of self-pity, so powerful I came close to bursting into tears. I really was in a bad way. Maybe, after all, I'd gone too far.

At five-thirty, on the dot, and being still alive, I began my sane new routine of moderate social drinking. I opened a beer.

I might have foregone it until a later day, but an unexpected pressure arose. In the afternoon a letter arrived from a Professor Chalmers at the University of Alberta inviting me to appear as a guest author at a writers' workshop for a couple of days — at a fee of $150 a day plus travel and expenses. Nothing like this had come my way before.

What had happened was, another writer had backed out for some reason, and on the recommendation of a drunken (albeit successful) poet we both knew I was being asked to take his place, which explained the short notice. The date was less than two weeks off. If I could confirm at once that I'd be available...

I read the letter with a sense of frustration and bitterness. It was like the plane with no food. Like Bill and Leona showing up for a party. Like the tire going flat. Like a bad joke. All the years when I was fit and ready to set off on any kind of junket they never asked me. They had to wait until now.

I had never been out west. I certainly wouldn't have paid my own money to go there, with Europe in the other direction; but still, a free trip, and a chance to add Alberta to my travels, to be able to say I'd been west of Ontario...

Not to mention the three hundred bucks. I didn't get money like that thrown my way every day.

And the exposure. A writer needed to get out and about, let the public know who he was. You had to promote yourself, it was practically an obligation in the trade. The quality of your writing didn't matter. It was the recognition factor that counted.

Also, I hated to let this professor down, the first one to throw me a bone. Already I was in his debt. And beyond that it might be a kind of feeler from the Academic Community, an opening for further opportunities of the sort. These people controlled most of what little money there was around. Readings, workshops, writer-in-residencies, grants.

I tried to imagine making the trip sober. Flying, meeting strangers, reading to an audience, handling questions, socializing...

The only thing I'd done sober in years was sit down in the morning and write; and in the past year I hadn't even done that.

There was no way around it. To accept the offer would be suicidal. One more bout with the bottle and I'd be dead. I might as well shoot myself, it would be a less painful end.

At 5:29 the pint of beer was on my desk, unopened, and my eyes were fixed on the second hand of my watch as it circled the final minute.

At 5:35 I was reconsidering the offer from Alberta. Less than half a pint of beer.... and all at once I was back in the game.

The rest period had worked. The beer had its flavour again. A mountain of despair lifted from my shoulders.... had already shifted before the cap was off the bottle.

I was only having one, it was true. Just the one today. That was the deal, otherwise I couldn't have allowed myself any.

I took my time finishing it. The soothing effect enabled me to do some rational thinking. I had to consider Eva's reaction to that letter, the fact it hadn't seemed to cause her any alarm. She'd merely said she'd like to go with me. She'd never been out west either.

It wasn't a bad idea. I couldn't always be thinking of myself, plotting to get away on my own and chase women. Life must get a little dull for her too, living out in the sticks.

And with her along to take care of me – being a trained nurse as she was – I'd be in good hands. She could do most of the talking, and see that I ate regularly, and got to bed on time...

My so-called career was involved. Where I stood now I wasn't exactly burning up the track. You had to expect a certain amount of pain and sacrifice. When it seemed you were at the bottom of your resources you just had to dig deeper.

Most likely I was babying myself, not nearly so sick as I thought. I didn't feel that awful bad at the moment.

I ran through it again. If I were to have only the occasional beer, when I desperately needed one – like before getting on the airplane – and during the flight – and before landing – and –

No! I'd have to be tougher than that on myself.

I called out to the kitchen: "What do you think? Should we go?"

"It would be nice. But it's up to you. If you think you'll feel well enough by then..."

"It's a couple of weeks from now. I'm just wondering if they'd pay your way."

"You could ask."

"If they won't then I'm definitely not going. I don't think we can afford it. Do you?"

She didn't reply.

"Of course there's the three hundred dollars I'll get. But I don't think that would cover your fare."

"Maybe they'd make up the difference."

"You think so?"

"You could call and find out."

It was hard to make up my mind. There were too many intangibles. I wasn't leaving without her, that much was certain; she'd have to be there to take care of me. The best course — all things considered — was to let the question of her fare decide the issue. It would then be out of my hands. They couldn't accuse me of giving a flat refusal.

Even if the professor balked I could always ask for another day or two to think it over.

How the hell could I know what I'd be like two weeks from now? I didn't have a crystal ball.

I picked up the phone. A sudden shadow of doom passed over me. Dylan Thomas... Brendan Behan... Walt Macbride... Except they wouldn't be writing biographies about me. I'd be buried among the Unknown Soldiers.

The phone rang and rang and nobody answered. I'd have to try again later. By now my pint of beer was finished. I put the empty in the box. One was all I could have, a deal was a deal. Relatively speaking I felt not too bad... I should be able to make it through the evening, and maybe have a second pint before going to bed. But enough for now. The words were going through my head as I took another bottle from the case under the bed and popped the cap, silently, so Eva wouldn't hear.

I shrugged, gave a little sigh.

It really was too much of a struggle. I reckoned I would just have to keep on drinking, for the time being. It was regrettable but what could I do? I'd tried. You couldn't accuse me of not putting up a fight. But a man has his limits.

I'd reached for that second pint like a robot, telling myself one thing and doing another.

Maybe it was a reality I just had to learn to live with. We were inseparable, me and booze. A genetic fact of life. Part of my destiny.

The thought comforted me. I finished the second pint, though it was nowhere as enjoyable as the first. The taste had gone funny, almost sickeningly bitter.

But I'd reached the decision I wasn't fighting this any longer. In my mind I'd returned to moderate drinking. That was Aristotle's motto, moderation, and it was going to be mine too. If anything was extreme it was total abstinence.

The thing to do now was sit down to a meal and a glass of wine.

I made a stab at eating, stuffing a couple of bites down my throat. And I had my glass of wine.

As soon as I left the table I returned to my desk out of sight of the kitchen and opened another beer. I took one drink and the effect was dramatic. A flash of heat lightning shot through my skull. My vision blurred and it felt as if a tube of hydrochloric acid had burst in my guts. I almost passed out. I set the bottle down and reeled towards the bed.

§

I stayed in bed until the next morning, though I didn't sleep. Different times I felt a force sucking me into a black unconsciousness, but it was too sudden and massive to be mere sleep. I fought back to the surface in terror. If I went down there I might never come back. Some instinct impelled me to resist, as though my life hinged on it.

So I kept awake, shaking and horrified, ripped by convulsions, levitating and plunging towards the abyss...

There was a loathsome smell about me, my breath, perhaps, or coming from my pores; an odour like the exhalations of a bloated corpse. It never left me while I was in bed.

My internal organs melted away, bowels, loins, testicles, turning into a steaming voluptuous broth...

§

In the early hours, with just the barest hint of light in the room, I had an experience that happened on and off for the next several days. I heard a radio playing. The first time it came from the kitchen, though there wasn't a radio out there, or anywhere else in the house for that matter. We didn't own one. The volume was low but I could make out that a man was speaking, being interviewed, responding to questions. I strained to hear the words. I recognized the voice — it was Brian Mulroney, one of the candidates for the leadership of the Conservative Party. I remembered they were having their leadership convention to replace Robert Stanfield. But what was Mulroney doing on the radio at that ungodly hour?

It wasn't a dream. I was absolutely wide awake. I sat up in bed, puzzled as to where the radio had come from. Had Bill and Leona left it behind? And why, if it had been left on overnight, hadn't I heard it before now?

I keyed up my ears to catch what was being said. It was like listening to a conversation through a wall — the voices audible and distinguishable, but only a few words and phrases I could make out. Mulroney was saying, "As I see the role of Prime Minister... Mr Trudeau... fitting the office to himself rather than himself to the office..." The woman doing the interview spoke too low for me to pick up her questions. Not that I cared, I had little or no interest in politics... It was the radio itself that interested me. How had it got there? Why had it suddenly started playing? Eva was asleep on the couch, hadn't moved all night, so she couldn't have turned it on.

I was as lucid as I'd ever been, fully alert to my surroundings. I pinched myself on the arm. There was no question I was awake.

I had to look at this calmly. I was aware such phenomena as hallucinations occur — but this couldn't be an hallucination. I distinctly *heard* the radio, as real as I heard the wind blowing outside. I rapped on the wall. That was a real sound. I listened to the radio.

That was real, too. External noise, not something in my head. It wasn't even in the same room.

Nor did I believe I'd flipped my lid. I was perfectly sensible of who I was and where I was and what I was doing here. And I was trying to examine the situation with cold logic.

I got up and went out to the kitchen to look for the radio. It seemed to be in the stove. In the oven, probably. But it wasn't, the oven was empty. Now I could hear it coming from the direction of the wood box. Then it stopped.

I was no sooner back in bed when it started again. I woke Eva.

"Do you hear that radio?"

"What radio?"

"Listen."

She listened carefully, and shook her head.

"You can't hear it?"

"No. "

Something funny was going on...

I had plenty of time to think about it, because over the next few days and nights I heard not only the radio in the kitchen but others in the walls, the floor, the ceiling, under the bed. One carried nothing but Morse Code. Another played endless rock & roll. A third had a ham radio frequency, with call letters from all over the world, staticky "Blah-blah-blah... Over... Blah-blah-blah... Over..." I picked up some college basketball scores from a station in Tennessee.

At times all the radios were going at once, but there was one station – the one I heard most often – which drowned out the others when it came on, and it always played the same song over and over.

Balls to your partner,
Arse against the wall,
If you don't get fucked on Saturday night
You'll never get fucked at all!

I was sure I'd never heard this song before, or if I had it was nowhere in my memory. The singer was a woman with a refined English accent, not unlike the Queen's — in fact that's who it sounded like — and she ran through hundreds of verses. It was an extremely lively performance. She was backed by a razzmatazz band and had a younger girl singing counterpoint, repeating over and over: "*Get your leather! Get your leather! Get your leather!*" There'd be a slue of verses, then sudden silence, broken by a man's voice: "*One! Two! Three! Four!*" The girl coming in, "*Get your leather! Get your leather! Get your leather!*" and the band jumping and the Queen belting out the chorus, "*Balls to your partner, Arse against the wall!...*"

The fillings in my teeth — I'd read about people whose fillings picked up radio waves. But in that case the sounds ought to be coming from inside my mouth, and they weren't...

The truth, when it finally dawned, went through me like a wintry chill.

The most plausible explanation — indeed the only possible explanation — was that the Air Force was beaming radio signals into the house in order to drive me insane.

They would have that kind of sophisticated technology today. And they had the motive... It all came to me in a flash. The letters I'd written, letters-to-the-editor about their fighter planes flying over my roof and their approach to the Base outside Bannonbridge... I created quite a public controversy, and to my surprise they actually altered their flight course to avoid not just my house but the entire area.

But they wouldn't forget something like that. I'd heard of the mutterings at the Base. An airman I'd met in the tavern had warned me... "Some of the guys in the mess were talking about accidents people can have... They consider you Public Enemy Number One. Myself I don't give a shit, I'm getting out next month anyway..."

I'd ridiculed the Canadian Forces as a kind of government make-work program. It was the way I did things. They'd disturbed my peace so I had to bludgeon them to death.

I'd been pretty naive to think they wouldn't retaliate.

Somehow they'd isolated a frequency peculiar to my brain, which explained why Eva wasn't affected...

I could feel a panic coming over me.

There was no way of fighting something like this. And no one would believe me if I tried to tell them. They'd say I was mad...

"Eva!" A cry of desperation. I couldn't handle it alone. She came in from the kitchen and held my hand and listened to me.

She was the greatest nurse in the world. Calm and gentle and understanding.

She admitted it was possible but most unlikely. In her opinion I was suffering from severe alcohol withdrawal. In other words, the DT's. I was merely hallucinating.

"But I'm not seeing things."

"They're called auditory hallucinations."

"Really?"

Of course! It had to be that. I'd even thought of it myself. I grabbed onto her diagnosis like a drowning man. All I'd needed was an authoritative opinion, and she was a medical person, she knew what she was talking about.

A weight lifted off me. I wasn't in the power of an evil force. I wasn't being driven mad.

I settled back and listened to the music. It wasn't bad entertainment in its way. It turned out to be a welcome distraction, all things considered. In that sea of agony it was the only refuge I had.

§

On Wednesday I sat down at the typewriter and with a spastic forefinger punched out a brief note to Professor Chalmers. I explained that I had to decline his offer because the date conflicted with a deadline I had to meet on an important magazine assignment. It wasn't the whole truth, but it was enough.

I didn't know how I was ever going to write that story for Janet. There were many black clouds in my sky and that was one of them. I'd been a fool to ever take it on in the first place. I'd been drunk, of course, drunk and cocksure. No problem.

The two-sentence letter I'd just written had taken half an hour and strung my nerves to the snapping point. At the end I was gasping for breath.

I was going to be found out, that's what was going to happen.

§

In the night I remembered something, a passage I'd read in William Burroughs's book *Junkie*. It had to do with a Mexican woman who'd done two weeks of heavy beer drinking and then died. I couldn't remember what she'd died of – cirrhosis? That seemed to be what got you in the end. But it was the mention of cat piss, the woman complaining about smelling cat piss before she died. Burroughs himself had had the same sensation after some particularly serious drinking.

It was the smell I had in my nostrils now, pungent and more powerful than the other nauseating odours that enveloped me. I thought at first the cat had done some spraying. But he wasn't around, El Gato, he was off on one of his periodic expeditions.

Still, the scent might have lingered behind. Though I hadn't noticed it before...

In the morning I went upstairs to my study and found what I was looking for in the book. The disease wasn't cirrhosis but uremia, or in Burroughs's case, incipient uremia, the early stages.

I then checked one of Eva's medical books. It didn't have much on the subject, but there was a long list of symptoms, and I had every one of them.

I went downstairs again. It took me a while to summon the courage to speak, to find the right words, and to control my voice. It had to be done offhandedly as befitted a subject that was of no great importance.

"You're some nurse, you are."

"What do you mean?"

"You should have been able to tell what's wrong with me."

"Why? What do you think it is?"

"It's called uremia."

"*Uremia*?" She looked startled. "What makes you think that?"

"I looked in one of your nursing books."

"Oh, it couldn't be. That's a serious illness."

"Well, for one thing I can't piss."

"You can't?"

She asked me to get the book, and I did, and she said, "Not that one, there's a better one."

I went back upstairs and got the other book, and she began reading, with me reading over her shoulder. Together we ran down the symptoms. It was the same, I had them all. And as my eye moved down the page it fell on this statement: *"Uremia is always fatal."*

My heart sank to the pit of my stomach. Cold fingers wrapped around it. My vision blurred, my head went into a spin. For a minute I thought I was going to pass out.

I had never believed, not actually believed, that I was that bad off – not me.

I was going to *die*?

I turned away from Eva and put on my coat and went outside. I walked down by the river. A harsh wind was blowing, lifting the fine snow off the fields and swirling it across the ice. I stood for a long time by the river. I didn't want to go back to the house, to have to face Eva, with us both knowing. She hadn't known what to say. She hadn't even been able to look up while I got my coat on and went out the door. It was as if in one decisive moment we'd been cast into different regions, different dimensions: she with the living, me with the dead.

Thirty-four years of age and finished. Done for. All over.

I was aware of an awful sense of desolation, a kind of desperate loneliness. I was going to die. The odd man out, as I'd so often felt myself – though never like this.

The tears welled up in my chest. I hurried away from the river bank, bolted before my feelings annihilated me.

I had to return to the house. There was no comfort there, nothing she could offer me, but I couldn't keep by myself...

She was sitting by the stove with the medical book still in her lap. Without a word I took to pacing the floor. I had to – it was one of the symptoms, extreme restlessness. I avoided her eyes which I knew would be pitying me.

§

She leafed through the book, and after a while she said:

"It's probably not uremia."

I stopped in my tracks. "What?"

"It could be something else."

A faint stirring of hope.

"Symptoms can be misleading... There are other possibilities..."

"Like what?"

"Well... I don't like to say this..."

"Go on."

"It could be... well, syphilis, for example."

"*Syphilis*?"

I stared at her in disbelief. I started pacing the floor again. Oh, I wasn't stupid, I knew what was coming.

"Syphilis isn't so bad. It can be treated."

"I know that."

Pause.

"Well?"

"Well what?"

"I'm not trying to put you on the spot. But if it *is* syphilis... Apart from anything else, it's a contagious disease, and I think I have the right to know..."

"To know what?"

"Did you sleep with someone in Montreal?"

I didn't answer.

"I'm only asking as a nurse. Would you rather it was uremia?"

"No. "

"You can tell me. I'm not going to be mad at you."

What could I do? There was no way I could slip out of this one. I was cornered like a rat.

Everything was going against me anyway.

"All right. Yes!"

"I knew it."

There it was, the note of triumph in her voice.

"What do you mean, you knew it."

"I could *smell* it off you." She almost snorted when she said it.

"Oh, come on." I turned away.

"You might at least have taken a shower before you came home."

"It was a couple of nights before... You couldn't have still..."

It wasn't enough I had to die, but to be humiliated in my last hours. Pettiness and degradation! It would be nicer if I showered before dying, it's true. I hadn't bothered, but... In those early mornings, shaking and sweating and gasping for breath — I could no more have showered than eaten a live chicken. It was thoughtless, of course...

"Who was she?"

She wasn't going to let up.

"Does it matter?"

"It matters a lot. I'd like to know what sort of woman she was."

"It wasn't a whore, if that's what you're worried about."

"That could be a matter of opinion."

I saw my reflection in the kitchen mirror. It would be hard to imagine a more abject figure. Bedraggled beard and hair, sad bleary eyes, an expression of absolute misery.

"Well?"

"All right." It felt like a betrayal, but I had to come out with it. "It was Janet."

She nodded. "I knew it would be her. I could have told you that before you ever left for Montreal."

"Then why did you ask?"

"I wanted to be sure."

"I see. So... what now?"

"Oh, I don't think you have anything to worry about. I'm sure she practices her promiscuity in the right circles."

"You mean I'm not likely to have... got anything."

"I wouldn't think so."

"That's wonderful. So all I've got is uremia. Instead of a curable disease I've got the fatal one. Nothing to worry about."

"I didn't mean it that way."

"No."

I stood before her like a whipped dog. There was no mercy in her. I thought, she must have bided her time for years, looking for this moment, to finally have me in her power. I awaited the recriminations. I was wobbled, staggered, but still conscious, still on my feet.

But nothing came. When she spoke again it was without rancour.

"I just wanted to know. I'm not angry with you. Really."

And some time later:

"Is it bothering you, what you told me?"

"I guess so."

Among other things.

"Never mind. I'm not going to mention it again. You can forget about it. Okay?"

I nodded. "Sure."

§

We took a walk up to see our friend Tommy Waggoner. We both needed to get out of the house, and besides, there was something I wanted to ask Tommy. He lived about a quarter mile up the road in a little smelt shanty. We went very slowly, Eva holding my arm.

Being out in the air helped. The bushes along the road were coated with ice, the sun glittering on the crystal branches. It was a beautiful day to look at and to breathe in. I had at least an intimation of what it was like to be alive, something in the mind, though I didn't feel it.

Tommy saw us coming through the gaping cracks in the half-doors, and before we could knock he hollered out: "Come in! Come in!"

He was a man of sixty and of huge size, about six-four and 250 pounds.

"Sit down! Make yourselves at home. I was wondering when you'd be up again. How are yez today?"

"Walt's not feeling too well," said Eva. "He's pretty sick."

"Sick, eh? That's too bad. Sit down, sit down." We were already seated, Eva on the only chair, me on the lower of the bunk beds beside him. "Have a beer."

"No thanks, Tommy."

"No?" He looked at me with surprise.

"He's sick," said Eva.

"Oh, I know he is. I thought so. I could tell by the look of him. You'd better have a beer."

I shook my head. "No."

"You sure?"

"I'll have one," said Eva. He opened her a pint from the case of Schooner at his feet and said, "Here you are, my little woman." There was just enough room for the three of us in his shack. It was only about eight feet square and had double bunks against the back wall and a small table and chair and a pot-bellied stove. The stove was crackling, and though you could see the snow outside through the cracks in the door it was stifling hot inside.

"Can I open the door some?"

"Go ahead. Go right ahead! You're warm, are you? I like to keep a good fire going. I was going to ask if you were warm enough. No, no, go ahead, open the door."

They were like stable doors, and I pushed the upper half open a bit. I didn't say anything for a while. They were both talkers, the two of them, and it was easy enough to sit back and let them gab away. Often that's all I did anyway.

There was something on my mind but I didn't like to give myself away.

More than once I opened my mouth and shut it. Then I began to get impatient. With these two there were no lulls.

Finally I broke in on Eva and said matter-of-factly:

"Tommy, by the way, do you still have your sore back?"

"Eh? What's that?"

"Didn't your back used to bother you? I remember you saying something..."

"Oh yes. It was good for a few years but it's acting up again. I don't know why, I don't do no lifting. But it's not as bad as a few years ago."

"Were you drinking much then?"

"Drinking? I guess I was drinking! I was working on road construction with Carvossa and Ashley's John and we were drunk on rum every day. The whole summer, for three months. I didn't fish that year 'cause I sold the boat I had. I was drinking two quarts of rum a day." He shook his head. "Oh, I was drinking all right!"

"And your back got sore?"

"Yes, and not just the back. My feet swoll up something awful and one day I couldn't get my boots off. I could hardly walk. It was so bad I went to see the doctor. I went up to see Dr. Moore in town and he had to cut my boots off with a knife." He grinned, looking at us from under gray bushy eyebrows. "When he got my boots off he looked at my feet and said, 'When was the last time you had a bath?' That's what he said. *'When was the last time you had a bath, sir?'* I told him, 'Oh, about two or three years ago.' He said, 'I believe it.' I'd been tramping around that dusty road all summer. I wasn't really working — I was a flagman, they had me there to wave the traffic through, and I never did that half the time. I was too busy drinking. Oh, I couldn't take a bath, I didn't have time. I didn't have a bathtub anyway. Dr. Moore looks at my feet and he says, 'So you're an alcoholic.' 'Me?' I says. 'Oh no,' I says, 'I'm no alcoholic, I work every day. I *work* every day, how could I be an alcoholic?' Oh, we did some terrible drinking that summer. He told me, he said, cut out the drinking and you'll get better. And he give me some pills and sent me home. I didn't take the pills, I don't know where they went. Carvossa's dog probably ate them. But I stopped drinking for a while. Two quarts of rum a day! I don't think I've been the same since. I think that's what ruined me. There's no need of that."

He coughed, a deep slushy cough like a bad cold breaking up. He couldn't get rid of it though he hadn't smoked in five years. His legs were wracked with arthritis, unsteady and halting when he walked. His stomach was bloated the size of a medicine ball. Eva had told me this last would be from liver trouble. And his sore lower back... That would be where his kidneys were...

Talking about ailments he told us of an operation he'd had for a hernia a few years before. It was when he was working in the woods in winter, after the fishing season was over. He used to tie the hernia in with an old piece of shirt, but sometimes it would work free and fall out, and the pain would knock him flat on his back. As time went on the hernia kept growing. "It was big, oh my! I guess it was. It was big as your head." He finally went to the hospital for an operation. Because of his asthma they couldn't put him to sleep and instead injected him with a local anesthetic. He had to lie on the operating table awake and watch the doctor cut him open and perform the operation.

"Were you scared?" said Eva.

"Scared? My little woman. I was scared I was going to thaw out." The big grin again, showing rugged yellow teeth. "I say, I was scared *I'd thaw out* before he got me sewed up again."

They let him out of hospital the next day and he took a taxi downriver. There'd been a storm the night before, and he found the door of his shanty blown open with three feet of snow drifted inside.

Some pints of beer he'd left lying around had frozen and burst and there was broken glass everywhere. Still stiff and hobbled from the operation he shoveled the shack out, and then rooted around in the snow for some wood to get a fire going. Everything was soaked from the snow as it melted.

He chuckled as he related this, enjoying the story, like it was all a joke.

Every month he bought a lottery ticket. That was his big dream, to win the lottery. He liked to talk about what he'd do with the millions if he won. How much he'd give to this one, how much to the other.

He had a generous heart. It was from a small woodlot he owned that I cut our wood for the winter every fall. Not to mention all the help he'd given me with my boat. And not once had I been able to make him take a penny.

The whole long winter he sat in that squalid shack with nothing to do but keep the fire going. I used to think, no wonder he drinks so much. I would too, in his place.

I remember him saying, "I had a case of beer the other night, only one case, and my little man I thought I was going to die, I was that sick. I was up the whole night puking. Blood pouring out of my nose... I didn't think I'd see the morning. I don't go to church but I said my prayers that night. Oh my, I guess I did."

I knew he wasn't exaggerating, because he wasn't in the habit of complaining. When he told me this he was standing on the steps of the liquor store about to go in. "But, you know, a man *might as well* be dead if he can't enjoy life some of the time. I say, he *might as well* be dead."

It was a tonic to see him, the way he could laugh and make a good story of his hardships. He'd been through a hell of a lot more than me, and here he was, still kicking. Nothing was going to make him knuckle under.

It made me ashamed of myself. I wasn't the only one with a sore back, but who was doing all the moaning and whining?

It was time I pulled up my socks and made a real effort at getting back to health.

§

I started as soon as we got home.

"I think I'll have something to eat," I said to Eva.

I gave it a good shot, stuffing a cracker and a few spoonfuls of soup into me. It was about as appetizing as a bowl of mud. But I kept it down.

And then I began shaking worse than ever.

"Why don't we have a game of cards," I said. A convalescent has to do something to keep his mind occupied.

Eva got the cards and we started a game of Crazy Eights, a simple game that wouldn't put too much strain on me.

We were not very far into the game when suddenly I set the cards down on the table.

Eva looked at me in alarm. "What's wrong?"

I was sniffing the air.

"What is it?"

"Oh God... Eva..." I could feel myself unravelling, as if the last threadbare string holding me together had given way.

The cat had still not returned and yet the smell of cat piss was unmistakable. It had to be coming from me.

I got to my feet and stumbled into the bed, afraid I was going to pass out before I got there. My brain was hot. Everything in front of me looked blurred.

She came and sat on the bed beside me and put her hand on my forehead, stroked my hair.

"What is it?"

"That smell...

"What smell?"

I told her about what I'd read in the Burroughs book. It was impossible to deceive myself any longer.

"It must have been the cat," she said. "He must have sprayed in the kitchen before he left."

"No, it's me. The smell wasn't there before. You didn't notice it."

"But I'm used to it. You know what the cat's like."

"It's me."

"I've been around hospitals enough to know the smell you mean. It's not the same."

I didn't believe her. She was just trying to soothe me. I sniffed at my wrists. I couldn't be sure. I had her smell my skin.

"It's my breath," I said

"Your breath is all right."

I knew she was lying. She saw the terror I was in, she'd say anything at all to comfort me. I couldn't forget the vapours rising from my pillow at night. My breath was ghastly.

How could I even pretend to fool myself, when after all this time I still couldn't have a piss. You didn't need to be a doctor to know you weren't supposed to keep all that piss inside you. My system was getting poisoned.

"Would you leave me alone for a while."

There was nothing she could do. I could see the helplessness in her eyes. It was no consolation to have her sit sadly beside me and watch me die.

"Don't you think you should go to the hospital?"

I shook my head. What would be the use? Their own medical books admitted my disease was fatal. There were no exceptions. At best I'd end up chained to a dialysis machine until it caught up and finished me.

Left alone what I did was start praying. It had been a long time since I'd thought about God. I'd pretty well chucked him out of my life in the same box with the Catholic Church. What I'd done, in fact, was set him aside for reconsideration in my old age when there was nothing else of interest to do. I didn't disbelieve in him. It was mainly that he didn't fit in with my ideas of life, what with all his rules and restrictions and everything.

Now all of a sudden I'd arrived at my old age, in a manner of speaking. My declining hours. I was in a real bind and there was no human power going to come to my rescue. It was my last resort.

So I prayed. What I said I'm not sure, not exactly, but it was along the lines of: "G o d I k n o w what it looks like I'm only doing this talking to you because I'm scared shitless I admit it I'm sorry! I haven't been a very good guy but I always believed in you it's not much I know but I'll do better I'll try I'll really try and change I'll if it's what you want I'll give it up I'll give up drinking for good I won't drink anymore if you save me from this I'll never touch another drop please help me I'm not ready to die just one more chance..."

§

I kept an empty jam jar by the bed, just in case, and that night in the dark the tiniest trickle came. In the morning I examined the jar and found about a thimbleful of murky orange fluid. I saved it and when I went again that afternoon I used a separate bottle and made a comparison. A little more than a thimbleful, and still a deep cloudy orange, but a shade less so. What went into a third bottle that evening might have filled a shot glass.

Friday night it happened. I awoke in the dark and got down on my knees and heard the water pouring into the bottle. It was like hearing angels sing.

Friday afternoon Eva heated the copper boiler full of water on the stove and filled the huge zinc washtub, and in the middle of the kitchen floor I had a bath. She said it would make me feel better, and otherwise wouldn't do any harm. I was too feeble to actually bathe myself so she had to do it for me.

I felt like a child being bathed by his mother. It felt good.

Sitting cross-legged I observed that the soles of my feet were completely covered with the dead white skin of large deflated blisters.

I had to laugh at how filthy I was.

"It's not funny!" said Eva. But her spirits were lifting too. It was as if a great black cloud had passed from over the house and the sun was shining again.

Once on the road to recovery my progress was remarkable. It was as though the only question had been whether I would live or die, and since I was to live then the sickness was no longer required. By Monday I was eating, washing, brushing my teeth and hair, and my beard was trimmed. The shakes left and within a week I'd completed the story for Janet.

As the days passed it was like emerging from a prolonged state of semiconsciousness, as if for years I'd been heavily sedated with drugs. I started eating breakfast in the morning, something I hadn't done since my teens: bacon, eggs, toast, hot chocolate... I'd forgotten how delicious food could be. I was able to remember the events of the day before, all of them, and not just in surreal snatches, confused with scenes from dreams. I could read and watch television without nodding off. My senses revived, I smelled the fresh air, the ice, the snow; and my vision improved, and my strength. I had vastly more energy and stamina. I could do small tasks without cursing and throwing objects. I *looked* better, my skin, eyes, the set of my mouth – I'd dropped years from my appearance. I looked alive for a change. I had never realized how much I'd been depriving myself by being pissed all the time.

§

Three months later I decided to have a drink. I knew it was a chancy business, but if you'd asked me why, I'd have said that death by drinking was perhaps not as bad as death by boredom. Living isolated in the country with nothing to do but read and watch television and throw darts finally got the best of me.

The early sense of well-being I'd experienced lasted only a few weeks. Good physical health is all well and fine, but once the novelty wears off what are you left with? The reality of my situation hit me. I was condemned to a life without fun. No more excitement, no more songs, no parties, no girls, no travel. None of these were possible without booze, not for me.

As a drinker I was a free spirit. As a teetotaller the picture was quite different: sombre, taciturn, timid, irritable, a bore to myself and others.

Stuck out in the woods as we were we had few visitors, but when anyone happened along I saw what a hopeless case I was. I didn't know how to relax. I had no spontaneity, no conversation. Eva had it all, and while she sipped her few beers and chatted and laughed I felt like a useless piece of furniture. People put a strain on me, and I knew if I could just have a *drink*..

The real me was bottled up and the cap was on the bottle. What was left was a nervous bundle of inhibitions.

I stopped talking to Eva. I don't know why, but I couldn't let her near me. I had an uneasy sense that my value as a person was diminishing daily. I became testy, snapping at her over trifles. I resented any kind of good mood she was in.

I couldn't get an erection for close to a month after sobering up. When it came back I ought to have been all right, except I had no self-confidence. I couldn't initiate anything. I was afraid she'd reject me. She seemed a total stranger, somebody who just happened to inhabit the same house.

I went into a depression I couldn't shake. My writing provided no relief, because I couldn't write; there seemed no point to it. All my vitality seeped away. I dragged myself around in a kind of emotional No Man's Land. It was as if my body had recovered but not my spirit. It was either dead or the next thing to it.

It appeared I was going to have to live out my days like a retired old man. Yet I wasn't very old, I might have a good many years left. A long life of reading, watching television, throwing darts. And not talking to anyone. No sex. No songs. No travel. No joy. A life that stretched before me like an endless desert.

One afternoon I drove to town for some groceries, and when it came time to return I didn't want to. I simply couldn't face another day exactly like the last. If I could have just one little pint of beer...

I hadn't forgotten the agony I'd gone through in January, but the impression had faded somewhat around the edges.

In the back of my mind I'd been considering for the past week whether or not one beer would kill me...

In retrospect I can see that once considered the deed was as good as done. It was only a question of time.

I felt my pulse quicken. It was almost sexual, the anticipation. The lure of the forbidden, the excitement of succumbing to temptation. I was firm, however, about having just the one. As I drove to my father's apartment in town my conscience kept saying, "You know you shouldn't do this," and another voice said, "Yes, you're right." Meanwhile I stepped on the gas to beat a red light. I got a beer from the fridge and drove down the shore road and parked looking out over the river. It was a beautiful fresh spring day. The ice had gone out and the water was a deep cold blue. The sun was shining. I had the beer in one hand and the opener in the other.

"I suppose this *is* a mistake... After all those vows I made..." And then I thought of the house in Rum River and it was more than I had in me to turn back now. "It's only an experiment," I told myself. "There's only one way to find out."

It was delicious. I savoured each small mouthful, and it was all there again, the sense of wholeness, the light streaming back into life, the glorious promises of the future... The fusing of dreams and reality... And all with just one pint of beer.

I wasn't seriously tempted to have another. I knew what I was doing. I drove leisurely home and there was no appreciable let-down as the effect wore off. The change in routine alone was a tonic. It was the first taste of excitement I'd had in several months.

And I felt reassured. For wasn't it a well-known fact that an alcoholic couldn't stop after one drink? A real alcoholic?

The next few days, being cautious, I stuck to fruit juices and soda pop, but the day after that I had another beer. And a few days later I had two. One, two, what was the difference? I had the situation in hand.

And then I ran into a girl I hadn't seen in years, not since university. I had harboured her among my fantasies over the years but I'd never expected to see her again. She'd returned home from Toronto.

And I *felt* something. A real emotion. It was fear, but having been in a zombie state for some time I welcomed the sensation. It was the pinch I needed to prove I was alive.

I was worried about the kind of impression I'd make, that's what it was. Would I be able to talk to her without a snifter or two under the belt?

I actually didn't run into her directly. Someone told me she was in town.

I had a beer first and gave her a call and invited her out to a tavern in Clifton. The tavern was as good a place as any to take a girl and talk over old times. Her name was Elena, a stunning blonde with a gorgeous figure – as I remembered.

In the tavern her big eyes looked into mine, and she told me about Jesus Christ and the surrender of one's life to God and the solace she'd found living among hermits. She had changed quite a lot, and in more ways than one. That breathtaking figure – What had happened to it? She was almost emaciated. And those great staring eyes...

Right away I was uneasy. I had hoped for something else. I began to think that maybe she was insane. I ordered another beer, my third of the day. I couldn't stop myself even though it was one over the limit. As I drank my thoughts grew more confused. I tried to talk about my soul and such things but nothing came out right, it was as if I'd forgotten how to express myself. Stumbling, groping for words, not knowing what to make of those eyes, trying to stare back at her. I came very close to ordering a fourth beer. I would have had she joined me but she said no.

The beer didn't taste so great anyway.

I drove her home and immediately sank into a despondency that lasted the rest of the day. All I could think of was death.

It was often in my thoughts, death. When Eva happened to remark that so-and-so had got cancer it was like an icy hand clutched my spleen. Cancer. Death. The mention of any fatal illness. Whatever it was it was going to get me too. The fears of that horrible week in winter came back. It was Death himself on my track, no matter what shape he might take.

After my experiment with drinking in taverns with evangelistic women – something to be avoided in the future – I stayed dry for a few days, and then went back to having one or two ales again, off and on.

Eva knew nothing about it. There was a chance she wouldn't understand so I refrained from telling her, for the time being.

In June (if you can fathom this) Janet phoned. Eva took the call and gave me a look as she passed the phone.

Janet had another story assignment for me. She said she was going to be taking a week's holiday in Prince Edward Island, and could I go over at the same time and do a piece on some fishermen? In other words, a nice opportunity to combine business with pleasure.

Eva hovered a minute by the door, then went back to her book in the kitchen.

I had no choice but to refuse. I told her Eva knew about us. It was true, and it carried some weight, but it wasn't the main reason; I could have got around it; but to travel and do interviews, and entertain a woman... Nobody could do those things sober, or even half-sober, or a quarter sober.

"How did she find out?" said Janet.

"Oh, you know," I said, keeping my voice down.

"You told her?"

"I guess so."

"Big mouth."

A thousand bucks payment and a week at the beach with an attractive woman, both out the window. It gave me something to think about on the subject of the rewards of sobriety.

In July two artist friends from Newfoundland showed up and stayed the night, on their way home after delivering some sculptures to Ontario. They were packing a gallon of wine and a quart of rum and a couple of cases of beer, and with everything there right under my nose I had to tell Eva I could drink okay now, socially, in moderation. I said I'd been having a drop now and then in town and everything was in order.

Her eyebrows rose, but she just said, "Oh?" And a little later she said, "I don't see why you can't, really. All you have to do is drink sensibly."

By now she'd probably had her fill of my sober personality.

"That's what I mean," I said. "I've learned my lesson."

To my friends Perry and Andrew I explained I was more or less on the wagon and would only be having a glass or so. And then I proceeded to drink eight or ten, or maybe twelve, I don't know how many; not to mention getting into the wine and rum. It was that kind of evening, I got caught up in the festive mood and my normal restraint went out the window.

Next morning I felt less than ideal, somewhat on the queasy side, but I suffered through it, with the help of a couple of pints of Schooner in the mid-afternoon.

The important thing was, though, upon subsequent reflection – the lesson I'd learned, you might say – was that I could get lit and it wouldn't necessarily kill me.

By fall I was at it every day, but holding the line at half a dozen pints, special occasions excepted. And then one day for some reason my kidneys ached. I heard the heavy gong of doom. The old terrors returned with a rush.

I put in a week of fearful and tedious abstinence before something came to mind. A biography of Ernest Hemingway I'd read. His kidneys had gone bad from drinking and his doctor had taken him off beer altogether, but... he'd allowed him a daily shot of whisky.

Well, that must be it! My problem was beer. So I tried a glass of rum and it worked just fine. Then the following afternoon I had two, and before long I was drinking a pint a day and heading towards a quart. That brought on a new experience. I was upstairs one day, out of sight of Eva, and having a guzzle of rum, when I began to feel myself coming apart at the seams. A huge sob rose to my throat. I thought I was going to collapse on the floor in tears. The strength drained clean out of me. It was as if I'd suddenly found myself hanging by my fingertips from a twenty-storey building and was losing my grip.

That's what it was. I was losing my grip. I was on the verge of a breakdown, a total emotional collapse. It was a horrifying sensation.

What *happened* when you broke down? If you let go... what then? A sudden snap? Raving, hysterical? I had a picture of Eva finding me on the floor like a lump of quivering jelly.

They'd lock me away for sure, that's what. Like Angela. In a panic I hung on for dear life.

I could expect no sympathy from Eva. She'd know the truth, what a helpless, hopeless mess I really was. She'd have the upper hand at last. The game would be up for me...

Shock treatments and experimental drugs. I'd never see the light of day again.

It was a desperate situation. I took deep breaths, wiped the cold sweat from my forehead. By sheer will − by the last ounce of it I had − I pulled myself back from the edge.

The experience left me shaken, but I'd learned something, a lesson of vital importance. It wasn't only death I had to fear but captivity. I had to be strong. It was simple as that. The weak went under, the strong survived. I must never give myself away.

§

I didn't touch another drop for about three weeks. At the end of that time, my fears having settled, it occurred to me that perhaps I could get away with drinking only wine. Beer and hard liquor were proven enemies... but wine after all was a civilized drink. If millions of Europeans could exist on a daily diet of it, why couldn't I have a casual glass or two?

It was the same story all over again. A little wine at first, then more, and then too much. Finally I decided what I really needed was a change of scenery. These all too familiar surroundings were driving me to drink. So in November I took a trip to Newfoundland. I was there a week and was roaring drunk the entire time, swilling down everything I could get my hands on. I had a hell of a spree, singing, partying, running the roads, and in the mornings drinking first thing out of bed to stave off the reckoning. It caught up with me of course. I got deathly sick and very scared. I knew I had to get home before I died, that one more day might do it. My kidneys hadn't failed — but could they hold out much longer? I made it back and in a couple of days tailed off the stuff, and quit again for good.

§

December 3, 1976. Eva has suggested AA and perhaps it's the sensible thing to do. But I've got a good reason for not going: I don't want to. Not yet anyway. I may be wrong but I see something like AA as the end of the line and the end of life. No booze, no life. Sit around with a bunch of over-the-hill alkies talking about the good old days, gone forever. They have a club house so I suppose I could take up throwing darts again. Wonderful.

I've still got a kick or two left in me.

A man likes to hang onto a little pride if he can. Crawling into AA like a drunken bum... What would they think? I know the way people think. If it's not disapproval it's disappointment. The look that comes over their faces... Ah, Macbride, we expected better of you. We thought you'd amount to something. And now look at you! *You miserable clump of shit.*

And what is there to life, while we're on the subject?

If you're too depressed to work, and too inept to philander, what's left?

And that's me sober.

I've had my experiences on the wagon, I know what it's like. It's no tour down the scenic highway with Miss Nude America on your lap. It's hard travelling; the lonesome road to nowhere.

So what am I left with? I don't want to make a case for the bottle because I can't, it's the very devil. But I'm caught between the devil and the briny deep.

I'm like Samuel Johnson, who said the only time he knew contentment in the moment was when he was drinking. I'm like that, I've got a discontented nature.

And like old Tommy said, if you can't enjoy yourself some of the time *you might as well* be dead.

December 6, 1976. You notice how social drinkers never knock back a mug of straight rum or rye but always put a mix in it, like Coca-Cola or ginger ale, something sweet and syrupy? *And they never run into trouble with alcohol.* It's in the hard drinker's nature to abhor these mixes. But I've been thinking about it... Could that be the crux of the problem? The lack of enough sugar getting into the blood? In all my drinking years I never ate or drank anything sweet and sugary, like cake, candy, ice cream, pop. I had no appetite for them. Well, then, what if it's the *sugar* that creates a balance and keeps a person sane and moderate? The secret of success with these social drinkers?

Of course I don't know. You can never know anything from theorizing. It's a thought, though.

The mix makes for a bigger drink, too; you can sip on it, draw it out longer. One jigger and lots of cola. If I were to make a point of always using mix...

I've got to have something to get up for in the morning! One bright spot in the day. And if you don't experiment how are you ever going to find out?

I know what it sounds like, but it's not a rationalization. There's a difference between a rationalization and a potential medical breakthrough.

ON THE ROCKS

Fourteen months later...

Like a rat gnawing its way out of my belly, that kind of fear. And over what?

We were in a hotel in Madrid, Eva and I. It was in 1978, towards the end of February. We'd come in on a late flight and I was tense and crabby, to say the least. I'd tried asking the cab driver to take us to a cheap hotel, but I couldn't make myself understood. In the years since we'd last been to Spain I'd forgotten all my Spanish words. Ah, ah, ah – hotel, sure, he could understand we were looking for a hotel, but I couldn't get across the "cheap" part. He drove us to the Ritz Hilton or the Astor Madrid, some great palace of a place with carpets on the sidewalk and a gold-braided doorman. "No, no! Too *mucho pesetas*. Drive on!" The meter running while he cruised the streets. Finally I lost my temper and blew up at him. He was deliberately not understanding me. "You fucking bastard!" He didn't know English, I could let it all out. Ranting, fuming, Eva shrinking into the corner. "Walt, for heaven's sake..."

I was like that travelling sober. On edge and short-tempered.

He took us to an old slum of a *pensione* in an alley, and I got out and beat on the door and nobody came.

"I think he's telling us it's too late, they're all locked up for the night," said Eva.

It was almost two-thirty in the morning.

"Since when do you speak Spanish?"

But she was right, it was the same impression I'd got from him, even though I didn't believe him. I waved him on, cursing bitterly. "You rotten prick!"

He eventually landed us at a hotel that still looked too big to me, a highrise off from the centre of the city. But Eva had had enough.

"I don't care what it costs!" Taking matters into her own hands. Well, it would be on her head.

It was her money, she was paying for the trip, so I suppose she figured she could do what she wanted.

Our other times in Spain we'd paid two or three bucks for a good room, and you couldn't have asked for better. But the country was changing. They'd got rid of Franco and brought in a democracy. New freedoms everywhere, freedom of speech, freedom to vote, and freedom to pillage poor unsuspecting wayfarers. Without batting an eye the guy behind the counter says – in good English – "Our rooms start at 3,100 pesetas."

I did a quick calculation. Fifty dollars!

What were we supposed to do? Walk out into the cold February night? Our taxi was gone, and in any case I didn't want to see that cabbie again. He'd come in with us, carried a couple of our bags, and then had a confab with one of the hoods at the hotel desk. Settling his cut for bringing in a few fish.

"We'll take it," Eva said.

"But... but..." In 1973 we'd rented a fully furnished villa on the sea for fifty bucks a month! And now, the same thing for one night?

It put the fear into me. Prices had gone haywire. Eva had about a thousand dollars to see us through the month. Me, I had a hundred tucked away for emergencies. Thirty days at fifty bucks a night, not to mention food and trains and so forth...

It didn't all hit me at once. It got me later, when I was in bed. That and other things.

§

Our trip had got off to a bad start, even before crossing the ocean. We'd taken the train to Halifax and booked into a another over-priced hotel (at Eva's insistence), and I never slept a wink. I was insomniacal anyway, when dry, but it was a foggy night and our hotel was by the harbour, and every two minutes a foghorn went off like Gabriel's trombone announcing the Hour of Judgment.

I told her we should have brought sleeping bags and camped out in the train station and saved all that hotel money.

But money meant nothing to her. She was a working woman and more in tune with the economy. She didn't share my outrage over prices and she wanted some comfort in her travels. Formerly, when it was me calling the shots, she'd had to tramp around for hours with a pack on her back while I checked out the low-cost establishments. We'd saved a lot of pesetas that way, though it's true we didn't always end up with the most lavish accommodations.

But now she was in charge, and we were travelling in style, and the cost be damned.

Speaking of dictators, there had been some changes made in the government of our own little household. After years of tailing around after me Eva had gone out and got herself a job writing ad copy for the local radio station. It goes back even further. I'd say it began when my kidneys quit and I nearly died; when I had to switch over from daily maintenance drinking to the binge system.

It wasn't by choice, this transition. Something had taken its toll, and I didn't have the staying power I'd once had. And without having a drink every day my self-confidence disappeared. Meanwhile, our money dried up – what little there was – and someone in the family had to go to work, and since it wasn't likely to be me it fell upon Eva.

She started small, but next thing she was hosting her own morning talk show; and a couple of months later she was Program Director; and within a year she was the Station Manager. A phenomenal rise.

I wasn't surprised. I'd always known she had it in her. I'd even encouraged her in the beginning, though not without misgivings. I'd heard a little voice whispering that matters might get out of hand – which they did.

Before long she bought a new house and a new car and we moved up from Rum River and into the heart of Bannonbridge.

And there we were, trapped with a mortgage and car payments and a job I didn't think she'd ever want to leave.

Being a radio personality naturally everybody knew her name, and it was great for the old ego when people would say to me, "Oh, yes, of course. You're Eva's husband."

§

We got out to the Halifax airport early, shortly after noon hour. Our fight was scheduled to leave at 2:30 in the afternoon. We were to fly to London and change planes for Madrid.

I'd heard some vague sounds about labour trouble at the airports in England, slowdowns and work-to-rule and suchlike. But I hadn't paid much attention; it wasn't something I wanted to hear. We'd bought our tickets well beforehand, to get the discount, and I suppose I just hoped the problem would go away at the right time.

The loudspeaker at Halifax airport said due to union difficulties at Heathrow Airport our flight would be delayed until five o'clock.

Then it was delayed till seven-thirty. And then ten-thirty. And then two the next morning. And so on.

Eva had brought a few books to read, and she kept her nose in one of these to put the time in. But I couldn't read while travelling. I was too nerved up.

I paced around the airport, muttering and cursing our bad luck. I noticed there was a bar in the place, as there generally was at an airport.

I couldn't help but think it would be nice to slip in for a cold one, just to pass the time.

There was no danger in one beer that I was aware of. These days I was even purer than a social drinker, I was a teetotaller. I hadn't had a drink in three months, not since November when I'd puked up a gallon of blood and thought I was a dead man again.

I never told Eva about that particular episode. I didn't tell her those kinds of things, or much of anything, for that matter. I was a guy who took care of his own problems. Anyway, my health wasn't the reason she'd laid down her rules. All she'd said was if I started in I'd be drunk and sick the whole month and ruin our nice holiday in Spain.

It was a hard charge to answer, due to my past escapades. But I knew she was wrong. It was like saying a guy could never change. She had a very pessimistic attitude.

Nobody likes to be talked down to, and naturally it made me mad, but I didn't have the moral authority to argue back at her. She held the purse strings and if I wanted to go to Spain I had to nod my head and keep my mouth shut.

"Will you promise? You've been doing so well."

"Sure, sure."

For three months I'd shown what kind of will power I had. In the beginning it was the stomach haemorrhage scare; but that faded, and then it was the promise of Spain. I had to get to Spain. I'd had a vision about Spain, and it was the only thing I lived for.

Prowling about the Halifax airport I was conscious of a knot in my stomach the size of a coconut. It's not easy setting off into the unknown, to a land where you don't speak the language, apart from a few words like *vino tinto, cerveza, gin y tonica,* etc. Though I'd done it before I'd been different then, courageous and resilient, not bone dry.

Once the will starts to crumble there's no gluing it back together again. The thought gets in your head like a maggot and begins to chew, and by then it's too late.

Yet I didn't give in without a struggle. I debated the issue thoroughly with myself, examined both sides in all fairness. The impossible ordeal ahead, as matters stood; the fact I had no intention of getting drunk; the reward that was due me for all these months of abstinence; the conviction that I was a man, not a mouse, and could make my own decisions; the knowledge that deep inside I'd meant to drink anyway, as soon as we'd got away from Bannonbridge.

I considered it all, and all things considered, there was really only one scruple holding me back.

Eva was sitting in the airport concourse with a clear view of the bar entrance. How could I get in there without her spotting me?

I was going to have to wait. Nature had to eventually take its course. I paced and sat and smoked one cigarette after another and paced some more. And at last she got up and headed for the washroom.

Being a woman she'd be in there a while, I figured; maybe quite a while, if she had a case of nervous diarrhoea from travelling. At all events I didn't need much time. I'd have preferred to relax over my beer, but beggars can't be choosers, and I was nothing if I wasn't a beggar these days.

The moment the door swung to behind her I was into the bar like a shot. "Give us a Molson!"

You might wonder why I didn't make it a triple rum, pour as much into me as quick as I could.

It was like this. I could handle a beer without going off the deep end — I could pull back after one. I wasn't out to get drunk. In fact, I'd *never* wanted to get drunk; what I sought was the lift to my spirits, the glow, the comfort, the surge of vitality; the sense of freedom and adventure.

I downed the pint quickly. It was good, no mistake about it! Right away, out of habit, my mind jumped ahead to the next one, wondering if I had time to fit it in. But wisdom prevailed. It was too risky, I was already pressing my luck just being in there.

I walked out the door... and straight into Eva. It gave me a start. She was standing square in front of me.

And the look on her face. I'd never seen it quite like that before. I had the sheepish grin on, and was trying to come up with a flippant remark, when she said, "I thought that's where you'd be."

"I just stepped in for — "

But she wasn't interested in what I'd stepped in for. She hissed at me like snake. She stared straight into my eyes and let me have it.

"So much for your word! If you think I'm taking this trip with you drunk you can think again. I've got a good mind to turn around and go home."

"Oh, come on now. It's not that bad. I just had one beer."

"Yes. If it was just the one. But it's always just the one. You'd better tell me now — Are you going to drink? Because if you are then you can go to Europe yourself. I'm not going with you."

It hadn't been laid out like this before. Like an ultimatum.

"Well?" she said.

There's nothing like an ultimatum for finding out who's boss.

She clearly meant business. I held my tongue while a tug of war went on in my head. I *wanted* to tell her to go to hell, that I'd be only too happy to go to Spain without her (I had the ticket she'd bought for me, after all). But upon reflection I knew I couldn't do it. I didn't need something like that on my conscience, sending her back home without her vacation.

"Well?" she demanded.

Besides which I didn't have the money to go on my own anyway.

"Okay, okay! I won't have any more. That's the end of it."

A long hateful glare from her. And by now the same back from me.

"I'm warning you," she said.

It was a hard swallow, too hard to go down all the way. It stuck in my craw like a piece of slag. It wasn't some five-year-old kid she was talking to — it was me, who'd once been the boss in this family; and who'd once had some pride. Nobody including her had ever told me what to do.

I stomped away from her. I didn't even want to stay on the same level of the building with her. I went up to the mezzanine. I lay down on a bench. I took stock.

I'd suffered humiliation long enough.

§

I had my Spanish *vision*, yes, but I was a realist. There was always the chance it mightn't come true. And then what? Back to our house, the big new house that Eva bought... Eva's house... Caged forever, while she was out in the world making a success of her life. Doing great at her job, getting promotions and raises, and going out for drinks with politicians, journalists and businessmen. Coming home at two or three in the morning. While I cooked dinner and ate my half and threw hers in the garbage. Then sat in front of the TV all evening.

My big achievement for the day being I didn't take a drink. And her telling her friends what a bore I was sober. I knew, I'd overheard her. I was no good sober and I was no good drunk.

Well, I was going to show her a thing or two. I'd try this trip and see if something didn't happen. And if it didn't...

From the depths of my anger came strength and courage. It was time to make plans for my future. I *knew* I could leave her.

Desperation is the true mother of invention. I needed a plan – and in a flash one appeared full blown. I'd go to New York! Or Los Angeles. No, I'd go to Toronto, where there was less competition. I could set up as a freelancer, make my fortune. Come up with brilliant ideas and sell them to all the high-paying magazines. Do research and interviews and pound the typewriter morning noon and night. No literary nonsense, no artistic pretensions, all for the buck. I'd get rich! And buy a penthouse. And a Mercedes convertible. And have all kinds of women. Women who were fast and loose. My life would be filled with work and pleasure.

And I could do it, too. I knew in my heart I had it in me. All I'd been missing was the incentive. Well, I had that now, thanks to Eva. When you've got nothing to lose there's nothing to stop you. Instead of being kicked around like a dog I'd take my fate into my own hands.

A sepulchral voice broke the air announcing our flight was delayed until two in the morning. Lovely.

At two o'clock it was delayed again until five-thirty. I didn't get any sleep. My mind was too busy working out the details of my future. The number of rooms in my penthouse, the furniture, the style of clothes I'd wear. The women. All kinds of women. Women who could treat a guy properly.

Not only did I not sleep, I didn't eat either. It never occurred to the airport or the airline to offer us a meal to tide us over.

When I heard our flight announcement I went downstairs and joined Eva. I was a different man, no longer the cur she'd become accustomed to, but a commanding personality. The foremost journalist in North America, if not the world. It must have puzzled her, this transformation. One day she'd understand.

She seemed to have got over her snit — no doubt repenting her harsh treatment of me. It wouldn't do to have a hostile travelling companion. She was going to have to depend on me whether she liked it or not. By her own admission she was a poor traveller.

She was forever telling people that she liked foreign places but hated getting to them. I knew from past expeditions her stomach got upset and she suffered from diarrhoea and couldn't eat. And what was worse, she couldn't drink. I used to wonder at that, because it seemed to me a couple of stiff ones first thing in the morning would set her straight.

She was also at a loss where foreign languages were concerned. She wouldn't even try the words for fear of embarrassing herself. It was easier to let me sound like a halfwit.

Being the man I had to accept the responsibility. It was my job to take care of everything: tickets, schedules, hotel rooms, ordering in restaurants, asking directions.

This talking in foreign tongues was not my idea of fun, but once I got some oil in the machinery I was as good as a native. I could whip off elaborate lines like *Hable una habitacion matrimonial por una noche?* all in one breath. *Donde este el estacion?* The bars I could find myself.

So far, however, on this present journey, she was the one who'd seen about the tickets and our hotel room in Halifax. She'd done it all and I hadn't done anything. But then, we weren't in foreign parts yet.

It occurs to me I might be giving the wrong impression. I don't want to be unfair, and imply she was the cranky type. We'd had a lot of great times in our day, before things changed. Even now, as a rule, she was good-natured, the kind who accepted the ups and downs of life and made the best of them. If anyone was the grump it was me. I thought I'd better say that.

But I'm not really talking about her. None of this has much to do with her, or anybody else. It has to do with my state of mind.

But at the time it didn't mean I was about to excuse her.

I used to get mad at her when she was cheerful. I'd wonder — what's going on? What's she doing behind my back? Why should she feel so good when my life's in such a mess?

When I came up to her where she was waiting she gave me a shy sort of look, like let's forget the hard words; but I'd been humiliated, and I wasn't the type to forget.

My face was set in stone. Without a word I picked up the bags and strode toward the boarding gate.

The plane was no sooner off the ground than they announced they'd be serving dinner. At six in the morning!

The stewardess asked us if we'd like wine with our meal. I didn't hesitate. I ordered a small bottle of red wine, a quarter-litre. "You want one?" I said to Eva with perfect civility.

She didn't dare. Wine only aggravated her stomach condition.

But observe: not a word of admonishment. She looked a mite dubious, but she didn't say anything. It wouldn't have mattered anyway. We were in the air now and she was stuck with me whatever I did.

§

I managed to sleep for a few hours on the plane, awakening as we approached England. We got in around seven in the morning, their time. Our flight for Madrid was scheduled for eight, which meant we had to hustle to make sure we caught it, busing around through the byways and back alleys of that meandering complex. But we needn't have been anxious. The airport workers were on semi-strike and our plane didn't get off until eleven that night.

The bus let us out and we followed the crowd to a waiting room. It was a dismal spot, a remote cranny in the bowels of Heathrow. The benches were wooden, dark and shiny from centuries of use. The few tiny windows were high on the wall and clouded with dust and grime. Flies buzzed around. Cobwebs hung from the corners of the ceiling.

I sat for as long as I could stand it, conscious of the bar just yards away, begging me to come in. Eva had her eye on me, giving me the stern look every time I got up and took a few paces in that direction.

Flesh and blood can endure only so much! The craving for a drink kept increasing by the minute. By this stage, having had little or no sleep or food, I was nervous, depressed, and fretful. I was absolutely certain I couldn't board an airplane in this condition. I'd done it in Halifax, sure, but then I'd been enraged. The rage was gone now, and I had nothing to sustain me.

It wasn't just the usual peril of engine failure or the wings falling off. It was the hi-jackers. Hi-jacking had become all the fashion in the past year or so.

My agitation wouldn't let me be still. I started to panic; the shadow of death loomed up; it grew larger than my fear of Eva. Without looking her way I got up and ran into the bar.

It was very crowded in there, and none too clean. With a glance I took in the sawdust on the floor, the half-barrels for tables, the low three-legged stools.

I had no English currency. I asked the bartender if he'd take Canadian money, and he said yes. I ordered a pint of bitter. He said that would be six dollars and a half. Dying Jesus! I thought inflation was bad in Canada. But the condition I was in, he could have got a lot more than that out of me. I passed him a ten and he gave me back a bunch of British change.

I drank my mug of beer while Eva glared at me from the waiting room. There was no wall between the two rooms, nothing to separate us but a wooden railing and a couple of posts.

When I finished I decided to do the right thing, and went out and invited her to join me; but she only pursed her lips the harder and shook her head.

So I returned and had another half-litre mug – what the British call a pint. I felt significantly better, except for her eyes boring through me. I took my time, drinking very slowly. I didn't quite have the courage to order a third. I didn't want to get her too riled at me.

Besides, it never hurt to show that like anyone else I could take the stuff or leave it. I could walk away if I wanted to.

§

We boarded the plane at nine that evening and spent two hours sitting on the runway before the strikers cleared us to take off. We couldn't smoke and they gave us nothing to eat or drink. All we could do was chew our fingernails and stare at the other passengers. While we waited the beer wore off. Nothing out the port holes but the night. Darkness and desolation.

§

In Madrid, as you'll remember, we found ourselves a hotel. With the delays and the cockeyed time difference it was hard to tell exactly how long we'd been travelling. But it was long enough when you haven't had any sleep.

My nerves were pretty much unravelled. I made a few restless turns around the room, then said, "I'm hungry, I'm going to go see if I can't find a sandwich. You want one?" At times like this you had to be able to improvise.

"No. I just want to take a bath and go to sleep."

"I'll be right back."

I took the elevator down to the lobby and found the same bandit behind the desk.

"I'd like to get a bottle of wine," I said.

"I'm sorry, sir. Everything's closed up now."

"Oh."

So I went back upstairs.

"Everything's closed. There's no food," I told Eva.

Nothing to do but call it a night.

I had a shower and climbed into the sack. There were two single beds, one for her and one for me.

It was very quiet in our room.

More than anything I wanted to get out of my bed and go over to hers.

I couldn't use sex for an excuse, it wouldn't have been seemly, not with her being exhausted and more or less disgusted with me. And me supposedly still holding a grudge against her. Even if I tried it, put my pride aside and crept over and crawled in with her, I was sure she'd just kick me out. "Oh, don't, I'm *tired*."

I stayed awake for hours, tossing and sweating. I was assailed by a host of fears. I was afraid we'd run out of money. I was afraid of the flight tomorrow to Valencia. I was afraid of the thugs in the lobby downstairs — that they'd be up to kill us for our traveller's cheques. Cut our bodies up and throw us in the sewer. I was afraid that they wouldn't kill Eva but just me; that she'd led me here to Spain in order to get rid of me, with these Spanish friends of hers, whom she'd met God knows where...

The last was a horrifying thought. It was too horrifying; I couldn't let myself believe it. But what did I know about her, really?

I was like a child lost at night in the woods. I listened for noises, terrified. If only I could hold onto her for comfort. She was right over there, I could hear her breathing. All I had to do was get up and go to her. She was only a few feet away.

Begging her, "*Let me in with you! Please...*"

"*You're not a baby anymore! You're six years old! It's time you learned to sleep alone. Stop that whining!*"

Returning to my cold bed...

No, I'd rather die first. I'd hang on by the last thread and take what was coming, suffer and die rather than have her do that to me.

§

It was almost dawn by the time I drifted off. An hour later Eva shook me awake. We had to get on our way to catch the flight to Valencia.

Our plane was an old twin-propeller job, and the passengers some of the hardest cases I'd ever set eyes on. Swarthy-faced shifty-eyed desperadoes. I pointed them out to Eva, a tremor in my voice. It wasn't my paranoia getting the better of me. She too, a normal person, was worried; I could see it in her face. I wasn't the only one who read the papers.

Flying in an airplane was enough by itself to test anyone's courage, as far as I was concerned; it was especially nerve-wracking in some rickety converted cargo transport left over from the Spanish Civil War.

But to have some maniac jump up with a hand grenade in one hand and a machine gun in the other...

That wouldn't be the end of it, either. It could go on for days or weeks. Flying to one airport after another and being turned away and taking off again. In constant dread of looking at a terrorist the wrong way and getting your head blown off. And if you stayed alive, the day coming when a squad of Israeli commandoes made their assault with guns blazing and hand grenades exploding. Blood and guts all over the place...

I sank my fingernails into the armrests as the plane strained to get off the ground, rattling and rolling, bouncing through the air.

How could I ever get through it? Terrorists were notoriously intolerant people. They were likely to be Arabs, Moslems, who didn't believe in alcohol. With them in charge I'd never find a chance to settle the nerves, wouldn't have a prayer of surviving. I craned my head to check out the stewardess. She was at the rear by the kitchen nook and the washrooms, getting ready to wheel a cart up the aisle.

I couldn't stand it any longer. If a skyjacking was about to take place I had to act quickly.

I'd narrowed my suspicions down to six definite cases. Any second now one of them might whip out a pistol and it would be too late. Something had to be done.

I whispered in Eva's ear and she nodded and I got up and headed for the rear of the plane.

I took the stewardess by the sleeve, said quietly:

"I'd like a bottle of wine."

Eva still hadn't turned around, and she was too far off to hear me.

"We'll be at your seat shortly," said the stewardess.

"Couldn't I have it now?"

She saw the urgency in my eyes and took pity on me. She must have sensed the straits we were in, that the inevitable was coming, meanwhile going about her duties fatalistically. She gave me a quarter-litre of red wine and a plastic glass. I filled the glass right in front of her and before she could say, "Sir, you can't − " I downed it in one gulp. The deed was done and I passed her the empty. Then I went into the can, which is where I'd told Eva I was going in the first place.

The threat was over. I felt the wine in my veins bring peace and security.

And so it was, my son, that with quick thinking and decisive action I was able to thwart the wicked hijackers. Preventing almost certain loss of dozens of innocent lives, including my own.

What a hero!

It wasn't a long flight from Madrid to Valencia, but under certain conditions minutes can seem like hours.

We came over Valencia from the wrong direction and had to make a 360 degree turn at the last minute. It was as if the pilot woke up and suddenly realized he was going the wrong way. With a wrench of the wheel he stood the plane on its side, one wing pointing straight up at the sky, the other down to the earth. If the lower windows had been open we'd have all poured out. It put a tremendous strain on the old machine, you could feel the nuts and bolts cracking and the guy wires screaming. We got shaken around like pebbles in a gourd.

When the plane levelled out I told Eva I had to go to the washroom again, pronto.

I beat it back to the kitchenette and bought two more bottles of wine off the attendant. I took the cork off one and tossed it off, direct from the bottle, and stashed the other in my pocket.

I returned to my seat in time to get my safety belt on and bounce in for a landing.

I drank the other bottle in a washroom in the airport.

§

It was around noon when we emerged from the airport. Though it was February it was like an early summer day. Madrid had been cold and shivery but here the air was mild, and there were oranges growing in front of the airport, and rows of tall palm trees.

There's something about the air, the atmosphere, of Southern Spain. It seems like a different sun than elsewhere, kindlier and more gentle.

We took the airport bus into Valencia.

I was still in command of myself, I should note. Although I'd sort of started drinking that didn't mean I had to carry on with it. I was feeling reasonably okay. In fact at this stage I was feeling pretty good. The plane rides were over and the weather was nice, and Eva herself was relieved to have got this far alive, and was treating me like an adult companion.

We arrived at the bus station and had to wait several hours for the bus to Denia, which was our destination. I left Eva parked on a bench in the station reading an Agatha Christie novel. This was her way of putting in time, reading. I was much too fidgety when travelling to sit down and read. I strolled around the depot, and up and down the street outside.

Across the street was a wall overlooking the great gully of the river Turia, its bed dry as a bone, with soccer nets set up and several games of soccer going on. And further off, on the other side, an ancient city gate still standing from medieval times.

My heart felt a twinge of happiness. It was nice to know the feeling, even if I could never retain it, with all I had to worry about. I felt so good for a few minutes that I got the idea to go into the depot and order a glass of wine.

Eva was sitting across the floor from the bar, where she couldn't help but see me. Yes, I was aware of that. But I decided to stop sneaking around and drink openly like a normal person. Even if I wasn't one I could at least drink like one.

I walked up to Eva and said, well, first I remarked on the sights I'd seen outside, establishing a friendly tone; then I said, by-the-by: "Would you like a glass of wine or something? I see a bar just over there. I might have one myself."

She hesitated. "Well, I suppose... I guess it wouldn't hurt. Do they have anything to eat?"

"Oh, they must!" I said this with great spirit, a man who had a buoyant and hearty outlook on life. Because that was how I felt now, the two of us making for the bar together.

I ordered her a glass of white wine and a saucer of *mejillones*. I passed on the food myself because with drinks being rationed it didn't pay to dampen the effect.

Eva sipped on her wine and ate her mussels, and I put my red wine away in a couple of sociable swallows; and then, still restless, and with an empty glass in front of me, I went outside again. I came in a little later and with a nod to Eva ordered another *vino tinto*.

They were small glasses, and there's not much kick to a dry wine. I was pacing myself, keeping everything well in hand.

In my walks I'd noticed a tiny makeshift bar, a kind of canteen, out back where the buses came and went.

With departure time drawing closer I took a stroll out there and ordered a double cognac. I got it down just in time to go fetch Eva and board our bus.

I don't know why I drank that one. I just did.

We got settled on the bus and headed along the coast towards Denia. The afternoon sun streamed through the window as through a magnifying glass. I kept telling myself, this is February – and the folks back home are buried in snow, the poor bastards.

I devoured the scenery along the road. The dry scrub ground and palm trees and prickly pear cactuses and orange groves. The brown stuccoed towns and white stuccoed seaside villas. The blue-green Mediterranean. It was beautiful! I was in Spain and the bus was piping traditional Spanish music (and what can better stir the romantic soul than Spanish music!). Rolling along in a near ecstatic state to dreams that were bound to come true.

§

We pulled into Denia, back where we'd been five years ago. Our original thought had been to be adventurous and try somewhere different, maybe travel down the coast toward Seville. But after the hotel tab in Madrid and the general rigours of the excursion thus far, we'd changed our minds.

We got off the bus and there happened to be a bar right there — and right everywhere, in that country — and since we hadn't had our first meal of the day yet we went in and had tortillas; and a glass of wine each, and a second one for me.

You can't eat in Spain without wine. Besides, Eva liked a drop of wine herself. And that's all it was, what we had, a drop. I could have upended a barrel and drained it, but always I had to let on I was like everyone else, that a glass or two was really all I wished for, it was plenty.

I'm not saying I didn't appreciate whatever nibble came along. But it was hard on the system, this shilly-shallying, neither drinking nor not-drinking. I'd feel fine for a little while, until the effect passed; then my spirits would plunge and the gloom come pouring over me. A cycle of ups and downs.

We walked down to the Villas Ferrer office and Eva rented us a villa. It was the same agency as the last time, but five years ago I'd been the one who'd done the renting. Mr. and Mrs. Macbride, the mister doing the talking. Now the shoe was on another foot, hers, and the pants on her legs.

I stood back in the corner studying a Grecian urn, glad enough in any case to let her handle the transaction. We'd reached our destination and the agent, Janet Ferrer, was English; so really, I wasn't needed. Eva was much better with people, anyway.

At this stage in my career I only dealt with the public if I had to, if I couldn't get out of it. Unless I had an urn or two in me there was a good chance I'd seize up and begin vibrating; and I didn't like the way people looked at me when this happened.

Still... even though I went along with the new state of affairs, it didn't mean I accepted it gracefully. I was conscious of how the mighty had fallen. I felt sad for myself having come to this. I was not happy with Eva for usurping my place. I harboured the thought that one day things would change; the worm turn and announce that, due to certain expectations having come true, he was no longer a washout but a man on the brink of a new life.

I wasn't thinking of my career in Toronto. I'd had second thoughts about that particular escape route.

Lying in bed in our Madrid hotel it had seemed the zaniest notion I'd come up with yet – in its way as frightening as the Spaniards conniving with Eva to slit my throat.

Selling my ideas to editors? Interviewing people? Writing horseshit about their lives? That wasn't me. I'd have to be drunk from the word go, just to consider it.

No, it was something before that. What you might call a vision I'd had, back in Bannonbridge – or close to Bannonbridge. On the road to the Bannon-bridge dump, to be exact.

Eva and Janet Ferrer were chatting away like old friends. It was decided we'd take a villa at El Oasses again, though for the sake of change we chose a different fish this time – *La Mabra* instead of *La Cavalla*. All the villas were named after fish.

The rent was still quite reasonable, a hundred and thirty a month; a jump from fifty dollars, but nothing like the hotel prices.

Now that we had a roof over our heads I could at least stop worrying about Eva's money running out.

Our next move was to rent a car for a couple of weeks. It was an inspiration I'd got on the bus, after the wine and the cognac, when it had seemed like a bright idea. Eva had no objections so long as she didn't have to drive herself. The cheap rental models had standard stick shifts and she could only handle an automatic. She was also put off by the drivers in Spain. She said she wouldn't take the wheel here in any kind of vehicle. I would have to do the driving. No problem!

I scribbled my name on the agreement and we loaded our bags into the miniature car – a tiny Seat 200 – and took off down the road to *El Oasses*.

§

I thought of all the exciting girls from France, England, Sweden, Germany and such countries who would have discovered this unspoilt patch of the Mediterranean, an oasis paradise.

I felt a fidgety anticipation as we turned onto the lane towards the sea. We pulled up and opened the villa and lugged our things in.

There was an elderly couple sitting in wicker chairs in front of the villa to the left of ours. They gave us a nod, and with a British accent the man remarked on it being a fine day.

It was that, we said.

Eva had things to do, unpacking, checking the place over, making the bed. It was chilly as a crypt inside and we lit the two gas heaters. I did that for her, then marched back and forth from one corner to another for a few minutes. I was restive. I had to get out and take a walk. I had to see.

I went down the lane to the breakwater, passing the five or six villas between ours and the sea. They were empty. The ones above us in the direction of the road were empty too, except for the old British chap and his wife, both of them well up in their sixties.

I stood on the steps above the beach and looked and listened. Not a sound but the waves tumbling onto the shore, the wind in the palms. The place was desolate. There was no one here; only an old Englishman and his wife. And suddenly I wanted to cry.

§

It had seemed such a sure thing, the day it came to me. I was driving out the Botsford Road, taking the garbage to the dump. I might as well have been taking myself with it from the way I was feeling. I was in the dumps before I ever got there.

I don't want to belabour this, but things at the time looked bleak. My purpose on earth had come down to making the bed and sweeping the floors and cooking dinner. I couldn't seem to do any writing — I had no spirit. You can't work when you're dejected like that. I couldn't write and I certainly couldn't do any honest work, the type that earns money.

Something had happened to the weather in Bannonbridge. Every day the sky was clouded over. Dark clouds, cold gray drizzle. Never a trace of sun.

I was often on the verge of tears. Moping around with that kind of pressure inside the chest, like a swollen tumour, trying to push the tears out. I couldn't cry, of course, at least not sober. When I was drunk I cried over anything and everything.

I remember watching a track meet on television. I was half in a trance – I'd been drunk for days – and as a girl cleared the bar in the high jump I burst into tears. It was just too moving.

The afternoon I went to the dump I remembered we were booked to head for Spain in February, compliments of Eva.

Looking back I can say she was doing this in large measure for me, though I didn't appreciate it. She knew how bored I was, and how little there was for me to occupy myself with in Bannonbridge.

Sure, she had a boyfriend or two, but that was only to square things up for the running around I'd done myself (and still tried to do, without success, when I was on the spree). And because I wasn't anything in the way of company anymore. If I wasn't drunk I was morose or grumpy. Who'd want to come home to someone like that?

She didn't have it easy. But I was too wrapped up in my personal misery to have any sympathy for her. All I could see was her success and her friends and my own dwindling significance.

My thoughts turned to Spain and better days. Our trip was several months off, but I could hold on till then. It wasn't as if I had any choice. Spain... I longed to be there again. Life had been better in Spain. And suddenly – no, it was gradually – I had a vision. Not a real one, like a religious vision, but inside my head. I thought, *I don't want to go on like this. I deserve more out of life than the deal I'm getting. It's because I'm stuck in this damned town, where I never wanted to be. It's Eva's fault, she's the one wants to be here, and since she's got the money she calls the tune. My problem is I'm tied to Eva's life. I have no room to expand.*

And then I saw it.

When we got to Spain. All of a sudden an apparition. A rich and beautiful girl... She's lying topless on the beach, and something happens, an enchantment. There's the static crackle of electricity... She falls in love with me! (Never mind the details, they could fill themselves in later). The days pass, and we find time to spend together, getting to know each other...

I can't get over this girl! She's an artist, she paints pictures, and yet she's the one who should be painted. She's got the body of a *Playboy* fold-out. Added to that she's sensitive, intelligent, well-read and good-humoured. You'd think she had everything, and yet... all these years something has been missing from her life... the man she's always dreamt of...

Eva doesn't see what's going on. To her I'm like a dog coming and going, and who notices a dog? I no longer count with her. She sees me as worthless, a discredit to the human race.

And to think I'd almost come to believe the same myself.

This girl and I continue to see each other on the quiet, days of poetic and erotic bliss... It seems our happiness will never end. Time is but a measure of our heartbeats. But all too soon...

I hear a voice. It's Eva announcing our stay is up, telling me I'd better hop to it, start toting those bags, buster, we have to get back home. "I've got work to do, unlike some people I know. I can't loaf around here forever."

The girl pleads with me not to leave. "Don't go!" she says. She begs me to throw in my lot with her, and share her fifteen bedroom villa, her servants and her swimming pool; her Mercedes, her Jaguar, and her Porsche. For you see, her late father was a billionaire, and on his death provided for her very well indeed.

Will I chance it? I give it sober thought, take account of all I'd be giving up, and the changes it will mean. And after a dramatic pause I say, "Yes." Tough decision.

Eva will have to be told.

I break the news to her as gently as possible, expressing the hope there'll be no recriminations on either side. It's simply time to move on. That's all.

Everything considered she'll be better off without me. I've only been a millstone around her neck. With me in the way she never dared bring any of her men friends home for the night. It was a nuisance maintaining that sort of decorum.

And this young lady that I found, she not only falls in love with me but with my work. She loves my stories. Says I'm the greatest undiscovered genius in the world. And that's not all! Being of an old and influential family with more contacts than an optical factory she soon introduces me to the chairmen and presidents of the great publishing houses, and in no time I have a million dollar contract, and am wealthy in my own right.

And when this happens she learns I haven't been with her just for her money. Even with all my own riches I choose to remain at her side, firm and faithful. Leave her for another? What kind of cad would do that? Our life together becomes more sublime than before, now that we're on an equal footing. I can no longer be mistaken for a leech. I've acquired self-respect.

It was a beautiful vision of things to come.

And knowing this, that I was going to escape in a matter of months, picked me up magnificently, as I drove to and from the dump that afternoon.

And it sustained me through the dark remaining days of autumn and the oppressive snows of winter, until the end of February, when my moment of salvation was at hand.

I remember lying on the living room couch, fetus-like, on a sub-zero winter afternoon, and feeling the sun in the window, and its deceptive warmth on my back. I was deep in the glooms, dead and empty, faced with another endless impossible day, and my vision returned to save me.

The sun I felt was the sun of Spain.

I was sunbathing on the roof terrace, sheltered from the sea air, with its touch of coolness, and the sun beamed down like a day in summer, warming, soothing. I wasn't thinking of anything. I felt curiously at peace.

And in the villas all around us were new friends, mostly pretty girls, and the girl of my dreams was with them. What nationality was she, British, American, Danish, German? We hadn't met yet. But someone told her I was a man of letters, and she should introduce herself. It was so rare she met a man who truly interested her...

She and her debutante friends, taking the sun, in their string bikinis... Then she left them, took a stroll down the beach and climbed the tiled stairs to our rooftop, where I was lying on the chaise alone, Eva having gone into town to the English library...

On this trip to Spain I had a lot to look forward to.

§

And lo, here I was, in Spain. Standing on the sea wall, looking around, listening. Very still. Nothing stirring but the waves and the breeze. Not a human in sight. No pretty girls. No girls of any description. No people, other than a decrepit old couple from England.

It was a brutal yank back into reality.

I didn't know what to do, where to turn. My stomach felt like I'd eaten ten pounds of ultra-sweet chocolate. A surge of sickening energy and no way to let it out. Total futility – that was it – my life in a nutshell. Once again the high hopes and the big letdown. I didn't know how I was going to endure it, a month of nothingness in this barren place. To come so far – to the Garden of Eden – and no one is home, only me.

The sun clouded over. I remembered that kind of sky, most likely it meant we were in for two weeks of rain. I'd spend them indoors, shivering before the gas heater, watching Eva drink wine and eat roast chickens, gazing at me with a complacent smile.

I could walk across the room and look out the window at the rain... But not really. Not with feet that weighed a ton. I couldn't possibly lift them.

There was only ONE thing to do.

God himself couldn't blame me.

I'd been praying and asking God for help with my drinking, and sometimes the liquor store was locked when I went to buy a bottle. Sometimes he intervened.

But he wasn't going to intervene today.

The *Bona Platya* was still where it had been, a little ways down the beach. My feet took me there. I ordered a double gin and took a table by the window and stared out at the water. The sea was roiled, dark foam-crested waves heaving onto the shore.

A few more drinks. When I got back I found Eva had been talking to the old English pair, and they had invited us to their villa that evening for a drink. Jolly good. That ought to be exciting.

But first we went to the *Trompeta Azul*, our other old haunt. We ordered spaghetti and wine. Eva said nothing about my drinking. She knew it was too late at this stage; she might as well just go along with it. And maybe, fond hope, she might even enjoy herself, as we'd done in the past.

We drank the wine and had sherry and cognacs. And amidst warnings to behave myself we went off to see old Mr. and Mrs. Weatherby.

I remember one event from that night, nothing else. In this scene – having most certainly drunk most of our hosts' liquor – I announced I had to take a leak and asked where the toilet was. Halfway up the stairs, my fly already undone, I slipped and tumbled back to the bottom.

An accident like that wouldn't normally have fazed me, but as I glanced up from the floor I caught the expression on their faces. Instead of enjoying a good laugh at my expense the old couple looked thoroughly disgusted.

If there was anything I disliked it was people who affected a superior attitude — something the British were notorious for.

I was getting tired of their stuffy mannerisms anyway. I'd almost crippled myself and the least they could have done was laugh. It was time to set a few matters straight.

Pulling myself to my feet I began somewhat as follows: "Though but a colonial ruffian..."

I can't remember my words, but I believe it was an inspired soliloquy, as I'd have described it. I delved into the sex lives of the British, with their neurotic perversions, repressions, frigidities, impotencies and what have you. And by way of punctuation — as the words poured out — I extracted my cock and shook it at them. I was still doing this as Eva dragged me out the door.

§

Though we remained next-door neighbours for another three days — before they packed up and moved — this aged couple didn't say another word to me.

But first there was the morning after. The torment as my memory awakened and my conscience attacked. There were only two options I could think of — I could commit suicide, or get out of bed and go into the living room.

I decided on the latter. In the living room I poured a large glass of brandy, then sat by the window and surveyed the morning gloom. I could see our little car parked across the lane, and knew it would still be sitting there two weeks later, for all the driving I'd be fit to do.

EARLIER TIMES

CAUGHT

I became the owner of a bicycle when I was ten years old, having inherited it from my sister Maria. In those days, in the nineteen forties and fifties, adults didn't ride bikes, and being in Grade 12 Maria considered herself an adult now and therefore too old for a bicycle.

It was a girl's bike, it's true, and there was a stigma of sorts attached to a boy riding a girl's bike, but I was so glad to have a bicycle of any kind that I didn't care. It was also a full-sized bike, meaning I couldn't sit on the seat and pedal – not at my size, not till I grew some; but on the other hand it had no crossbar and I was able to stand upright and pedal. With a full-sized *boys* bike someone my size had to stick one leg under the crossbar to do it.

At that time I had a friend in another part of town named Jeremy Duval, who also had a bike, but his was a younger boy's bike, and *he* had no problem sitting and pedalling. Nor did he have to worry if he outgrew it, as his father was the local bank manager and would just buy him a bigger one when that time came.

Jeremy was in my class at St. Cecilia's, and being a rather puny "rich kid" was subject to getting picked on a lot. Nobody in my class picked on me because I had a gift for rough and tumble schoolyard wrestling, and could more than defend myself. I was blessed in that regard, because it wasn't how smart you were or anything else that gave you status at school and immunity from bullying, it was who and how many of your classmates you could beat; and as it turned out, I could beat them all.

I was also a "good guy", like the Lone Ranger and Superman and Batman and the other heroes of comic books and movie serials, and it was in that capacity that I'd at times step in and rescue Jeremy and other weaker boys when they were in peril, if I happened to be around.

Besides the above-mentioned cowboys and super-heroes, my sister Alice had set an example for me when I was three or four years old. One day a girl next door and her friends began pushing me around and scaring me. Alice was there too, and when she saw what they were up to she lit into them.

"You leave him alone, he's only little!"

She gave the girl a shove and knocked her down. It was all it took, the girls saw she meant business and stopped bothering me. It was the only time Alice she did something like this for me, but I never forgot it.

Like myself Jeremy was a big reader of boys' mystery and adventure novels. He had a large collection of the Hardy Boys series, my favourites, and would lend them to me one at a time, which I suppose had a good deal to do with my ongoing friendship with him.

One summer afternoon I called for him, and we biked around town and ended up by the wharves and the railroad tracks. Neither of us was supposed to be down there, but that was where we were.

Our bikes were our horses, and when we set out I said to Jeremy, "I'll be the Lone Ranger and you be Tonto."

"I don't want to be no friggin' Tonto. I'm Tom Mix."

"Hi-Yo Silver away!"

"Dig dirt, Tony!"

So the Lone Ranger and Tom Mix were riding along the tracks looking for train robbers, and came to a boxcar on a siding by one of the sheds. That was too inviting for me to pass up. I reined in my horse against it and lifting myself out of the saddle climbed up the iron ladder and sat on the boxcar roof and waited for Jeremy to creep up the ladder behind me. I could see the determination in his face, it was a bold move for him. He liked to pretend he wasn't afraid but he was, about just about everything.

We were on a level with an open second floor window in the warehouse and climbed through. Inside it was like a huge loft with sacks of animal feed piled to the ceiling and the floor covered with a sweet-smelling powder. We crawled on hands and knees to a hatch in the floor and peered down. There were three men loading a truck at a bay on the floor below.

I could hear Jeremy breathing by my ear. "They'll see us," he whispered. "We better go."

A man looked up and we hurried back out the window and onto the roof of the boxcar. I went down the ladder first and when my feet hit the ground there was a man standing by our bikes. He caught hold of my wrist.

"What were you kids doing up there?"

He was a rough-looking man in a dirty tan windbreaker with a stubble of beard on his face. He wasn't one of the ones we'd seen in the warehouse. They couldn't have got here that fast anyway.

Jeremy came down right after me but the man ignored him, and Jeremy jumped on his bike and took off. I tried to pull away but the man held tight.

"You know that's against the law?"

"We weren't doing anything. We were just playing."

"Yeah, playing. I saw you coming out of that window. What'd you steal?"

"Nothing."

"You're in real trouble, sonny. You know it's against the law to break and enter? I'm going to have to take you off to the police station."

"I didn't do anything – honest!"

It was a sickening feeling, getting caught. One minute you're playing and the next everything's different and you know you're in for it.

"You better come with me."

"What for? Lemme go!"

His big hand had my wrist like a clamp, pulling me after him. I tried to dig in my heels and squirm away.

"What's the matter? You don't wanta go to jail?"

"No. I have to go home."

"You should've thought of that before."

"Lemme go... I didn't do anything..." But I had, that was the trouble. I wasn't supposed to be climbing on boxcars or sneaking into buildings. I knew if my mother found out I'd get it. And when she discovered I'd been arrested, that I was down in the lockup . . .

"Please, I won't do it again."

"That don't matter. You broke the law."

"I didn't steal anything."

"You didn't, eh?" He was looking up and down the tracks. There wasn't a soul in sight.

"I promise I won't do it again."

"Sure, sonny. That's what they all say."

"I won't, honest I won't."

"I ain't so sure about that." He squinted down at me. "It's not like I'm a mean guy or nothing, but the law's the law. I might get in trouble myself if I let you off."

"Please. We were just playing."

He glanced around again, as if his mind wasn't completely made up, and I felt a momentary hope.

"I'll tell you what," he said. "I'm gonna have to think about it. What we better do, you come on over here with me and we'll have a little talk. Maybe you're not such a bad kid."

I dragged my feet along after him, still in his grip. We crossed the tracks and made for an old boathouse almost hidden in the trees and bushes on the riverbank.

"Where're we going?"

"Just over here."

"What for?"

"You want to go to jail or you want to talk?"

"I want to go home."

"In a little while – maybe. If you're a good kid and don't give me no trouble. I got to think about it."

"My bike's back there, someone might take it."

"Don't worry about it."

If I lost my bike... I could see my mother, the fit she'd take, the rage on her face. "Where's the stick! You're going to get it, mister."

The boathouse was padlocked, and we sat up against one of the big double doors facing the river. The ground was a mess of broken glass and bottle caps and smelled like piss. There'd been a wharf there once, but all that was left were some old rotting logs sticking out into the river.

"Here. Sit closer to me," the man said.

"Let go my wrist. It hurts."

"Don't try and run away."

He released his grip and put his arm around my shoulder, pinching tightly with his fingers. With his other hand he took a wine bottle from beneath his belt.

"How old are you, sonny?"

"Ten."

He put the bottle to his mouth, took a long gurgling drink, wiped his lips and let out a deep sigh.

My heart was like lead in the pit of my stomach.

"Y'know, kid, maybe I won't have to turn you in. I should but maybe I won't. We could be friends, you and me. What do you think? You want to be my friend?"

"Sure."

"That's good. I'd give you a drink but you're too young to drink. Do you drink?"

"No."

"You can have one if you want."

"I don't want one. I'm not allowed."

"No." He let out a hoarse rough laugh, and started coughing. "You wouldn't have a smoke on you? Naw, you wouldn't smoke." He pulled me closer. "You know, you're a good-looking kid. You be nice to me and maybe I can help you. I wouldn't like to see you get in trouble."

"I didn't do anything. Let me go, okay?"

"It depends."

He took another drink and set the bottle at his feet and for a moment he said nothing. Then he leaned his face over mine. "Do you like me?" he said. There was an awful stink on his breath. I turned my face away.

"Eh? Do you like me?"

"Sure, I guess so."

He squeezed my shoulder.

"So you like me?"

"Yeah."

He grinned.

"How much do you like me? C'mon, tell me."

"I don't know."

"Sure you do. Tell me."

"Can't I go now? Jeremy's waiting for me, I have to get my bike and I have to go home and – "

"Not yet. We're gonna be friends, okay? I ain't a bad guy once you get to know me." He tipped the bottle again, screwed the cap back on. Then he said:

"Do you love me?"

I didn't know what he was talking about. I was getting more scared by the minute.

He had his arm tight around me, leaning down over me. He was huge and dirty and all over me, breathing sour wine in my face, holding me so I couldn't move. I felt smothered by him.

I knew I should tell him what he wanted, anything to get on his good side, and yet I didn't know what to do. There was a difference between humouring someone and telling an out-and-out lie.

"Eh? Do you love me, kid?"

But I had to get out of there.

"Don't be shy. Go on, tell me."

"I guess so."

"Say it."

"I love you. Now can I go?"

I tried to move but he only squeezed tighter.

"That's sweet, kid."

All around there was nothing but sunlight. I could see out on the river, the ferry boat just starting its crossing from the other side, a flash of sun on a car window. Everything bright and quiet and peaceful. A normal safe world where everyone was going about their business – everyone but me. It was like I was trapped in a dark hole. Doomed.

"Gimme a little kiss," he said. "C'mon, just a little kiss, okay?"

His eyes were watery and shining. I was terrified, I didn't know precisely what the danger was, but it was bad, all right. I tried to shrink away from him.

It never occurred to me to yell for help. How could I yell for help when I'd been caught? I'd been caught before, I'd been caught robbing the nuns' apple orchard, and the next day was hauled into the principal's office at school, had to face Sister O'Hara. I was terrified then, too, sick to my stomach. But was I supposed to yell for help? When they caught you there was no help.

"Please. Let me go, will you. I'm supposed to be home, my mother said..."

"Gimme a kiss. C'mon, be nice to me."

"I don't want to."

"C'mon, kid. You wanta go to jail or what?"

He hovered over me, waiting.

"Can I go then?"

"Sure. Just gimme a kiss first."

I leaned up and touched the stubbly beard with my lips.

"There." I started to get up.

"Hey, hold on," he said, pulling me back. "That's not a kiss. A real one. On the mouth."

"I don't want to – I want to go home!"

He jammed his open mouth against mine. His lips were wet and heavy, sloppy, like a mouthful of greasy fat. He had me in a bear hug that almost suffocated me. I tried to twist my face away from that stinking wetness swamping my mouth. I pushed my hands against his face and got my mouth free.

"Stop it! Lemme go!" There were tears in my eyes, I couldn't help it. I was sobbing. "I want to go home, you said I could!" I couldn't hold it in any longer.

"Don't cry. Cut that out! I'm gonna let you go." He was breathing hard, eyes glistening. "In just a minute."

"You said I could!"

Suddenly I heard Jeremy hollering. "Walt! Hey, Walt! Where are you?"

"Don't answer!" the man said.

Jeremy shouted again. I couldn't see him because we were hidden from the tracks by the boathouse and the trees.

"He's looking for me. My friend's over there. I have to go!"

"No, you don't."

"I want to go home . . . My mother said I have to be home. She'll be looking for me."

"Does she know you were breaking into places? She'd give you a lickin' for that, I bet."

"I want to go home!"

Jeremy again. "Walt? Hey, Walt?"

He was over by the boxcar, I could tell by where his voice was coming from. Jeremy. I felt an enormous wave of sorrow for myself. Why couldn't it be Jeremy here? Why hadn't the man grabbed Jeremy instead of me? Why did it always have to be me who got caught? Everything seemed hopeless. The man was having another drink of wine, still with his arm around my shoulder. I thought of making a break for it, suddenly twisting away and running . . . but even if I got away I'd never have time to stop for my bike. The man would get my bike and you just didn't lose a bike every day. My mother . . . The thought of my mother made my despair even worse.

The man's hand was on my fly, his fingers undoing the buttons, sliding down inside my shorts. I grabbed his arm.

"I want to go home!" I'd been sobbing before, but now I broke out crying aloud and yelling at the

154

man to let me free. "I have to go home! My mother wants me!"

"Shuttup! Pipe down, I said!"

"I want my mother!"

"Stop it!" He put his hand over my mouth.

"Hey, Walt!" Jeremy was still there. "Walt, where are you? What's going on?"

The man hesitated. There was a flustered look on his face. I squirmed for all I was worth. His grip loosened and I struggled to my feet.

"Okay, okay!" he said. "You can go now." He got up too, fumbled for his bottle of wine. "And keep your mouth shut. The cops find out about you – "

But I wasn't listening. I was running, racing through the trees and wiping the tears off my face, heading for the tracks. I got to the boxcar where I'd left my bike but it wasn't there. Then I saw Jeremy. He was standing at the corner of the alley leading up to Harbour Street, signalling to me. When I got to him I saw the two bikes in the alley. He'd wheeled mine away.

"What happened?" His eyes were as round as quarters.

"Nothing." I wiped my face with my sleeve. "Let's get out of here."

"What'd he do?"

"He wouldn't let me go. He said he was going to have us arrested." I had trouble finding my voice. I tried to force a grin. "He wouldn't let me go so I let on I was crying."

I didn't tell him anything else. I was still shaken, and embarrassed because he'd seen my tears.

In fact I never mentioned any of it to anyone,

155

above all not to my mother. I didn't tell my mother about trouble I'd brought on myself by being where I shouldn't, like down by the tracks and climbing up on boxcars and into shed windows; not unless there was no way around it. If she found out that was when the stick would come out of the woodbox and I'd get a good licking. Or so I thought.

To me it was like in the movies: if you fell into their clutches bad men did bad things to you. But that something could be done about it in my case, or that it all wasn't my fault anyway for disobeying my mother, I didn't know. At age ten I didn't know very much. The incident had scared the life out of me and I'd cried like a little baby and if there was anything I knew that I could compare it to it was like what would have happened to Tom Sawyer if Injun Joe had got hold of him.

UNCLE VIC

Sully left for Boston in early May, 1961, while I still had a couple of weeks left in my sophomore year at St. Timothy's University. He wasn't long gone before he wrote telling me he'd struck paydirt. His rich uncle lived in a house the size of Buckingham Palace, he said, and – "get this, Sam!" – it was stocked with every known brand of liquor, not to mention some nobody had ever heard of, and all free for the taking. His cousin Linda was dying to meet me. She was a knock-out, a Marilyn Monroe look-alike and, as he put it, "horny as hell."

I'm not going to gloss over Sully's vocabulary. His education had been badly neglected, but he was what he was, and in the long run it's a man's character that counts.

My name isn't Sam, it's Walt Macbride, as you know, but Sully liked Sam better. We'd called each other George and Sam for a few days once, carrying on like a couple of old Bannonbridge codgers, and he just kept on doing it.

"I told her a wack of lies abowt what a great guy you are Sam," he wrote, "so if you dont get lade it wont be my fawlt." His uncle Vic could snap his fingers and we'd have our choice of jobs – the high-paying temporary kind we were looking for. He'd be working already except he was waiting for me to get down there first, so we could start together...

I was on my way the day after my final exam. I took the early morning SMT bus to Saint John, got another to the border, and from there transferred to a Greyhound for the final leg down through the States. It was a sixteen hour ride. I was stiff as a board when I called him from the terminal in the heart of Boston.

"Hi, Sully," I said.

"Hello, Sam."

"How's it going?"

"So so. Could be worse."

"Well, anyway, I made it. I'm here."

"Where?"

"In Boston. Where do you think?"

"No kidding? What're you doing in Boston, Sam?"

"Cut it out. Look, I'm beat, I can barely move. Get over here and pick me up."

"Where'd you say you were?"

"At the bus station."

Silence on the other end.

"Sully?"

"Yeah, Sam?"

"I said I'm here. Come on and get me."

"I don't have a car, Sam. Even if I did, I don't have a license."

"Look, I'm not in the mood."

"Hold on. I'll check with Uncle Vic." There was a clunk from the phone, followed by muffled voices. "Sam? He's too tired to drive. He says to take the bus."

"The bus? What bus? I just got off the bus."

"No, a city bus."

"How do I do that?"

He went away and came back again.

"Forget the bus, he says you'd only get lost. Your best bet is a taxi."

"Hey, come on. I already spent eighteen bucks on this lousy trip."

"He says it won't cost much. You're not too far away."

"I don't want to waste money on a taxi."

"I know. But I guess you'll have to, Sam. What can I say?"

"You were supposed to pick me up here with you uncle. That's what you said in your letter."

"I know, Sam. But the situation's a little different now."

"What do you mean?"

He whispered something.

"What? I can't hear you? Speak up."

"I'll tell you later. You better get that taxi. I'll see you when you get here."

"You... dog fucker! How much is it going cost me?"

"Just a sec." Voices off the phone again, talking to his uncle. "He says a couple of bucks at the most."

"A couple of bucks! You're going to make me spend a couple of bucks just to get from the bus station..."

Oh, it was nearby, all right. It was so far away the cab driver had never heard of the street, didn't know where it was, drove all over Boston trying to find it. He was a big fat black man with a stub of cigar stuck in his mouth. "I know that street's around here somewhere..."

I worked myself into a frenzy, twisting, squirming, swearing under my breath. Watching my money tick away. I told the cabbie if he didn't find the place soon I wasn't paying him. I was on the point of shoving his cigar down his throat when he reached over and shut the meter off, said he wouldn't charge me the rest of the way. Two minutes later he found the address.

Ten dollars and forty-five cents... I threw the money at him and slammed the door.

Sully was waiting on the sidewalk. I put my hands around his throat and choked him to death. That's what I felt like doing. I could hardly speak I was so mad. In those days ten bucks was a good two days pay for some people. My old man among them.

"Don't look at me, Sam. It's not my fault." It was that cheapskate uncle of his, he said. Afraid it might cost him twenty-five cents for gas if he had to drive to the bus station.

"What're you talking about?" All the stuff he'd written me about his Italian uncle, how rich and generous he was, dying to lavish his wealth on us...

"Did I say that?"

"Boys, I feel like smashing you one."

"I know, I know. I don't like it either. Anyway, put your pack on the veranda and let's get out of here. Before they see you."

"Before they see me?"

"I'll tell you later. They're all crazy. You'll find out. Let's take a walk."

160

"What the hell's going on? I don't want to take any walk."

"It's okay. I got a bottle of wine. I stole it off the old bastard, he makes it himself."

That was different. A drink wouldn't hurt at all right now.

We were in a quiet residential area with only the occasional streetlight. Darkened houses, yards, trees, hedges. We ducked in behind a hedge and Sully brought the bottle out from under his jacket. There was a cork in the bottle and we had no corkscrew. I had to dig it out piece by piece with my pocket knife, bits of cork falling into the wine. I took a mighty swig and suddenly my eyes filled with tears. I gasped, choked, spit, spewed. It wasn't wine, it was vinegar!

"Sam, what's the matter?"

He took the bottle and sniffed. "Holy shit! I must've got the wrong stuff. It's dark down in that cellar."

§

Uncle Vic's financial empire turned out to be a barber shop with four chairs, and his palace a sprawling, run-down old house in a part of Boston called Newton. There were two boys in the family, one sixteen and the other twelve, both shy, sly and gawky. The gorgeous daughter was a scrawny thirteen-year-old with an oversized nose and an adenoidal voice. Mrs. Vic, Sully's mother's sister, was a bag of bones. She was constantly racing round the house with a haunted look in her eye, waiting hand and foot on her husband.

It was sickening the way Sully sucked up to them. He never missed a chance to go on about how great it was to be a rich American — the car, the furniture, the carpets, the appliances. Pointing everything out to me in a loud voice so his uncle could hear.

He must have felt he had to do it — put on the poor relation act, the awestruck sod-kicker from Canada — so they'd be too flattered to kick him out. He'd been leeching off them by now for several weeks, and bringing me in didn't help matters. It was obvious neither of us was welcome.

The first thing I noticed about Sully was his beard, the fact he didn't have it any longer. It surprised me considering one of the reasons we'd left Bannonbridge was so we could do things like grow our beards in peace, without all the small town pressure.

I asked him what happened, why he'd shaved.

"I don't know, Sam. No particular reason. It was starting to itch in the heat. I'll grow it back quick enough. Hey! Wait'll I tell you..." And he went on to another subject.

I'd arrived there on a Friday night. On Sunday morning at the breakfast table I could feel some funny looks coming my way, along with a snickering from the kids.

Uncle Vic said: "Don't they have razor blades back in Canada!" This brought a big laugh from all the family. "You're not one of them beatniks, I hope?"

Later that morning, as Sully and I were sitting around the living room, the family burst in on us, armed with scissors and a hair clipper and an electric razor.

I glanced at Sully who gave an apologetic shrug and slumped deeper into his chair.

So Sully's beard had itched and he'd just decided to take it off. No particular reason.

They circled round me, grinning and snorting and feinting with their weapons. It had to be some kind of joke, I thought. A stupid hint. I decided to humour them and play along. Jumping out of my chair I stood with my back against the wall, in a defensive position, like Bull Curry, the wrestler. Suddenly the daughter let out a screech and lunged at me. I caught her by the arms and pinned them to her sides. Then they all charged, wild-eyed and screaming.

It was like a gang-rape. They weren't fooling! In an instant my dander was up, and I fought back like my virtue was at stake, laying about and sending family members flying in all directions. I flung the younger son at the mother and the two of them crashed to the floor in a heap. I threw the daughter on top of them. I had the older son in a headlock when Uncle Vic cried, "Take it easy! We're only kidding! You don't have to get mad!"

"You're not shaving me, boy!"

"It was a joke!"

His wife untangled herself and got shakily to her feet. She tried to laugh. "Can't you take a joke?" she said.

I let go of the kid and managed to calm down somewhat, get a hold on myself. Sure, they were just putting me on, it was all a misunderstanding, ha ha! What fun. No hard feelings. I laughed along, but inside I was fit to be tied. The minute Sully and I were alone

I said, "I don't know about you, but I'm getting the hell out of here."

"I'm with you, Sam. I told you they were cracked. The same thing happened to me, only they didn't wait so long. Boys, if I'd had somewhere else to stay, I'd have pounded the shit out of them. But I had to stick it out till you showed up."

§

At the dinner table that night the mood was subdued, with Uncle Vic lowering at us from under his bushy brows. When Uncle Vic was silent, everyone was silent. When Uncle Vic talked, they were still silent, unless he made a wisecrack which they had to laugh at. It didn't appear there'd be any wisecracks or laughter, until we announced we planned to hit the road in the morning. Then the atmosphere took a turn for the better.

"Well, we hate to see you go," said Uncle Vic, suddenly beaming, "but all things considered... You know, times are tough and jobs are scarce, especially in Boston. And for guys without work permits... So you're on your way back home, then?"

"We thought we'd try New York," I said.

"New York!" He had his mouth full of spaghetti, strands hanging down his chin, and his jaws gaped open. "Did I hear you say New York?" He looked around the table for confirmation, and the family — taking their cue — rolled their eyes and snickered.

New York! We couldn't go to New York. A couple of kids like us? We wouldn't last a day. It was the biggest goddamn city in the world, with more criminals per square foot than you'd find in the whole of Canada. Murderers, muggers, dope addicts, pimps... We'd have our throats cut the minute we stepped off the bus.

"We weren't going to take the bus," I said. "We were thinking of hitchhiking. We thought maybe you could tell us how to get to the highway – "

"Hitchhiking!"

Where the hell did we come from? Hitchhiking! Didn't we know hitchhiking was illegal in America? Did we want to get arrested? Thrown in jail and deported, never allowed in the States again? Only bums and vagrants hitchhiked anyway – people too goddamn lazy to work for a living so they could pay their way like everyone else.

"I know what I'm talking about, believe me. It's a tough world out there. The place for you guys is back home with your families. You'll only get in trouble drifting around like a couple of deadbeats."

After dinner he led us into his private den. It was a good-sized room furnished with a TV and a sofa and a big soft easy chair and a desk and some shelves stacked with books and magazines. It was his hideaway, he said, where he could get away from the family and relax.

Pointing us to the couch he poured himself a glass of brandy and sank into the easy chair. He lit a cigar and blew a cloud of smoke over us. He was clearly in an expansive mood, now that we were leaving.

Looking at me over the rim of his glass, he said, "Percy tells me you got a college education."

Percy was Sully's real name, Percy Sullivan.

"Well, kind of. Part of one," I said.

"A great thing, education," said Uncle Vic. "I missed out on it myself, but it don't mean I don't respect it. I'm American born and bred, but my folks come from the old country – you know the story – big family, hard times, the Depression, scratching for a bite to eat. Us kids had to get out and earn a buck soon as we could. Education took second place. You know what I mean?"

We nodded. "That Depression must've been something," said Sully. "The old – I mean, my father, he told me about – "

"Now, I don't mean I been a failure in life. I worked hard, and if I say so myself, I think I done okay, all things considered..."

He paused and took a pull on his cigar.

"*Okay?*" said Sully. "Okay, he says!"

"For a guy that had to pull himself up by his bootstraps. Not too goddamn bad. But with a college education... Who knows? I was a smart kid back in grade school. I think I might've done pretty good in college. But that's life and you can't change the past. Right, boys?"

"That's right," said Sully. "You know, I never thought of it like that. You can't change the past. The past is gone, and – "

"Don't get me wrong, now. I been to school. I went to Saint Theresa's for six years – only that ain't the school I learned the most from. I'm talking about the toughest school in America... The education I got there, money can't buy. Maybe you guys never heard of it. It's called – *the school of Hard Knocks.*" He grinned and took a swig of brandy. When we stopped exclaiming he went on: "I read a lot, you know that? I always been a great reader, I like to improve my mind. But I never had the training like you get in college. Percy tells me you're quite the writer."

I looked at Sully.

"Yeah, Sam's written all kinds of stuff. Tell him, Sam."

"He says you even sold some stories to magazines," said Uncle Vic.

"Come on, Sam. Don't be modest. Tell him about those articles you had in those magazines."

"That true?" said Uncle Vic.

"I seen them," said Sully. "He's practically famous. Another Mickey Spillane."

"Which magazines? Maybe I know them," said Uncle Vic. "I read a lot of magazines. Don't get me wrong, now, I'm not being nosy. But what's the pay like? It must be pretty good."

It was like being caught in quicksand, getting sucked into one of Sully's lies. You'd never think an Armistice Day poem in our local weekly would have made such an impression on him.

"The pay? Oh, I don't know, not that much, I guess."

"How much? Don't be shy."

"Well, you know... They aren't big magazines..." I had to play along. It was like a game, putting someone on, and anyway, I couldn't just show Sully up. *Don't listen to him! Your nephew's a liar, a born liar!* "Not like *Time* or *Life* or anything. Ha ha! It's different up north... We don't have the big population and everything... "

"But the average. A thousand? Two thousand?"

167

"No, no. Not that high."

"Five hundred?"

"Uh, maybe, yeah, five hundred..." Sinking deeper into the muck. "Something like that. Roughly speaking. About five hundred. More or less."

Uncle Vic nodded, pouring himself another brandy. He was quiet for a minute, thinking.

"You know," he said at last, "it's quite a coincidence, you being a writer. I'm going to tell you boys something I never told no one else. I don't know if you're ready for this, but here goes." He leaned forward, drawing us into his confidence. "I'm a man of the world, okay? You look at me and you say – there's a guy with both feet square on the ground. A hard-nosed businessman. Am I right? You wouldn't think... You're not going to believe this, so get ready. What you don't know is, this same guy had a dream, a beautiful dream since childhood, a secret ambition... And what he always dreamt of becoming was..."

We waited. Sully said, "You don't mean..."

Uncle Vic nodded. "You guessed it. *A writer.* Just like your friend here."

He sat back to let us recover from the shock.

"I knew you'd be surprised. But it's no word of lie. I had a teacher once, a hell of a good teacher, Miss Giancana, and it was her put the idea in my head. I was just a kid in Grade Six, but she saw something in me. She said to me, 'Vic' – I remember her very words – 'Vic,' she said, 'you got a flair for writing.' A *flair* – that was the word she used. She'd have us write things, little stories, what they called essays, and I did one about the Fourth of July that bowled her over. She told me it was the best in the class. A hell of a woman... You know, I still think of her today sometimes. I learned more from that woman than all my other teachers put together. She wasn't just smart, she had *wisdom*, and wisdom ain't something that grows on trees. There's one thing she told me I'll never forget, a piece of advice I'm going to pass on to you guys. You ready for this?"

We nodded.

"She says, 'Vic, never use a public toilet without covering the seat with toilet paper. There's no telling who was there before you — what disease you'll pick up.' Now, young as I was, it stuck in my mind, and I never forgot it. To this day I don't sit on a strange toilet without putting paper on the seat."

He settled back and, as he'd been doing at intervals since dinner, raised a leg and farted, without batting an eye. I could see Sully staring at the floor, his lip between his teeth. He shook his head slowly. "Jeez, that's... You know, it's the kind of thing a guy wouldn't think of. None of our teachers ever told us that. Did they, Sam?"

I had a sudden fit of coughing and choking behind my hand.

Uncle Vic was lost in his reminiscences. "I'm telling you, that woman was a genius. And she was only a Grade Six teacher! It's what I mean about education. Who knows what I missed by not going to college? Miss Giancana said to me, she says, 'Vic, when you grow up you ought to be a writer.' And, you know, in my heart I guess it's what I hoped I'd be. I been thinking of it lately, and the reason is — I'll tell you why — it's the *stories* — I got a hundred stories in my head. It come to me the other day, when Percy was

169

talking about you. A *hundred* stories? A thousand! In my shop I hear things you wouldn't believe. One guy was telling me he was on his roof putting up this TV antenna and he slipped and fell off. Two or three stories high, straight to the ground. He should've been killed, right? But get this. He landed on his dog! One of them big Saint Bernards. He got up and walked away, no broken bones, not a scratch."

I glanced out of the side of my eye at Sully. He was sucking in his lips and making strange sounds, shaking his head back and forth. "Not a scratch..." he was saying. "What a story!... Jeez!... Right off the roof..."

"You get it?" said Uncle Vic. "Man's best friend. Saves his master's life. So what do you think?" he said to me. Before I could answer he shifted in his chair and ripped another one.

I could feel my belly shaking, like a volcano was going to blow out my mouth. I got my hand up just in time to cover another choking fit.

"Something in my throat," I gasped.

"I bet the dog got some scare," said Sully, seeing Uncle Vic staring at me. "Guy falling out of the sky like that."

"You wanta believe it! The dog was flattened, busted his back right in two. But the guy, nothing. You see what I mean? If I had the time to write, if I could get stuff like this down on paper I'd make myself a bundle. But where's the time? I got a business to run, a family to support. You understand what I'm saying?" He heaved out of his chair and poured himself another drink. He'd already had a bottle of wine with his dinner, and neither then nor now did it cross his mind that Sully and I might appreciate a drop ourselves. Back in his chair he took a guzzle and belched.

"It's like fate or something, you being a writer and showing up here," he said. "See, I had this idea for years, in the back of my mind, but I never run into someone like yourself. Then I got thinking about it lately, and out of the blue who should appear but Mr. Writer himself! Don't tell me the age of miracles is over. A guy with your education and a smart head on his shoulders? Who don't have a family or a business to tie him up? It's got to be fate." He tapped me on the knee, showing his teeth in a broad grin. "Okay, I'm not one to beat around the bush. I'll put it to you straight. How does fifty-fifty sound?"

"Eh?"

"A partnership! We form a team, we work together. I give you the stories and you take it from there, shine them up a bit, get them to the right magazines. And we split down the middle, fifty-fifty. What do you say?"

I couldn't think of anything to say.

"I know, I know," he said. "It's kind of sudden, but it's a great idea, right? It'll be easy, you get the stories ready made, all you do is fix up the spelling, the sentences and things, add a word here and there. We use your contacts and sell them to the magazines. You know that side of it. So it's a deal?"

"Gee... I don't know... I'd have to think about it. It's pretty sudden, like you say. A partnership..."

"It's a new idea. Two heads better than one. We're going to make a lot of money, don't worry."

When I still hesitated, he said:

"You see a problem?"

171

"Well, we're leaving tomorrow, for one thing."

"Yeah, but you're going back home, right?"

"We don't know. We might go anywhere."

"It don't matter. Soon as you get where you're going send me your address. We can do it by mail. I'll ship some stories off to you and you can start right to work. And when the cheques come rolling in send me my half. I trust you. You're an honest guy, I can see it in your face, otherwise I wouldn't be talking to you."

He was a hard man to refuse. We were still guests in his house. We were going to need a drive from him somewhere in the morning, the highway, the bus terminal. And he kept pressing me, wouldn't let up.

So I said, "Okay, it's a deal."

Later, before going to sleep, Sully and I discussed our destination in the light of what Uncle Vic had told us about hitchhiking and New York and so forth. The knifings and shootings and work permits and deportation...

Though we didn't like to admit it he'd sowed some fear in us. We were already fed up with the United States, anyway. The people here were just a bunch of chiselling cigar-smoking con artists, from the taxi drivers on up. We decided to forget New York and take a bus on up to Montreal and then hitchhike to Toronto. From Beantown to Frogtown to Hogtown, as Sully put it.

Sully said, "Are you really going to go partners with that old bastard?"

"Are you kidding?"

"What'd you think of his dog story? I thought he was going to say... The guy fell off the roof and on

172

the way down he cut a fart and it blew him back up again. Like a rocket ship. Jet propulsion."

"That's not bad, Sully."

"I got a hundred of them. A thousand."

TEN AND THREE

In the morning Sully and I took the bus to Montreal, and once there found a room for the night on Rue St. Antoine. Normally rooms rented by the week but the janitor let us have this one for a dollar-fifty a night. We only stayed one night. There were workmen gutting the inside of the building, and when we moved in they had half our ceiling knocked out and part of one wall. Everything was covered with plaster dust, including the bed, which wasn't much of a bed to begin with. It was an old iron bed with a mattress that sagged to the floor. We were given a moth-eaten army blanket for a cover and a couple of bags of cement for pillows.

The man who rented us the room mightn't have been the janitor. When we thought about it later it seemed more like he was the foreman of the work crew. Everybody disappeared at supper time and there was just us in the building. The front door was left unlocked.

Even though we were from New Brunswick and not big city boys we thought we were getting a poor deal for our money.

That evening we walked around Montreal, feeling foreign and out of place since we didn't speak French. After a while we got tired of walking the streets and went back to our room.

We figured it was like we'd heard somebody say once, that if you were English you couldn't find work in Quebec, and so next morning we left Montreal and thumbed to Toronto.

In Toronto we were lucky enough to find a large clean room on Jarvis Street for eight dollars a week. People spoke English in Toronto but work was still hard to come by. We went through the Help Wanted ads and found that they all asked for people with experience.

After a few days I gathered my courage and telephoned about a couple of positions as dishwashers. The man wanted to know if we had experience, and I told him a lie. I said yes, we'd worked in some restaurants back home in New Brunswick. He said to come by next morning for an interview.

We didn't have an alarm clock so we stayed up all night for fear of sleeping in, and set off in plenty of time for our interview. I knew Sully felt the same as I did, untrained, inexperienced, unqualified. I could tell by how we dragged our feet and got there too late to bother going in. It was with a sense of relief that we turned around and went back home to bed.

A few days later, after some pestering from me, Sully made a call and actually got hired over the phone as a house painter, having convinced the man he had five years experience. He'd done a little painting with his father and figured he knew enough to fake it on the job. I thought we were set now. There was no need for the both of us to work, not with the good money painters made.

I stayed up that night and woke Sully at six in the morning, then went to bed myself. I was still asleep when he came straggling in at noon to say he hadn't been able to find the man's address. I knew he hadn't even tried.

After that, seeing that work was pretty much unattainable, we gave up and put the time in wandering about the city and lying in the sun in parks and going to triple-bill movies. We drank beer and played gin rummy all night and slept until mid-afternoon. It all became like a habit.

§

Down on Dundas Street just off Jarvis there was a greasy spoon called The One Spot that seemed to have an attraction for us. It wasn't the restaurant itself so much but the locale, the general atmosphere around the place. I guess we had an itch to take a walk on the wild side of life, mix with the outcasts of society.

There was a current of vice and excitement in the air, and it was easy to imagine we were a couple of desperate types ourselves.

Across the street from The One Spot stood an old clapboard building with a veranda running across the front and a small red neon sign over the door that said *Hotel*. We often noticed couples going in, but never coming out together. We observed the same girls in The One Spot and saw them strolling up and down Dundas. We might have been from down east but we weren't stupid. We had a good idea what was going on.

One night a girl came out of the hotel and went reeling along the veranda, staggering and stumbling and finally collapsing onto the railing. After some discussion Sully and I crossed the street to check on her, but by the time we got there another girl had appeared and was trying to help her stand up.

I said, "What's wrong, she drunk?"

"It's okay. Claudette, get up! You can't stay here."

"I'm not fuck-ing drunk." She was a tough-looking blonde about eighteen, with a French accent. She sounded as drunk as she looked, which was about as drunk as you can get. She muttered, "Doze fuck-ing goofball." Then she shouted at the top of her lungs, "Fuck-ing goofball!"

"For Christsake, Claudette! You wanta bring the goddamn cops?"

"I don' give fuck!"

The girl helping her was about the same age, dark-haired and quite trimly put together and not that bad-looking. I nudged Sully. Here were a couple of girls now, which was what we were looking for, when you got down to it – the main reason we were prowling the streets. The big blonde would be a nice match for Sully. I waited for him to say something, get the ball rolling. But he seemed to have lost his tongue.

That's the way he was. The only time you could get him to shut up was when you wanted him to talk.

Since it was left to me, I said to the dark-haired girl, "Need a hand? Can we – "

"No, just fuck off, it's none of your business." She looked around anxiously. Across the street a man came out of The One Spot and she called to him. "Jimmy! Come here a minute."

The guy had a flat cap pulled low over his eyes. He sauntered over and the girl said a few words to him, and then the two of them pried the blonde from the railing. With her arms draped around their necks they lugged her off down the street, all the while trying to get her to keep quiet.

Sully said, "I think they're a coupla whores."

"I think you're right," I said.

"I wouldn't mind fucking them, especially the little one. I wonder what they charge in this town?"

I'd never thought about it, in this town or any town. All I knew was, if you had to pay for it you must be pretty hard up. Anyone worth his salt could get it for nothing, not to mention any time he wanted it. Sully and I had never paid for it.

Which isn't to say we'd ever got it for free, either. We'd just never got it, period.

"Whatever they charge we can't afford it," I said.

§

We were sober that night, but a couple of nights later we weren't. We bought two quarts of wine and from the first drink all Sully could talk about was getting his hide. I got a kick out of watching him jump around the room, groaning and holding his crutch. "I gotta get laid! I gotta, Sam, I gotta get me skin! I can't stand it no more. I'm gonna do it, Sam!"

I didn't believe him. I'd heard him enough times before, he was long on talk and short on action.

"What do you plan to pay for it with?" I said.

"I can pay. We still got enough money. So what do you say, Sam, are you with me? Don't be chicken."

"I'm not chicken. It's just we're going to be broke in a week as it is."

"I don't care. I'll write the old lady tomorrow and hit her up. She's not going to let her only son starve."

After a few more belts of Golden Diana I had a change of heart, and thought maybe with a little egging on he might even try and go through with it, which would be something I wouldn't want to miss. By the time we left our room I was as much into the spirit of the thing as he was. It was Sully's night to howl and I was with him all the way, in the moral support department. If he pulled it off, maybe I'd take the plunge myself. That's what I told him, anyway, laughing up my sleeve.

We took what was left of the second bottle with us, under my jacket, and finished it in the toilet of The One Spot. Then we stepped out on the street ready for action. For a while nothing happened. It was dark along that stretch, just the one streetlamp halfway down the block, and a patch of light on the sidewalk in front of the snack bar. A couple of shadowy characters drifted by, neither one a girl.

Sully peered at his watch.

"It don't look good, Sam. They're not out tonight."

"We only just got here."

"Yeah, but it don't matter. We're not going to find nothing tonight. It's too quiet. The cops must've been around or something. We might as well fuck off."

"We haven't been here five minutes."

"Five minutes shit. It's been longer than that."

"Six at the most."

"Well, I'm not going to stand here like a dummy all night."

"You're getting cold feet, Sully. That's what's happening. You want to chicken out."

"Fuck you. I'm here, ain't I? So where's the fuckin' broads. You see any?

"Take it easy. What's the big rush?"

"We're wasting our time, that's all. We oughta get something else to drink. If one don't come along —"

"Look!"

"What?"

She was almost upon us before we saw her, only about twenty yards away, stepping briskly along with her heels clicking on the pavement.

I hissed at Sully. "This is it! Now's your chance!"

Out of the corner of his mouth he said, "That's not one."

"It is! It has to be."

"Naw, I can tell."

"C'mon!"

The girl drew abreast of us and tossed us a quick glance and passed on by. Sully never budged. Because of the dark I wasn't able to get a close look at her, but she was obviously young. I prodded Sully to get him to go after her.

"Lay off, Sam! I tell you, she's not one."

"You're chicken."

"Look who's talking. You go ask her."

"Me?"

"Yeah, if you know so much about it. You think I'm supposed to go up to some strange broad and ask her for a fuck? How much she charge? She'd call the cops."

"She's a whore, for Christsake."

"She's not."

"How do you know?"

"I can tell."

"Bullshit."

"Anyway, she's gone now. You blew your chance."

"She was probably a waitress or something."

"Oh yeah. A waitress. Strutting along down here in that tight little dress."

"Look, Sam, if she was peddling her arse she'd have done something. She just walked right by. She's got to let a guy know."

"You have to *ask*."

"You know all about it, eh? Done it a hundred times. Ask what?"

"How much she charges. What do you think?"

"Okay. So I say, how much? And what if it's too fuckin' much?"

"Tell her to forget it. Tell her you were just curious. It's simple."

"Sure, for you it's simple. It's simple as long as I'm the one's got to do it."

"Well that's what you came down here for, wasn't it? It was your idea."

"Anyway, I wasn't ready, she went by too fast. So that's that. I say we go find something to drink."

"Sully!"

"What?"

"She's coming back. It's the same one, I think. Sully, look — "

"I see her. Jesus Christ, I'm not blind."

"Okay, now this time don't screw it up."

As she approached she had to pass in front of the snack bar's lighted window and I got a better look at her face. I recognized her. It was the dark-haired girl from the hotel the other night. I poked Sully in the ribs. "It's — "

"Yeah, yeah. I know."

She was walking more slowly, and threw us another sidelong look, but not quite so brief as the last one. I gave Sully a shove. He leaned forward, then rocked back on his heels and stayed there, firmly anchored. I knew he wasn't going to do it. The girl went on by. And all at once — without a thought or conscious decision of any kind — I was taking off after her, as if pulled by a magnetic force. I just went. In a few strides I was beside her, and like an old hand at the game said, "Hi, how ya doing?" Falling into step with her. "Nice weather we're having," I said.

She gave me the once over.

"You looking for something?" she said.

"I don't know. Maybe."

"A little fun, maybe?"

"Maybe." Then it came out, slick as oil, as if I did this kind of thing every day. "How much?" *How much*! God, that was sophistication. Right down to business.

182

"Ten and three."

"Ten and....?" I didn't get it. "How's that again?"

"Ten and three."

"Yeah, I know. Ten and three."

"Well?"

"What's this ten and three?"

"You have to pay for the room too. The room'll cost you three bucks."

"Oh."

There wasn't a whole lot of seductive charm about her. She had a harsh voice and a sharp manner. But she was young, and if she wasn't entirely beautiful I'd seen many who were worse. There was no mistaking she had a good shape.

Thirteen bucks was a lot of money, but I couldn't turn back now, not after coming this far.

"Okay, where do we go?"

She glanced up and down the street. "Over there." We crossed the street to the hotel where I'd first seen her on the veranda with the doped-up French girl. I followed her in. There was no lobby, just a hallway at the foot of a staircase where a small counter had been set up. Behind the counter a wrinkled old man in wire-rimmed glasses was reading a pocket novel. He looked up and nodded to the girl. She turned to me. "Well? Are you going to get the room or not?"

The man swivelled the open register towards me. I hadn't expected the formality. I knew from movies you weren't supposed to sign your own name, but as I held the pen my mind went blank. I couldn't very well put down John Smith. The pen was on the paper when inspiration came to the rescue and I wrote

Sully's name, Percy Sullivan. My hand trembled as I gave the man the three dollars.

The girl took the key and went up the steep set of stairs with me at her heels, eyes level with her shapely behind, my excitement building. We walked along a dusky corridor and she let us into a room and flicked on the light. It was what you'd expect, simple and unpretentious. The kind of setting you might end up in if your life went all wrong, before you shot yourself. Peeling wallpaper, cracked ceiling, sway-backed iron bed, scarred chest of drawers, wooden chair. As soon as we were inside she said, "The money," holding her hand out.

"You want it now?"

"Yes, now. What do you think?"

"I figured I'd pay later."

She shook her head. "Let's have it. The money first."

It was a situation where you naturally had to be mistrustful. I couldn't let her see I didn't know my way around. Maybe only suckers paid first. She'd take my money and then... what? Pull a fast one, skip out on me somehow?

She stood just inside the open door with her arms crossed, waiting impatiently. She obviously wasn't going to give an inch.

As an old hand at this stuff I would probably know you were supposed to pay in advance...

I took out my wallet and handed her the ten. She put it in her purse and then turned to leave.

"Hey!" I almost jumped on her.

"What's the matter?"

"Where do you think you're going?"

"To the bathroom."

"What for? I mean what bathroom?"

"The one down the hall. Look, take it easy. I'm not going to run away."

"You better not. Okay, but don't be long."

I stood in the doorway until I saw her coming back, then went and sat on the bed. She locked the door behind her and put her purse on the bureau.

"Well, are you going to leave your clothes on?" she said.

"Oh." I whipped off my things while she stood fussing at her hair in the wall mirror above the bureau. It was the first time I'd been naked in front of a girl, but I didn't feel all that shy about it or anything. Maybe I would have if I hadn't been drinking. I felt a bit stripped down, that was all, like a bird without its feathers, or a cowboy without his guns.

Stretching out on the bed I kept my eyes glued on her every second of the way, afraid of missing something.

This was the part I'd pictured in my mind for years, the stuff of countless daydreams. Alone in a bedroom with a girl while she takes off her clothes piece by piece, her dress, her slip, her bra, her tiny panties...

Suddenly the room went black. I sat bolt upright, a delayed image of her hand going to the wall switch.

"Hey!"

"What?"

"Put the light on."

"I don't want it on."

"I can't see."

"Are you scared in the dark?"

"I can't see you. I want to see you."

"You seen me."

"Yeah, but..."

"I don't leave the light on."

"Why not?"

"Because I don't."

"Jeez..."

I could hear the rustling of clothes, and then felt the bed give as she lay beside me. "Move over," she said. It was so dark I couldn't even make out her silhouette; I couldn't see a blessed thing. I thought, this must be what you got at the ten and three level, you had to start out in the dark. Luckily we were only getting into the preliminaries. I could put the light on later, once we got to know each other.

I reached out to touch her, at last about to explore a girl totally naked. I felt again. I began groping like a blind man, running my hand down her body until my fingers struck skin. I had the picture now – she still had her clothes on! All she'd done was pull her dress up around her waist.

She was making a mockery of my fantasies. I stopped where I was and tried to reason with her.

"You got your dress on," I said.

"I know."

"Aren't you going to take it off?"

"No."

"Why not?"

"Because I'm not going to. I don't do that."

"Why?"

"Because I don't."

"I took *my* clothes off."

She didn't answer.

"So how about it," I said.

"No."

"Why not?"

"What's the difference? You can't see me anyway."

"We could turn the light on."

"No! No lights."

"Well, if I can't see you there's no reason you can't take your dress off."

"I said no. Now do you want to fuck or not? Or do you just want to talk?"

"Well, jeez..." Muttering. "You're pretty hard to get along with." I put my hand on her belly and slid it downwards and when I reached the crucial point she grabbed my wrist.

"No touching."

"No touching?"

"You heard me. If you want to fuck, fuck. But that's it."

"Cripes..."

There was nothing for it but to climb on top of her. Her legs were spread and I felt her grip as she put the business end in place. It slipped in easily. Soft and moist and warm in there... And then the instinctive movement. In and out, in and out... I'd never had a lesson in my life, but who cared? I was going at it like I'd been doing it all my life. Right into it! Bounding away like there was no tomorrow.

I breathed in the perfume she wore, its heavy fragrance, like a mass of funeral flowers. Her cheek against mine, soft and smooth. I nibbled at her ear lobe. I wanted to know everything. I reached down to examine what was going on below. She caught my hand again.

"No."

"Why?"

"Because."

"Why not?"

"Just don't, okay?"

I didn't let it bother me. Her little regulations. I felt a rush of amorous warmth for her. She was under me, and I was inside her, and she wasn't really as tough as she made out, I could sense it. When I kissed her on the mouth there was a hesitation before she murmured a muffled protest and turned her face aside. She didn't do that either, kissing.

How could she not be feeling what I was feeling? True, I'd paid for her, but still, this was me, not just some guy off the street. It was a landmark occasion. My passion had to include her, it was too great for me alone.

I was riding along on a tide of emotion, when suddenly, for whatever reason, she responded, a little at first and then more; she was no longer just a passive body beneath me, but moving, alive. She was as soon as lively as I was, letting out little gasps, clinging to me, the two of us galloping along in grand style. I had no idea what I was doing but something was working. At the end, as we burned up the homestretch and crossed the finish line, it was all tremors and shudders and moans. She gripped me like a vice before sinking back limply.

For a while, after, she stayed in my arms. I felt wholly at peace, not a thought in my head.

She stirred presently. I felt the bed lift and then the light went on. I waited for her to get undressed and come back to bed so we could snuggle naked under the sheets. But instead she pulled on her panties and smoothed down her dress. She stepped into her high heels. I stared uncomprehendingly.

"What are you doing?"

"I have to go."

"Go where? What for?"

"I have to."

"You mean that's it?"

"Wasn't it enough?"

"But..." Goddamn it, there could be no such thing as enough. I didn't want her to leave... You'd think I was in love, the disappointment I felt. I assumed I'd have her for the night — I thought that's how it went. We'd taken a hotel room, and that's what hotel rooms were for, you spent the night in them.

But she didn't go immediately. She stood in front of the mirror and fixed her hair, and after that she sat on the bed beside me and we talked. She was different from what she'd been earlier, hardly the same girl at all. She asked where I was from, what I was doing in Toronto. I explained how I was looking for work but hadn't found any yet. I told her a bit about my big ideas, that I'd like to work for a newspaper some day and become a foreign correspondent. In a strange switch of roles she said, "You know, you're a nice guy. You shouldn't have to do this."

"Why not? I liked it!"

"I mean spend your money if you don't have a job. You're nice-looking. Don't you have a girlfriend?"

"Not now. I had one back home for a while, but not anymore. Can't you stay the night?"

She shook her head. "But *you* should. You paid for the room. You might as well keep it."

"You mean stay here alone?"

"Well, you paid for it."

I had a thought. "If I stayed would you come back later?"

She appeared to think about it. "I don't think so. No, I can't."

"I wish you would."

"Why?"

"Well, because I wish you would."

"Why?"

"Because I like you."

She gave me a long look. "You don't really."

"Yes, I do. So *will* you."

She paused again before answering, but then she said, "I have to be somewhere."

"Well, I'm not going to spend the night here by myself."

We were silent a moment. "Do you go to The Brown Derby?" she said.

"The bar?" Sully and I had walked by it quite a few times. "No, not yet."

"I'm in there quite a lot."

"Yeah?"

"Most nights."

I waited but she didn't say anything else. "Yeah, well," I said. And then, for some stupid reason, in case I was misinterpreting her, I said in a kind of rough voice, "I hope you don't think I can pay for this every night."

It was the wrong thing to come out with, I knew it at once. Her expression changed, as if I'd pushed her away. I laughed nervously. "Okay, maybe I'll see you there. Sure, why not."

"It's up to you."

"I'd like to," I said. "It's just that I hate to see you go now."

She got up from the bed and with a last glance in the mirror went to the door, opened it and paused to look back. Then she returned and kissed me on the mouth. For a moment she looked questioningly into my eyes. Then she was gone.

What was I to think? A man of my vast experience?

Experienced or not, naturally I felt she'd taken to me. The way she studied me, the hints she gave. Something had been going through her mind...

She wasn't a machine. Ten and three work couldn't be everything to her. She was human, too, and a young guy like me, about her age, drifting about with no job, and who didn't treat her like dirt... Maybe she was looking for something in her life. It was conceivable.

I didn't *know*, but it was a possibility.

§

I found Sully waiting for me across the street. He was in an agitated state, jumping up and down and gesturing and making faces. He was babbling away even before I got close enough to hear him.

"Slow down," I said. "What's wrong with you?"

From what I could gather he'd kicked himself when I'd walked off with his woman, just as he was about to pick her up. He'd cursed and called me down to the lowest, then tore off trying to find another one for himself. He'd been up and down Dundas and Jarvis and all the way over to Yonge. He'd propositioned half a dozen girls but none of them were whores.

"You should've seen their faces, Sam! I'm lucky I didn't get arrested. I was so desperate I stopped a taxi and asked the driver, I said, 'Where can a guy get put in this town?' He must've thought I was nuts. *Get put*, for fucksake! Nobody says that, only that halfwit Harris back home. The guy looked at me like I had a screw loose and drove off. You should've seen me, Sam. I was so goddamn horny! Oh, you're a great friend, you are. I was set to grab that one and you cut me out. How was she? Where'd she go? Let's go find her. I'll take seconds, I ain't proud."

"It's too late, Sully. She's gone. You missed your chance."

"What was it — I mean what was she like? C'mon, tell me."

"Oh, you know."

"C'mon, Sam!"

"Well, let's see..." Feeling like a man of the world. "Well, it's hard to describe. But it was great, Sully. You have to try it."

"What all did you do?"

"What do you think?"

"I don't mean that. Tell me everything. You prick! What was she like?"

So I told him about the ten and three, and going into the hotel, and the way she was to begin with, the no lights and everything, and leaving her dress on, and how after a while she turned more friendly.

"We hit it off once she got to know me," I said. "She said she wants to see me again, only I don't think she'll charge me next time."

"Go on. Bullshit!"

"It's true. She said to meet her at the Brown Derby."

"Maybe she's there now. Let's go see if we can find her. I'll take a free one from her."

"She's not going to give you a free one, Sully."

"I'll pay. I don't give a fuck."

"She won't be there now. She's got other business."

"So are you going to see her again? You quiff. Some guys get all the breaks."

I was enjoying my superiority to the hilt. "Who knows? Maybe I'll drop in one of these nights, if I'm not too busy. I'll have to wait and see."

And wait I did. I waited and waited and waited. And that was all I did. It wasn't the same the next day or the days after, once I'd had time to consider the situation.

It had nothing to do with my conscience. I can't say I felt the least shade of guilt or regret, no matter how deadly a sin I'd committed. I was at peace with my deed. I don't know why, but it was true.

What held me back was wondering if my imagination hadn't got the better of me. What if I'd read her wrong and she hadn't meant what I'd thought she'd meant? A girl like her met all kinds of men. Why would she single me out for special favours? I had to be kidding myself.

Besides which, getting hooked up with a prostitute was not something a man did every day. It was one thing to have a drink and go out for a night on the town, but when the sun came up next morning you were looking at a different picture. It took a certain type of character to fit into a whore's world, and I wasn't sure I could measure up. I wouldn't be *bad* enough for her. She'd be onto me before I could turn around twice. Assuming she was interested in the first place.

I had some other excuses of the everyday variety, the kind I could acknowledge and tell to Sully. What if they wouldn't serve me at the Derby? I was still underage and even the beard I'd been growing couldn't hide my youthful face. Sully knew what it was like. Sometimes they'd serve me and not him at a bar, and sometimes vice-versa, and sometimes neither of us. In the grand scale of things it was one of the worst embarrassments you could face in life, being shown up as a boy in a man's world.

And to top matters off, it was time to tighten the belt. I couldn't afford to go paying bar prices for a drink – especially now, after the ten and three.

As I mulled over all these particulars the days slipped by. The door to opportunity doesn't stay open forever, and after a period you realize it's too late, that you've left it too long.

I happened to see her once again, by chance a couple of weeks later. She was walking up Yonge Street on the arm of some fat old geezer in a suit and tie. He was staggering and laughing while she tried to keep him on course. I know she recognized me – our eyes met, and I saw it. I gave her a nod and a stupid grin, but she didn't nod or smile back. She froze me with a look that was cold as – I was going to say a whore's heart – and turned her head away and kept on going. And that was that for that.

WONDERLAND

I woke up three times. I was in jail. I had been told I was due out the following day, but today a guard came to inform me I'd been charged with rape.

Rape! Why would I rape someone, a gentleman like myself? It was preposterous. And yet I could get twenty years if they made it stick.

I was in this jail over a minor misdeed, a simple bar fight. It was just a trumped-up charge. The police were stumped and needed a patsy, and who better than some bum out of the drunk tank, as they took me for? Nobody would care.

There was a movie crew on location at the jail, and the inmates were told they could watch part of the movie being filmed. I went out into the yard and stood around with the rest of the inmates. When the filming was over the actors came over on our side of the rope cordon and circulated, chatting with the prisoners and each other. I got into a conversation with one of them, a bit-part player, and in the general confusion we strolled away from the set and out through the gates and onto the road.

It was night. Having been locked up in a cell for so long I had some trouble at first expressing myself, but the actor was patient and I believe we got along well enough. He was interested in playing me in a movie about my life.

At one point I saw a highway patrolman staring at me. He unstraddled his motorcycle and walked in our direction, hesitated, then returned to his motorcycle.

I noticed quite a few policemen stationed about, as if positioned strategically. They were on rooftops, in cars, in alleyways and doorways.

I left the actor and went back to the prison. At the gate I was set upon by a gang of newspaper photographers and then the guards grabbed me and rushed me to my cell. I had been under close observation all the time.

Being accused of rape I shouldn't have been permitted to leave my cell. Apparently one of the guards had gotten careless.

I was informed the further charge of jailbreak had been added to my sheet.

I argued I hadn't known about any restrictions and had only followed the crowd. But I might as well have saved my breath. They didn't listen to a word I said.

I remained in my cell till the trial arrived, several days later.

I was brought before three judges. Previous to my arrival at court I had debated whether to hire a lawyer or not. I was afraid of picking someone with inferior abilities, or one with little interest in my case.

If I was found guilty it wouldn't be the lawyer who'd spend the next twenty years in prison.

So I decided to represent myself.

It wasn't long before I discovered I'd made a mistake. The old saying is right, a client who represents himself has a fool for a lawyer.

The court procedure was so complicated that for some time I could scarcely identify whether I was the accused or not, let alone convince the jury of my innocence.

The climax came when the woman I was supposed to have raped was called to the stand to identify her assailant.

I'd never seen her before. She was blotchy-faced and frizzy-haired and so fat she could barely squeeze into the witness box. A five hundred pound woman.

I thought, "Surely she won't claim I was the man who did it." But to my horror she pointed directly my way and said, "*That's him — he's the one!*"

I protested. I told the judges she recognized me only because the newspapers had displayed my picture as the man "Charged With Rape." I said it had worked on her mind, that probably she didn't know what her attacker looked like at all. But no one was listening. The judges declared me out of order and the trial moved along as though I hadn't spoken.

I'd as much as called the girl a liar, when it was obvious everyone pitied her as "a poor unfortunate." It was a bad move, I saw that now. I realized I'd have to be more subtle in the future, more lawyer-like.

It was a bad stroke for me that the newspapers had got hold of my picture. Someone must have tipped them off that night when I returned from my walk with the actor. I remember the camera bulbs flashing from all directions and giving me such a start that I dived under some bushes and hid. It was all very ridiculous and undignified. The photographers dragging me out by my heels and pulling at my cap, trying to get a better shot of my face. They were such a nuisance that finally I took the cap off and told them to take all the pictures they wanted.

The guards never lifted a finger to stop them. They waited until the photographers were finished and then hauled me off to my cell.

§

I was sure I could prove I'd been somewhere else when the rape occurred, it was only a matter of producing some witnesses. The trouble was, I didn't have any, and didn't know how to go about getting them. I kicked myself again for not getting proper legal counsel. In my desperation I asked a man at the next table if was a lawyer.

"Yes," he said. "It so happens I am."

"I suppose you're here to observe the trial? I guess it's quite interesting, so much news coverage and everything."

"I'm working for the prosecution."

"Oh. Well, do you know where I could find a lawyer? I have to dig up some witnesses and they won't let me out to look for them. Besides, I don't understand the court procedure. When I try to speak no one listens. They tell me I'm irrelevant and out of order."

"It's too late now."

"It is?"

"Oh yes. Much too late."

The courtroom was in a modern building and very high up. It occupied the entire sixty-sixth floor and had large plate-glass windows on all sides. Whichever way you looked you could see the peaks and upper stories of other towering obelisk-type structures.

I had just finished speaking with the lawyer when an amazing thing happened. An airliner flying low and obviously in trouble veered towards us and went by with only a few yards to spare. I could see the strained face of the pilot as he tried to navigate through the forest of skyscrapers. It was a hopeless endeavour. In a matter of seconds the plane rammed head-on into the top of one of the other buildings. We couldn't hear it, our walls and windows were sound-proofed, but we saw the explosion. The building tottered and like a great pillar fell over sideways and crashed into another building, carrying it down with it. Before long there were skyscrapers tumbling in all directions like dominoes. And then fires began to break out...

It was nothing short of a miracle that our own highrise was spared, at least for the time being. Seeing those gigantic structures toppling slowly to their destruction sent a panic through the courtroom. Everyone began to scramble for the exits, judges, lawyers, guards, witnesses, and myself with the rest of them. It happened three elevators were kept in readiness during trials and these were instantly jammed. There was also a stairway, and I ran for this.

I was among the first to reach it and had a free passage before me. I wasn't thinking of escaping the law; I was in as much a panic as the rest.

I was able to gain the street and from there dodge through falling bricks and fiery obstructions and get clear of the disaster area.

It wasn't until a number of hours later that the chain reaction of falling buildings had spent itself, but by then the fires were out of control and threatened to devour the entire city. Firemen worked to isolate the fire in its huge cradle, prepared to sacrifice this sizeable area if the rest of the city could be saved.

I made my way to the top floor of a building at the edge of the fire ring and witnessed the spectacle of the firemen at work. They were in constant motion, biting off the flames whenever they appeared at a window, a door, on a roof; hurling the fire back in on itself, until it would have nothing to feed on but itself and eventually be its own death.

You can imagine the difficulty of spot-fighting a fire like this, but it was the only possible method, since the ring of destruction was such a large one, and the buildings of such tremendous size, and the number of firemen naturally limited.

I was astounded at their methods and their bravery. They worked in squads of three, swinging on long ropes suspended from God-knows-where, moving from trouble-spot to trouble-spot, sixty and seventy dizzying stories above the ground. They would enter a burning window, deal with the flames and immediately leap out onto a rope. The air was full of these ropes, like jungle vines in a Tarzan movie. Men swinging through the air and others hanging onto their legs...

When they leapt from a window they didn't always make it. Many fell screaming to the streets, sending the firemen below scattering like ants.

Flames raging, smoke rising volcanically to the sky... Acrobatic firefighters swinging from building to building... Shrieking bodies dragged from the rubble and loaded onto ambulances...

I went close to the open window and looked down. I was on the thirty-seventh floor, and my spine trembled at the height — while across the way men worked recklessly at heights twice as high. At one point three of them came soaring over, faces soot-blackened and sweaty, carrying in their free hands axes and extinguishers and gas masks. Cursing wildly they looked around, then attached themselves to another rope and flew away. I gathered they were inspecting the building for fear some sparks might have carried over.

I turned my gaze across the street again, just in time to see a rope snap and three other men hurtle downward and land with a silent smack on the pavement. One of them fell on a spectator running with his eyes turned upward. Workers scooped up the bodies and threw them into the back of a truck. Another man in cover-alls came along and set to work mopping up the blood stains.

I left the window and started downstairs. Several floors down I passed a couple of Africans in tribal robes discussing whether they should join the firemen. One remarked that the work was hard. "It is," said the other. "But work is work, and the money's good."

I wondered how anyone could witness such scenes and even consider becoming a firefighter.

When I reached the street I went for a stroll through the unravaged part of the city and soon succeeded in getting myself lost. I spent hours climbing up and down stairs and ladders, exploring narrow streets, trying to find something familiar. I knew the prison was not part of the destroyed section and I intended to return there, as an indication of my innocence. Eventually I ran into two young men who said they were going to the prison together, and I said I would go along with them since I didn't know the way.

We walked a long time and many miles, and were no longer in the city but on a small unpaved road in the wilderness. We came to a pond and the two young men said we would stop here for a swim.

"It's too cold to swim," I said. "It's only early April."

They said I didn't have to join them. I stood on the bank while they undressed and walked solemnly into the water. When they were waist deep one of them sat in the water over his head. The second young man stood beside him, and when his friend began to rise to the surface pushed him under and held him there.

"Hey!" I called. "He's going to drown."

"I know."

"Don't hold him under the water. He'll drown."

"I know. He wants to. He asked me to help him."

203

Well, I thought, he must have at that, because he wasn't resisting. I left them and continued down the road. It couldn't have been the way to the prison after all.

But it didn't matter. I'd find out where I was going when I got there.

CARNIVAL

It was November of 1963 and late at night and I was standing in a cold pelting rain beneath a streetlight on the edge of town. I stuck my thumb out and a car pulled to a stop. I staggered up to it and got in. Why I was hitchhiking or where I thought I was going I couldn't say. No doubt I had some idea in my head but it wasn't one I ever remembered.

The car let me off and I was out on the highway walking. I walked for the longest time, wandering from one side of the road to the other, until it occurred to me I didn't know if I was going away from town or towards it. I wanted to go home now. It was lonesome out in the dark and rain where there were no people and no houses. I changed direction several times with an increasing sense of desperation. Peering upward I thought I saw the lights of town reflected on the sky, miles and miles away, and I splashed along in that direction. Whenever a car came along I put my thumb out. One of them stopped. I got in and argued stubbornly with a man and woman over the way back to Bannonbridge. They insisted I was headed in the wrong direction. Finally I said I believed them, though I didn't. I didn't trust them. They let me out on the highway again, and I resumed walking.

By now I was completely bewildered. I came to a motel where the owner was just locking up. Rather impatiently he told me Bannonbridge was fifteen miles away. I asked him to call me a taxi. He said he didn't have time. I hadn't a cent in my pockets so I don't know how I intended to pay the fare. There was a phone booth by the road. The man gave me a dime and I found a number in the yellow pages and called the cab, giving the name of the motel. For a while I sat on the floor of the phone booth with my legs in a puddle outside. Then I got to my feet and began walking again, hitchhiking the few cars that passed.

Staggering down a road that seemed endless my mind was fixed on reaching my bed where I could sleep and sleep forever. I thought it would be pleasant to be dead. I could be easily enough, all I had to do was step out in front of a car. It was tempting. A car came up behind me and I didn't turn or move off to the shoulder of the road and it swerved and rushed past missing me by inches. A step to the left – that's all it would have taken.

I wanted desperately to get to my bed. Warmth, sleep... a blissful oblivion. To disappear where no one could come after me. That was death, too, wasn't it? If I got run down I wouldn't care.

I heard another car and turned and extended my thumb and there was a roar and splash as it shot by. Then a screeching of brakes. Reversing recklessly the car swerved back to where I stood. There were four young guys in the car. They knew me, and they were whooping and laughing, in high spirits. They gave me a drink of wine which I didn't need or want, since I was as drunk as I could get already. They were all drunk, too, but not in the same way. They drove me to my door and sped off with a squeal of tires.

Going up the stairs I felt for my glasses but my coat pockets were empty. So I've lost them, I thought. But it didn't seem important. I could find some way to get another pair, should I ever need them, or anything else. I must have lost them in the fight. It was all very indistinct. I didn't feel bruised though I remembered being on the ground and knowing the guy was kicking me. And I knew I'd started the fight.

I woke in the middle of the night and vomited on the floor beside the bed. Tomorrow, I thought, I'll decide whether I've had enough or not. I don't *have* to put up with this. The thought was comforting. and I fell easily back to sleep...

§

Whether I'll die or not I don't know. I think I'll die like my friend Sully, and someone will wrap me up and carry me after dark and throw me into the shallow river. When I threw Sully in he didn't float as I expected. He rested on the bottom below the wharf, in full view of anyone looking down.

I was late arriving when I said I would come over. I brought the book he asked for, but he was already dead.

Two people came back to life the night I threw Sully into the river: my mother who kept in the

207

background saying nothing, and my former girlfriend the beautiful Corinne (who'd left me because I sometimes took a drink as if that was a crime), though I hadn't known until then that she was dead too. She was undressing before me, removing a nun's habit. She came over to me and let me kiss her breasts, and then she slipped off her panties and I kissed her all over. I wanted to make love to her but she shook her head. "Mommy said no, I couldn't." Her perfumed breasts, the soft touch of her thighs against mine... It was maddening. I could feel my head spin. "If only you would," said. I wanted to cry I desired her so much.

I was downtown, walking the streets, and I knew it was my turn. I had desecrated death and I had to die, as Sully had. He laughed at me cruelly as though I were his murderer. I knew I had to die, because Sully was alive again and laughing at me, running towards me. No one else could see him. My time was come, I was out of my mind, beyond recovery. But I wouldn't give in without a fight. l was too angry to die like a lamb. I threw Sully through one of the windows of Grogan's Grill. The people walking by didn't care, they didn't so much as turn their heads. Sully looked out the window laughing. He knew I was beaten. Laughing at me. I couldn't stand how everyone ignored me. I caught hold of a man walking along the sidewalk and threw him through the window, too. But it didn't help, still nobody noticed me. I assaulted more people, heaving them through the window until they piled up in the restaurant in a heap of arms and legs; but it was all for nothing; I couldn't catch anyone's attention; the bypassers continued to look straight ahead as if I wasn't there. So

I would go home to bed then, and die as Sully died, smiling sadly in my bed.

The outer wall is gone from my room, and the wind blows in on me, chilling me to the bone. I put a jacket on, my black leather jacket that I haven't worn since I outgrew it in high school. This should help me, I'll walk outdoors with my jacket on for protection, it will keep me warm and shield me from the people out there. But the futility of it stops me, and I take it off. I'm afraid to die of coldness; I'm not afraid of the cold but I think that's the way Sully died. I'd better dress warm. I pull on my heavy winter underwear, an army shirt, a wool sweater. The wind storming into my room makes me shiver.

§

I found my glasses in the morning, they were in my pants pocket. One of the arms was missing but I was still able to wear them in lopsided fashion. I had two classes that morning but didn't make it to the first one. I went to the second only to let it be known I was on my feet and not afraid to show myself. Naturally the story of my fight was all over St. Timothy's. With only a few hundred students word soon got around. Nobody missed anything. I could feel the eyes on me as I walked along the hall, the murmurings from behind. But no one spoke to me directly.

At noon I went home and fixed dinner. It was all I could do to eat, forcing the food down to show I didn't have a hangover. The old man must have heard me throwing up in the night, but of course he said nothing. Nothing existed if it wasn't mentioned. He lived a philosophy that apparently worked for him and it wasn't my place to mess with it. A kind of Buddhism, maybe, a meditative state beyond reach of the material world.

After washing the dishes I went into my room and lay down. I was bruised and sore from the fight but it didn't matter. No doubt I'd been humiliated. Taking on a guy twice my size when I was falling-down drunk. I must have put up a pathetic show.

Not so long ago I'd have gone back at him when I was in better shape, out of pride. But now I didn't want to. There was a difference... I had no distinct memory of who the guy was, for one thing. I'd never seen him before. And I'd been the instigator. I knew how I pushed people when I was drunk.

But it wasn't that. The spirit was gone out of me. If I wasn't lit up from the bottle I felt depressed. I didn't want to fight anyone. I didn't have the strength.

When Sully was around I hadn't cared so much what people thought of me, because Sully and I, we'd been able to lean on each other. It was them and us.

But now it was all of them and only me. The burden of being alone on the outside was getting heavier. I began to wonder if I was right... If it was worth being a majority of one.

I was starting to see myself as everyone else saw me: a troublesome misfit. A guy with a few screws missing.

In any case, I decided not to kill myself, no matter how depressed I got. I found a way out, an insight that came to the rescue as I lay on my bed. It was like a revelation.

If life's not worth living (this is what it was) then don't worry, because you don't have to *really* live it. You don't have to die either, not right now. It's like a hole card. You *can* go if you want, but you have the choice of sticking around for a while. Knowing you can escape anytime is enough, so why not stay for the show? Look on it as a spectacle, a carnival, a circus. Like you've come here from another planet. And it's not your world, it's *theirs*. You don't have to be involved. Let them have the problems... It's the strain of making your way that kills you. Trying hard and taking it all to heart. Trying to show everyone...

§

Some months went by. I'd stopped being a Catholic in my mind, but I was still going to mass now and then, so as not to cause any trouble. With the old man being the church sexton I thought it best to keep up appearances. You never could tell. They might fire him if they thought his son was some kind of heathen.

I went to an afternoon mass. Father Clery in his sermon dealt with something specific for a change, instead of the usual holy platitudes that sent you daydreaming. "There's a play on Broadway now about the late Pope Pius XII, which is based on a lie... The idea that during the Second World War the Pope didn't stand up against Nazism as he should have ... This, I tell you, is a *lie*! And an especially vile one in view of the holiness of Pius XII...

"It is heartening, then, that recently Pope Paul published his first encyclical in which he condemned organized atheism, atheistic Communism... ensuring that the same accusations can never be brought against him in the future..."

There had been freezing rain throughout the day, and on my way home the cars coming from church crept along beside me, wheels spinning on the ice, barely keeping pace with me.

I was home in five minutes. The hall of our old apartment building has a ten-watt bulb hanging from a cord, but it still shows up the grimy wallpaper, the worn linoleum floor, the stained plaster ceiling. There's no light in the staircase to the upstairs apartment, and when I reached the top my hand struck cloth and I knocked the old man's felt hat off the bannister post, sending it rolling down the steps. With a curse I ran and retrieved it.

With the hat in my hand I paused. I had the feeling I was in somebody's movie, following a script that kept a step ahead of me, like in a dream. This sensation is always with me, as if I'm on camera, being monitored.

If it's true, if there's direction to everything I do, how does it explain knocking a hat down a stairs? Surely that has no significance. The whole puzzle of life could centre on the simplest incident.

I have a fear it might *not* all make sense one of these days. I seem to believe it will, for some reason.

The old man was waiting for his supper. I put some soup on and we ate in our usual silence, and then I went to my room and stretched out on the bed and read for a few hours. Every so often I had to put the book down with a groan, because I couldn't get the events of a certain night out of my mind. A fiend kept pricking my conscience, sticking its pitchfork in. *You're a jerk, Macbride, a complete screw-up. All you know how to do is alienate people. No wonder they can't stand you...*

I wasn't hungover. I didn't have that excuse. But the self-loathing was still with me.

My anti-suicide philosophy saved my life. It was a remedy I could always turn to. It was a wonderful thing, but it didn't actually prevent me from again getting caught up in life.

You might say I got caught up in life's carnival. Or more exactly, the annual St. Timothy's Winter Carnival.

It was held in February, and the final event of the festivities was a stage performance by the folk-singers Ian and Sylvia. I hadn't bought a ticket for the show, nor for any of the other events throughout the week, and this only made matters worse, why they all got down on me as they did. Not that I gave a goddamn. At least that's what I told myself. As if I was squirming with remorse for the exercise.

I'd been drinking that day and on impulse decided to take in the concert. The fact I was broke after buying my wine made no difference. I could be resourceful when drinking. Nothing fazed me, no obstacle was too great.

The concert was a big affair up at the Exhibition Building. I hung around the entrance waiting for an inspiration, when several cars pulled up and the Chancellor of the university himself, Monseigneur Hagen, got out with an entourage of priests and professors. Without hesitation I strode towards them like a one-man welcoming delegation and chatting at the Monseigneur walked past the ticket window as

213

part of the party. Once inside I took a seat in the back row. The lights went down and I slipped my wine bottle from beneath my coat, and throughout the show sat back and nipped on it contentedly.

At the break, after a little nosing around, I was able to learn where the reception for the entertainers was going to be held. I knew there had to be one. I didn't want to miss it because my wine was about gone and there'd be free drinks; and besides, being half-drunk, I was in a mood for socializing.

When the applause died for the last encore I made straight for backstage. Everyone was milling around, the students keeping at a safe distance from the singing stars, obviously in awe of them – but not me. Seeing an opening I drew Ian and Sylvia aside and said I'd be happy to conduct them to the banquet being laid on in their honour. It turned out they were hungry and thirsty and eager to get going. I ushered them to the parking lot and twenty minutes later found myself seated at the head table with Monseigneur Hagen and the president of the Students Union and Ian and Sylvia and their back-up guitarist, a young fellow named Monty.

On the drive over I'd confessed everything. Booze was like a truth serum with me, especially when I thought the truth would make an impression. What was there to worry about? We were all renegades and radicals, as well as famous personalities. I knew they'd side with me – and they did. As folk singers they couldn't very well align themselves with the Establishment.

As I sat centre stage guzzling my second double rum I was aware of an undercurrent of grumbling from the tables around me. They'd worked hard, the Carnival Committee, and this was their pay-off – an exclusive bash with the celebrated singers and recording artists. Only, who's sitting at the head table between Ian and Sylvia? Macbride! It was bad enough he never worked a minute for the Carnival, but he hadn't even bought a ticket to the damned thing.

Muttering in their teeth, casting black looks my way. They were itching to throw me out, but they couldn't, not with decorum. Not seeing I was on such good terms with the performers, who seemed to find the situation amusing.

I was not to remember a great deal of that night, I got so drunk. At one point the head of the Carnival Committee (whose place I'd taken at the head table) crept seething with rage to my chair and whispered some vicious things in my ear. Then he said the least I could do was consider myself on assignment for the college paper and interview Ian and Sylvia. Apparently some price had to be levied on me. I said it would be a pleasure.

The guitarist, Monty, was a carefree good-natured lad. He was sitting beside the Monseigneur and every so often he'd lift his leg and let rip a fart. The Monseigneur didn't stick around long, once the drinking got going in earnest.

I enjoyed the evening no end, while it was happening. I'm sure I did. But next day I felt terrible about it, writhing and twisting as it all came back on me. I hated making enemies, even of people I didn't like. But that's the way it was. I could hardly turn around without doing something wrong, or failing to do something right...

And I had that accursed interview to write. I'd forgotten most of what they said. But you didn't catch me that easily. As soon as I could I sat at my typewriter and made something up. I invented pretty well most of it. But that's journalism.

§

Around nine last night I set the book I was reading aside and went out for a coffee. Someone had my little corner booth, the one where I was in the habit of hiding myself, so I took another near the lunch counter. There were three young girls sitting on stools with their backs to the counter, facing my way. I knew them by sight, but no more; they'd have been children to me a year ago, but like Corinne they must have grown up fast. They were about fifteen years old.

One was as dusky as an Eskimo and quite a beauty. She was wearing tight slacks and a short imitation leopard skin coat, what they used to call a "shorty coat." I surveyed them over the lip of my coffee cup. Suddenly the dark girl called out, "Wally!" signalling for me to come over. I raised my eyebrows – me? Not many people called me Wally, because I wouldn't answer them if they did. I didn't like that variation of my name.

A reply sprang into my head: "No, no, my dear, you come here. And the name's Walt." Only I didn't have it in me, not drinking coffee. It wasn't Mr. Hyde out tonight.

I got up, half-glancing around to see if there was another "Wally" in the house. Strangely, the girl was looking away from me as I drew near, and continued to look elsewhere when I was standing directly in front of her. I realized then that I must have made a mistake. But I was here now, and had to go through with it, with something. The other two girls were staring at me questioningly... I couldn't just turn around and walk back to my seat.

"Did you call me?"

I might have been non-existent, a spirit, a ghost. It was unnerving. I repeated myself, conscious of my muscles tensing, my body beginning to tremble. At last her brown eyes focused on me. She said, "What?"

"I thought you ... Did you call me?" Of course she hadn't, I knew that now, but what else could I say? Had I been hearing things?

"No." She seemed surprised, as if it was the last thing she'd think of doing. She eyed me suspiciously.

"Didn't you..." I wished I could just walk away, gracefully somehow, but I was in too deep. "You called somebody," I said. "It sounded like Wally."

She thought about it. "No."

I appealed silently to the other girls, defenceless, not finding the words to straighten things out. They exchanged glances, giving me the same perplexed look as the dark girl. I raised my eyes to the ceiling. "Listen," I said, trying suddenly to be aggressive, "you think I'm hallucinating or something? Don't act so dense. You called somebody. It sounded like Wally."

"Oh! *Polly*," one of the girls said. She seemed glad she could help, and smiled sympathetically. Then they all understood. The dark girl had called to Polly, a friend sitting in one of the other booths.

The one with the dark skin, the beautiful one, made a face and dismissed me, but the other two were more merciful. They wanted to be kind to this pitiful figure in front of them. I mumbled with a weak grin that the name was close — "Only one letter difference," I said, holding up one finger. "That is... in the sound... the spelling..." I backed away and turned and walked to my booth. Trying to appear casual and unconcerned. A few minutes later the girls got up and left.

I didn't sit down in an angry flush and begin cursing under my breath. I rolled a cigarette and smoked it calmly, making a blank of my mind, my expression. This defense of course could only be temporary. The reaction when it came took full possession of me, like an inner explosion of self-hatred — for my ineptness, my self-consciousness, my bumbling lack of composure. And worst of all, that I would let such a paltry misunderstanding upset me so severely, as it was doing now.

No, I *couldn't* be just one person. For someone inside me was pouring a stream of scalding curses and bitter derision over another of my selves. It was madness. You'd think I'd get used to these awkward episodes, they happened almost every day. I couldn't speak to anyone without my mouth going dry and my knees threatening to buckle. My scalp tightening, eyes shifting, tongue seizing up. I couldn't understand it. When I was a youngster I'd been the most gregarious kid in town. Now I acted like I was terrified of humanity.

Walking home my mind was filled with fighting off phantom attackers, leaping out of the shadows at me. I pictured it vividly. How they'd throw me down, rip off my clothes and chase me naked through the streets...

What would I do? What revenge would I take on them?

I just wanted to get away. That's all I wanted. Get away to a place where I'd never be found and no one would know me.

A CASE OF IDENTITY

One day, in the mid-sixties, when I was a young bard living in Montreal, I was over visiting my girlfriend Eva, who'd just made up her mind to rent a television.

She showed me the ad in the newspaper and said, "Would you call them up? You're better at that sort of thing."

I didn't think I was, but since she said so I got on the phone to the rental company and asked them to deliver one of their 18-inch sets.

"What's the name?" the man said.

"Stuart," I said, giving Eva's last name.

"Okay, Mr. Stuart, we'll have it there this afternoon."

"He thinks I'm Mr. Stuart," I said to Eva as I hung up the phone.

She laughed.

"They'll bring it this afternoon," I said.

"I have to be at the hospital by four-thirty." Eva was a recent nursing graduate and had just started her first job at the Royal Victoria Hospital.

At three o'clock she was in the bathroom getting ready for work. I heard her call out: "If they come before I'm dressed you can sign the papers, okay?"

"They might want your signature," I said.

"Sign it *E. Stuart*. They won't know the difference."

She closed the bathroom door.

About half an hour later later the buzzer sounded. It was the men with the television. One man carried it in and stood holding it while the other sat down at the kitchen table with a handful of papers.

"Mr. Stuart?" he said. He was about forty, a big hearty man with a deep voice.

"Yes," I said. "Put it over here." The other man, who was younger, placed the set on a small table Eva had cleared off.

He plugged it in and it worked well enough. For an 18-inch set, however, it looked suspiciously like a 16-incher. The man with the papers admitted this was so. "We have an 18 down in the truck but it's two dollars a month more," he said.

I protested. "That's not what your ad said."

He shrugged.

"Look, I'll show you," I said. "I have the ad right here."

"They probably printed it wrong."

I chewed my finger for a minute, scrutinizing the television, trying to decide whether or not to keep it. I didn't like being cheated. On the other hand the picture was fairly good, and I hated making tough decisions. So I gave in.

"Okay, I'll take it."

"Fine." He sorted out the papers and began filling in the information: size of set, its cost, how long I'd want it, the date, and so on. "Your first name?" he asked.

"E. Stuart. The initial will do."

"E.?"

"Yes."

"Edward, I bet." He grinned at me.

"No."

"Eric?"

I shook my head.

There was a pause. I felt a twinge of uneasiness.

"E. Stuart," he muttered, writing it in. "Occupation?"

"Well, uh. As a matter of fact... "

"You're employed, aren't you?"

"Certainly. That is... I mean, I inherited... You see, my father died and left me some money... I'm kind of taking it easy these days. Ha! Ha!" Nervous little laugh.

It wasn't entirely the truth, to the extent that my father hadn't actually left me anything, and in fact hadn't died yet; but as an occupation "poet" doesn't generally make a big impression, especially to someone renting you something.

He congratulated me on my good fortune. "But I still have to fill in employment here... I'll just put self-employed. That ought to do. Now, Mr. Stuart, do you have some form of identification?" I felt my heart drop. "A driver's license, maybe, something to show who you are."

"A driver's license... Well, no, I don't drive. So I guess I don't have one."

"All right. What about a credit card?"

"A credit... I'm sorry, I don't have one of those either. I never buy on credit."

"Very wise. But you must have something in your wallet."

"Oh yes. I keep my money there."

"Nothing else? No identification?"

"I don't believe so."

"Why don't you check and see?"

"I'm pretty sure there's nothing."

He gave me a peculiar look. "Do you have a birth certificate?" Seeing me hesitate, he said, "You were born, I assume?"

"Oh yes. I was born — I mean, of course. But..." I could feel myself sweating.

"Are you trying to say you have no identification? None at all?"

"Well, I do, yes, but... You see..." I wiped my forehead. "As a matter of fact..." I walked to the bathroom door, stopped, came back. I stood by the table and tried to think. For a minute nobody spoke, the two of them watching me. "Look, I might as well tell you," I said. "It's like this. The television isn't for me. I mean, I called you but it's for my girlfriend, and she's getting dressed to go to work now. She's a nurse. So we thought we'd save some trouble — It's for *her*, you see. She's E. Stuart, not me." The older man chewed thoughtfully on his pen. "Just a minute," I said.

I went to the bathroom door, gave a knock and peeped in. "Are you dressed yet? You'd better get dressed and come out and sign this thing." She was standing before the mirror in her bra and half-slip.

"What's wrong?" she said.

I closed the door and went back to the kitchen. "She'll be out in a minute."

"You mean the set's not for you?" the man said. "Let's get this straight. Who is it for?"

"My girlfriend. I thought I'd take care of it, so she could get dressed – " I looked at him helplessly.

"I see. Okay," he nodded. "So it's for *Miss* E. Stuart?"

"Yes."

"And she's a nurse."

"Yes."

He crossed out the "self-employed" and the "Mr." and wrote in "nurse" and "Miss."

In the meantime Eva had got into her uniform, and she came out of the bathroom. "Hi," she said.

"So you're Miss Stuart," the man said. "Your boyfriend was telling us *he's* Miss Stuart and that he's a nurse." His partner guffawed and my face got red. "But I don't know what to think. He's not really a nurse, is he?"

"No, he's not a nurse," Eva said.

I forced a grin, or a grotesque excuse for one, trying to go along with it as best I could.

Eva took the pen and signed her name, and I scribbled mine to one side as a witness. The man said some more clever things about my being a nurse and then left with his partner.

"What was that all about?" said Eva. "You didn't really tell them you were a nurse?"

"No, I didn't. Are you ready to go now?" I said.

I didn't talk to her all the way to the hospital.

UP THE ROAD

LADY LUCK

I'm thinking back to when Eva and I were living on our 38-foot converted fishing boat, the Black North. *I'd got a writing grant from the Canada Council that year, 1972, and besides the boat and a trip to Spain I'd bought a second-hand half-ton truck and later in the year a broken-down old house without plumbing and other amenities and the acre of land it was on. You could get a lot with $4,000 back then and still have a bit left over.*

It wasn't the kind of house women ordinarily dream about, but Eva wanted a house and this was what she could find in our price range.

Before that, however, we lived on the boat, and it was on our first voyage downriver from Bannonbridge that I ran into Tommy Waggoner at the Bayside wharf. Since I'd only bought the boat a week before it was nothing short of an act of God and the tide running right that I got to the wharf without crashing into it.

As I was securing the rope I looked up and saw a big old fellow on the wharf watching me. He was wearing a dirty undershirt and greasy work pants and a pair of old work boots with the laces undone. His hair was gray and cut in a brush cut. After staring at me for some minutes he said, "Out for a little cruise, are you?"

"Yeah, just sailing around."

"Well, watch out you don't drown yourself. I say, you better watch out you don't drown yourself!"

My first impression wasn't a very good one. I had the feeling he didn't like me on sight, probably taking me for some useless pleasure-boater.

Useless I might have been, but the boat wasn't a pleasure to me yet — it still made me nervous, though not half as much as it made Eva. The bottle of rum I kept handy and which she would see me nip on didn't seem to have the settling effect on her that it had on me.

We saw Tommy again that night staggering along the wharf and climbing down the ladder onto his fishing boat, which was next to ours. Halfway down he slipped and did a back flip onto the deck. We heard him cursing and getting to his feet and lurching into the cuddy.

Next morning I noticed him sitting on the gunnel with his chin on his hands, staring out at the water. Since I was having a beer myself I did the natural thing and offered him one. He appeared to weigh the offer, then he said, "Well, now, I wouldn't mind one at all, to settle the stomach. But I didn't think you drank."

"No?" I said, wondering where he'd got that idea.

I stepped across onto his boat, and we talked for a while, and it turned out he'd taken me for the man who owned the boat before me — the one I'd bought it from for $650. This fellow was a teetotaller from the Air Base in Bannonbridge, and he'd made some belittling comments one day when he saw Tommy lying on the wharf half-cut.

"That man was no sailor," said Tommy. "He was scairt of the water. Scairt to leave the wharf if there was a breeze in the air. But he thought he was high and mighty. I offered him a beer first time he come down here and he said, 'I don't want your beer. Look at you, you're drunk! Take your beer someplace else and quit bothering people.' I took you for him, see?"

"He doesn't have a beard," I said.

"No? Well, I thought he might've grown one. That was last summer. I forgot his face, but I knew the boat."

Later that day Eva and I sailed off to Merganser Island to dig some clams, and when we got back the tide was coming in strong and there was a crowd of young people hanging about on the wharf. I made a terrible job of it trying to get the boat docked. Every time I came at the wharf the tide swept me past and I had to circle round and make another pass and the same thing happened. After the third attempt all the kids were pointing and laughing at me.

As I approached for a fourth run at it I saw Tommy at the edge of the crowd, and catching my eye he made a slight circling motion with his hand, very quietly so no one could see. I didn't get it right away, but then I understood, and instead of heading straight towards the wharf I wheeled around first and came into it against the tide — which anyone but me would have known to begin with.

I was still embarrassed and had to suffer the hoots of that gang of teenagers, knowing all about boats as they did. Had it not been for Tommy I could have been out there until the tide changed entertaining them.

We spent a lot of time at Bayside and Rum River and Wilawac Bay, and got to be good friends with Tommy. If he wasn't on his fishing boat he was holed up in his little shanty near the mouth of Rum River. In the off-seasons I often drove down from Bannonbridge to see him.

What I got to know about boats I learned half from trial and error and half from him. He gave me an anchor when I lost mine, and lent me a compass when I voyaged to PEI and Nova Scotia. He built me a bearing for the drive shaft when the old one rotted away. Things like that. He never charged me for anything.

He also provided a place where I could haul her up for the winter, in the field just below where Agnes lived...

§

Agnes in her high white boots and her long hair streaming behind her, running through the grass towards us screaming, "Take that boat out of there! You can't keep your boat there. This is private property! Get that goddamned boat off my property!" From a distance, with her miniskirt and white boots and trailing blonde hair, you'd take her for a teenager; but up closer the lines on her face told you she was older than that, at least in her forties.

Tommy wouldn't hear of me putting the boat anywhere else. No, I had to haul it up in the field beside his shack where he could keep an eye on it over the winter. He didn't tell me anything about Agnes until the boat was already ashore.

She stopped about twenty yards away and continued to scream. "You goddamned bastard, take that boat off my property. I'll call the Mounties!"

"Don't mind her," said Tommy, wedging another log under the keel. "She don't own the land. I got permission from Bill Watt. It's his land, not hers."

He got up and stood beside me, hands on his hips, belly like a great watermelon bursting through his shirt.

"I didn't say you could put that boat there!" yelled Agnes.

Tommy hollered hack at her. "What's that, quiff? I say, what're you howlin' about, quiff? Get out of here, you crazy fool, don't let people see what a goddamned fool you are!"

She stopped jumping up and down. "Tommy! Don't you curse at me like that!"

"Get back in the house, quiff! Get back in the house!"

"Don't you swear at me! I'll get the Mounties! I don't want that goddamned boat on my property! I don't know who owns that boat! I never said you could put it there."

"You're making a fool of yourself. Get in the house. You shouldn't be allowed out."

She continued to scream at us, but Tommy hollered her down. "What's that, quiff? What're you screeching about, quiff? Eh, quiff?"

She was hopping about like a swarm of wasps was after her. Then she ran full speed back to the house and stopped at the kitchen door. "I'll fix you, Tommy! You can't talk to me like that!"

"Get in there, quiff!"

"I'll fix you, you son of a whore!"

When she was gone I said to Tommy, "Maybe I should move the boat somewhere else."

"No, no, don't mind the *Fool*, don't mind her. You got permission, it's not her land. She thinks it is but it's not and it's never gonna be. A creature like her should be chained up. Talking to a stranger like that, someone she don't even know, yelling her head off at him. There's no one else around here behaves like her. Supposing it was her land, what harm's an old boat going to do it? It's just for the winter. There's only going to be snow in the field."

That wasn't the end of the matter. A week later, when I saw Tommy again, he told me Agnes had phoned the Mounties and laid a charge of *assault* against him, and it had cost him fifty dollars to have a lawyer defend him in court. At the trial, which lasted only a few minutes, the judge gave Agnes a severe tongue-lashing for wasting the court's time and for being a nuisance to the RCMP. She was bound over for a year to keep the peace. The charges against Tommy were thrown out.

It was by no means the first time the Mounties had had to deal with Agnes's complaints, and they hoped this would teach her a lesson. But it cost Tommy fifty dollars all the same.

Agnes was infuriated, but she kept relatively quiet over the winter, and left my boat alone, and I got it safely into the water in the spring. I used to anchor in Rum River just off her place and every day we were there you could see her charging about her yard screeching, "Kitty! Kitty! Kitty!" at the top of her lungs.

She was forever chasing after her cat. A peculiar woman.

§

What Tommy lived in wasn't even a shack, it was an old rough-shingled smelt shanty, measuring eight feet by eight feet, and just high enough for him to stand up in. It had a double bunk, which took up half the space, a potbellied stove, a tiny table the size of a TV table, and a wooden chair with no back. With Tommy alone in there it was crowded. He usually sat on the bottom bunk with his elbows on his knees, reaching over every so often to place a stick of wood in the stove.

He used the stove for cooking, so he had it going the year round. Even in the winter the shanty was unbearably hot, despite the draughts and winds coming in through the half-doors, which were only crudely fitted together. When the weather was mild he left the upper half of the door open so he could see out over the river from his bunk. His clothes and cooking things and food supplies were thrown on the upper bunk. There were no windows in the place. He'd been living there by himself for the past twenty-odd years.

§

My father, Joe Macbride, was from down in those parts, originally, and had known Tommy. I used to drop in to see him whenever I was in town, and when I mentioned I'd met Tommy, he said, "You mean Bad Tommy? What devilry is he up to now?"

233

"Why do you call him Bad Tommy?"

"Arrgh..." He didn't like talking, and questions in particular were always tough for him. I could see he regretted the opening he'd given me.

"Why?" I said.

Another growl.

"What'd he do?"

"He was younger than me... I didn't know him that well..."

"What kind of things, though?"

He mulled it over, considering all the angles. He said, "Nothing. Oh, I guess he's all right."

When I kept at him he said, "Well... drinking... fighting... always landing in trouble."

He grinned. Despite himself I could see he felt good we'd had such a long conversation.

§

It was no problem getting Tommy to talk. He loved company, living in that shanty all by himself. He could go on for hours about everything happening down-river, and if you started to leave there was always something else he could find to say. Agnes was one of his favourite topics...

She was the daughter of Bill Watt, the man who owned the field where I'd kept my boat over the winter. Some years back she'd married Tommy's nephew, Hazen Urquhart, and after the wedding they'd moved in with her father who not so long after moved out.

I knew Bill to see him. I'd overheard him one day talking to a couple of tourists fishing off the wharf at Bayside. He was telling them stories, and one of them said, "You're a great old fellow. What's your name?"

"Bill. They used to call me Wild Bill."

"Wild Bill!"

"That was when I was young. I guess I'm not too wild now."

He was in his sixties, a few years older than Tommy, and had suffered several heart attacks, along with some rough times during the six months he lived with his daughter and son-in-law. He was only a shadow of the man he'd once been.

Tommy's shanty was on Bill's property, directly across the road from the house, and there were no other neighbours within a quarter of a mile. Bill had told him he could stay there as long as he liked.

But then Agnes moved in and decided the property was hers, since she expected her father to die soon and leave it to her, anyway. With Tommy not paying any rent she wanted him out. She'd been at him about it for years, but the more she hounded him the harder he dug in his heels.

If she'd put it to him in a nice way he might have left, but her threats only brought out the contrary streak in him. Even when he had the money to move to a better place – when the government closed the salmon fishery and bought out his license – he stayed, just to spite her. And the longer he stayed the more it enraged her.

§

Hazen was Agnes's second husband. Her first, Burton Appleby, drowned in a storm while out fishing. During that first marriage she'd lived down the river on a farm not far from Bayside, about a mile from Carvossa's place.

According to Tommy, Agnes's first husband was a fine decent man — "A real good lad, and you know, him and the Fool used to fight every day. Now here she is, married to Hazen the Ape who's a no-good son of a whore, and they never fight at all, they get along great. It's funny that, now, ain't it?"

Tommy had no use for Hazen, but most people said he wasn't so bad. Not the brightest man around, and no match for his wife, when it came to who wore the pants in the house; but he was a good worker, a hardworking fisherman.

Tommy called him the Ape because of the way he walked, stooped-shouldered and with long dangling arms. Sometimes he called him the Tramp.

"What do you call him the Tramp for?" I asked him.

"Because that's what he is. You know a man by the company he keeps. Only a tramp could marry a woman like that one. I used to *like* him, you know? But that was before he got married, before I saw what he was made of. I thought there was nothing wrong with him. I say, I thought there was nothing *wrong* with him, but I didn't know him well enough. When they got married I give him a wedding present of fifty dollars because he's my nephew. But I'm awful sorry now that I did, I wish I had it back. He'd have a long wait today if he expected me to give him something. I wouldn't piss down his throat if his guts were on fire."

§

One year there was an outbreak of TB in the area, and Agnes spread the word about that Tommy was "the carrier." For a time Tommy was an outcast, no one would go near him, except to tell him he'd better get down to the Sanatorium in Saint John before he had an accident. People were worried about their children catching it.

The fact was, Tommy had gone to the hospital in Bannonbridge not so long before this on account of his asthma, and they'd checked him for TB and found no trace of it.

"And the Fool knew it, too," he said. "I told her. She come screeching at me one day saying I was the carrier, and I told her I'd just been to the hospital. But that didn't stop her. She got on the phone and the next thing everyone in the parish was saying I was the one causing the TB. It was pretty bad for a while. I wasn't going to no Sanatorium, I knew I didn't have TB and I didn't see why I had to prove something I already knew. Oh, it got serious, some of them around here were set to shoot me. In the end, to keep the peace, I went up to the hospital with Carvossa and got X-rayed again and I had no more TB than you have. The Fool was hoping someone would blow my head off with a shotgun. Or else I'd go to Saint John and she'd have her chance to burn my place down. I knew that — she went and done it anyway, a few months later. She thought she had me with the TB, but when she didn't she burnt me out later anyway. I owned a nice little trailer then, I'd just bought it and was into it no more than a month. It was all wired for 'lectricity, I had

237

lights and a hotplate and a 'lectric kettle. Then I had to be away for two weeks, I was in jail, to tell the truth. The Fisheries men caught me with some lobsters out of season and towed my boat all the way upriver to Bannonbridge. I thought they'd take my boat but they just fined me, and when I couldn't pay the fine they put me in the lock-up for two weeks. I didn't mind, I had a good place to sleep and they give me lots of grub. But when I got out and come back down-river my trailer was burnt to the ground — nothing left but ashes. It wasn't hard to figure who done it, but I couldn't prove nothing. I had no *proof*. Her and the Ape thought that'd chase me off, I'd crawl away and find a hole somewhere else to live in, but they was wrong. I wouldn't give them the satisfaction. I still had my little shanty, they forgot to burn that while they were at it. It's what I lived in before I got the trailer, and I kept it to store my nets in. So I just moved my nets over to Carvossa's shed and moved myself back into the shanty, like I used to be, and I been here ever since. Course if I win the lottery I'll move, I'd be foolish to stay then. But one thing I'll do is buy this piece of land from Bill and see what kind of a tune they sing then. I'd do it just to see their faces."

§

Wild Bill, who wasn't very wild anymore, had survived six months in the house with his daughter before leaving to live with his sister at Waggoner's Point. He'd got along well enough at first, until Agnes came upon his will while ferreting through his papers. When she read the contents she hit the ceiling. Her father had left her the house and the land it stood on, right enough, but the money he had in the bank and his other properties – including a valuable hundred acres along the highway – he had made over to his only brother and sister. Agnes flew at Bill and according to Tommy beat him half to death. Hazen had to pull her off him. After she'd cooled down some she demanded he rewrite the will and leave her everything. She was his only living child, wasn't she? And wasn't she taking care of him now in his old age? She deserved every last penny and inch of ground he owned.

After experiencing her in action Bill was in no hurry to revise his will. He was afraid if he did, giving her everything, she'd have him in his grave before the ink was dry. When he wouldn't make a new will, Agnes stopped being the dutiful daughter. She wouldn't let him eat at the table, giving him the scraps that were left over, like an animal. She wouldn't wash his clothes or clean his room or let her kids go near him. The only words he heard out of her were screams about his ingratitude. She wouldn't allow him out of the house, either – not unless he agreed to change his will.

She tore up the old will, which got Bill quite worried. He knew if he died without one she'd be his legal heir. And with the treatment he was getting he mightn't last long...

But he was lucky. Agnes and Hazen took the kids to Church one Sunday morning and while they were away he jimmied a window open and hobbled over to Tommy's shack. He told Tommy the whole story. From Tommy's he got a drive to his sister's in Waggoner's Point, and that's where he stayed.

Agnes tried her best to get him back, putting on a different face, acting friendly to him again, but Bill knew better. He wanted to live out his remaining days in peace, didn't want to be bothered about her. He let her and Hazen stay in the house and meanwhile made up a new will, keeping the contents to himself. But according to Tommy he'd cut Agnes out altogether, and when he died the house would go to his brother Bert. "And Bert'll kick them out of there quick enough. He's not like Bill, not the way Bill is now. You'll hear some howlin' when that day comes. But the Fool don't realize it, she still thinks the house is hers."

§

Agnes never let her kids go near Tommy. They used to wander over to his shack regularly, but she stopped them, telling the world she was afraid he might "try something with them."

"That's the way the woman thinks," said Tommy. "As if I'd do something like that with little children. My God, the woman's mental... I give her a good scare once, though, one day when I'd had enough of her, not long after she burnt my trailer. She was walking from the barn to the house with a pail of milk, and I was sitting out front drinking rum. I thought I'd give her something to think about. I had a twenty-two at the time, and I got it out and took aim and shot a hole in the pail she was carrying. She dropped it and run – Oh, you should've seen her go!

And the screeches — She thought I was shooting at her, and that I missed and hit the pail. But I wasn't. If I was aiming for her she wouldn't be around to bother no one today. She got the Mounties down about that, she wanted me arrested for attempted murder, but I told them I was only doing target practice, shooting at a tin can and I never knew she was there. I said I never seen her at all. If it'd been someone else besides the Fool they might've taken me in, but she used to have them down every second day about some nonsense or other and they knew what she was like. She was always bothering them, up until she took me to court last fall, about your boat. The Mounties just told me to get rid of the gun. I sold it and that's all there was to it. It shut her up for a few weeks... She was afraid of me then for a while. She hardly showed her face outside the door. But it didn't take her long to get back to her normal self."

§

Driving with Tommy you couldn't pass anyone on the road. "Stop, stop," he'd say, "give this poor little man a lift." No matter how many there were we'd pile them in. Sometimes I'll have the whole back of the truck full, as well as the cab.

We picked up one big strapping fellow who didn't have much to say, and when we let him off I asked Tommy who he was.

"That's young Paul MacGougan, I stayed at his mother's place one winter when I was fishing smelts. A nice little fellow, but to tell you the truth he's not too wise, sort of half-stupid, retarded, you know." To Tommy everyone was "little."

A friend of mine from Montreal was passing through in the summer and stayed a few days with us on the boat. I introduced him to Tommy, and later, when he was gone back, Tommy said, "Where's your little friend now?" My little friend stood six-feet-ten.

Tommy himself was not as tall as that, not by six inches, but then he outweighed Matthew by a considerable margin; it was his lifetime habit of seeing people as being smaller than himself.

§

He'd won a hundred dollars in the previous lottery, but that didn't impress him. He said he mustn't have prayed hard enough, and this time he was going to pray harder to see if he could up his winnings.

"I believe in prayers," he said. "I pray every day. Do you suppose if I prayed hard enough I might win the million dollars?"

"It can't hurt any."

"I pray, but I don't go to church. I don't believe in any church. As far as I can see one's no different from another. They all preach the same things when you come down to it. But I *belong* to a church. You have to belong to a church... When you die you need someone to bury you. I belong to the English Church. I give the minister some money every now and then so he won't forget to bury me when I die."

Not so long ago a Jehovah's Witness came to visit him.

"Good-day, sir, I work for Jesus," the man announced. Tommy was having a few and invited him in, though he would have done so anyway, drunk or sober. "Sit down, sit down," he said. "I'm on *unemployment* myself."

After sermonizing a while the Witness said, "Can I read you something from the Bible, sir?"

"Don't bother, no, don't trouble yourself. I don't have a Bible here."

"No bother at all. I'll get mine from the truck."

Telling me about it, Tommy said, "He started reading and I thought he was never going to stop. He must've read for over an hour. I wanted to have a beer but I didn't like to open one in front of him. Then the Carvossa fellow come along. He seen the truck parked outside and thought it was yours, and he strolled in the door carrying three pints of beer, one for each of us. The Jehovah Witness looked at him with his mouth open, and then he said, 'Don't open that beer, whatever you do! I'm reading the word of the Lord. Don't open that beer in front of the Holy Bible!' So Carvossa sat down to wait for him to finish. He was kind of shaky too, hungover, you could see he was dying for a drink. The man started reading again and I thought he was going to stay all day, I thought he'd never wind down. I didn't know what to do to get rid of him. Finally I told him there was a couple up the road who'd be real happy to see him, Byron and Shirley Appleby. He perked up at that, closed his book, and ran out and drove off to their place."

"I don't think I know them."

"Oh, nobody knows them, they never talk to no one, they're like two hermits. They wouldn't let their own mother in the door. They're brother and sister, they've lived there thirty years together, and there's not been a soul set foot inside their house except themselves."

§

Knowing how hard up I was Tommy insisted I take thirty dollars out of his hundred dollar prize, though he hadn't promised me any share before the draw. "Go on, take it, it's no good to me. I'd only spend it on rum anyway."

I took the money and bought three ten-dollar tickets on the following lottery and told him I'd split the take with him, should I happen to win.

"Well, I'll do the same with you," he said.

He bought seven tickets himself, using up the rest of the hundred dollars.

"And if we don't win, that old boat and truck of mine are going up for sale," I said. "They should bring me in five or six hundred. And then I don't know what."

"Oh, we might get lucky. If I hit the jackpot I'll give you half a million, and I'll give Carvossa a thousand."

"Only a thousand?"

"I don't want to give him any more, he'd only drink it all. He'd just waste it anyway. A thousand's enough for him. I say, a thousand should be plenty for him! That's what I told him I'd give him."

He'd only told Carvossa that to torment him, to see how he'd react. Promising him a thousand dollars out of a half million windfall. Carvossa had to choke it down, because a thousand was a thousand, it was better than nothing. He couldn't throw a thousand dollars back in someone's face.

When I saw Carvossa next he was into the rum and had enlarged Tommy's provision fiftyfold. "He's gonna give you half and he's giving me fifty thousand," he said.

"What'll you do with your money, Carvossa?"

"I'll buy a couple of nice big boats and fish lobsters. I'll buy five big new boats and set myself up in business. And I'll buy you a new boat, too."

"Well, now, if we win you won't have to do that, I'll be looking pretty good myself with half a million."

"That's true, you're right. But even if I don't get no money I'm going to have a new boat built anyway, a nice forty-foot drift boat — and I'll give it to you. That's right, you can have it. I'll just use it now and then, because I don't really need it myself. I'll give it to you. Honest to God."

Well, with a man as generous as that, how could I refrain from giving him a cut from my half million when we won?

When I told Tommy about it he said, "Oh, the Carvossa fellow's pretty cute, he's sly. He's not gonna leave nothing to chance."

§

"The Carvossa fellow," Tommy was telling me, "come over one day and said, he said to me — 'You know what I heard, Tommy, there's a story going around about Clara and Stirling McCann. The reason

245

she don't have nothing to do with him no more, why she kicked him out of the house, is she caught him fucking one of MacGougan's cows. So help me God.'

"The Carvossa fellow told me that. 'She caught him fucking one of MacGougan's cows.' Course I don't pay attention to that kind of nonsense, I'd never repeat a story like that. But Carvossa, he got Stirling to drive him to the liquor store and Stirling was talking to him and feeling sorry for himself about Clara kicking him out. 'I don't know what to do about that woman,' he says. And Carvossa says, 'You're better off without her, she's been going around telling people – she told *Tommy* that she caught you fucking one of MacGougan's cows – '"

Every time Tommy used the expression it was followed by an evil little chuckle.

"He said *I* told *him* the story, said it was me putting the tale around. When Stirling heard that he come prancing up to my place and he beat on the door, oh, he was awful mad, he wanted to know what I was doing telling Carvossa he was *fucking MacGougan's cows* – hee hee –

"But I set him straight. It was the other way around – it was the Carvossa fellow told me. I wouldn't go spreading a story like that. I'd heard it before, Freeman Waggoner told me the same thing two weeks before Carvossa did, but I said it was just foolishness. I wouldn't repeat a story like that. Only foolishness.

"So Stirling went and got Carvossa and brought him over, and the Carvossa fellow admitted it was him told me, and I wasn't the one to blame. He had to admit it, he couldn't go and deny it to my face.

"But, oh, Stirling was some mad, he come prancing up the road, doing some awful bouncing. You can't blame the poor bugger. You don't suppose that story's true, do you?"

§

When he was a boy the nearest store from Tommy's home was three miles away, which meant he had to walk six miles to get the groceries. He remembered one snowy day in December, the laugh the store owner had when he arrived out of the snow wearing a big pair of woolen mitts his mother had knit for him and not a thing on his feet. He said his feet were as tough as Gerard Poirier's steaks, thick callouses on the soles from having to go barefoot. He'd tramp through the woods in the dead of winter snaring rabbits with just old rags and newspapers wrapped around his feet. The first pair of boots he had in his life he bought for himself when he was fourteen and working on a farm. He lived with the farmer and was paid a hundred dollars a year. All his life it had been pretty hard times. "My little man," he said to me, "I seen more dinnertimes than dinners — and more suppertimes than suppers, too. And I'm not the only one, oh no, there was lots like me around here, and worse. I seen some of those Frenchmen down the river, they'd go a month without eating. I started work when I was seven, out fishing with my father, and I was earning my own living on my own when I was fourteen. And I've worked ever since, right up till they put the salmon ban on two summers ago. Now I work enough to get unemployment but that's about all. I

247

remember working as a grown man and earning ninety cents a day – and it took a good man to get that. Most made less. There was one year me and old Merle Trowbridge worked the whole winter fishing smelts, out on the ice the full time, and in the spring what do you think we had to show for it? I had seventy-five cents and Merle had a dollar and a quarter. That's what we had to show for a winter's fishing, and the only money we spent was for grub. In the spring Merle took our earnings and went into town and bought a couple of jugs of wine. It was all we got out of it.

"Year after year I had nothing at all. I used to have to work for nothing, going round from farm to farm cutting wood just for my food and a place to sleep. Once the wood was cut I'd have to leave and go to another place and do the same. I was like a tramp. I had to do it, there was nothing else. A man had to keep alive. Nobody had any money to pay you. Jobs that paid were awful scarce."

§

When the government put the ban on commercial salmon fishing and bought up the licenses, Tommy sold his boat. At first he said he'd got $2,000 for it, but later he told me the truth. "I say I sold it, but I didn't sell it, I give it away. All I got was $800 for it, I sold it when I was drinking. Only a month before I turned down twenty-five hundred dollars, and then when I was drunk and didn't know what I was doing I sold it to two guys from Bouctouche. I was supposed to get two thousand, but all they give me was eight hundred and a promise of the rest. But I never seen another cent, and I never will. They come with a truck while I was up in town and hauled it away to Bouctouche, my tools and everything in it, propane stove and tank and a couple of good nets. And they didn't pay to have it hauled either. The trucker come to see me later and I had to give him sixty dollars for taking my own boat away when I wasn't there."

"You shouldn't have paid him."

"I had to. I must've said I would when I was drunk, and if I said I would I had to do it. It was a new boat almost, only two years old, and with a new marine engine in it, too. It was the first good boat I owned. I used to have those old things — pukka-puks we called them, 'cause of how the engine sounded, the one cylinder. They was more trouble ... and leak? My little man, don't talk. There was no 'lectric pumps then either, you did all your pumping by hand. I spent half my life pumping out old boats. I must've bailed that whole river out a dozen times over."

§

Tommy's legs were bad, so arthritic he could barely walk. He hobbled to the truck and labouriously lifted himself in.

As we drove along he waved to everyone we passed, his big paw flapping loosely at the wrist like an infant's. On this side of Cuttersfield, a ragged community strung out along the road, he rolled down the window and hollered, "Joby! Hey, Joby! Where you working today? I say, where you working today, Joby?"

A scrawny little man turned his head and gave us a sour look as we drove by. He was sitting against the side of a shed with a wine bottle beside him. He was called Joe B. to distinguish him from his father, Joe T. Bransfield, and from other Joe Bransfields in the area, of which there were quite a few: Old Joe, Young Joe, Little Joe, Ashley's Joe...

"Joby must have the day off," said Tommy.

"He was telling me that a man can't work and drink too," I said. "He said you have to make your choice. You can't do both."

"He said that, did he? Joby said that? I didn't know he was that smart."

Near Heathland, another vaguely defined community, we passed a weather-beaten gabled house propped up by three great logs under the eaves.

"That's where old Vincie lives," said Tommy, in answer to my question. "Poor old Vincie lives there all alone now. That's him up ahead on the road. Slow down, slow down."

An old fellow in a ragged overcoat was inching his way along the shoulder of the road. "Give him a lift. Stop." I pulled over and Tommy shouted out the window, "Vincie! How's she goin' today? Get in, get in!"

He looked up at us, ashen and blotchy, his eyes lifeless as pebbles.

"Get in, man, get in!" Tommy had the door open and moved over beside me to make room. It was all the old-timer could do to climb into the cab. He was shaking and trembling like he had the palsy.

"Are you going far, Vincie?"

Vincie didn't appear to hear him,

"I say, are you going far?"

"Yes...Yes," he said at last, as we drove off. "Quite far."

"We're going to the Bay. Will that suit you?"

"Yes... "

"I say is that far enough, Vincie?"

He gave no indication that he recognized Tommy. His voice was just audible, a feeble whisper. He hadn't been hitchhiking. I wondered if he'd set out to creep the entire eight miles to Baie-Sainte-Lucille or if he was actually on his way somewhere else.

"How's your eyesight? Can you see at all, now?" said Tommy.

No reply.

"I say, how's your eyes? Can you see any better?"

"No, I can't hardly see a thing."

"The poor man's almost blind," said Tommy to me. "He used to be a great carpenter, Vincie, but now he's too blind to work. Ain't that right, Vincie?"

"Yes... I was helping Harry McCann... put the ceiling on his kitchen... but I had to quit. Couldn't see what I was doing."

Before long we approached the first houses of Baie-Sainte-Lucille, and Tommy said, "I suppose you're going to the Co-op, Vincie?"

I glanced over and saw the devilish grin on Tommy's face. Vincie hadn't shaved for some days and his whiskery ashen face looked the picture of death. His cheeks were sunken and the skin drawn back tightly from his teeth.

"I say, are you going to the Co-op, Vincie?"

"Yes," he whispered. "The Co-op."

251

"I thought that's where you were headed for. We'll drop you off at the Co-op and pick you up on the way back. How'll that suit you?"

Vincie said nothing. We crossed the Bass River bridge and when we neared the Co-op I put my foot on the brake. Tommy said, "No, no, don't stop here, we don't need nothing here. You're going to the liquor store, Vincie?"

"Yes... Oh yes."

"Keep going, keep going."

The liquor store was roughly in the middle of Baie-Sainte-Lucille, a raggletaggle fishing village beaded along the highway for a couple of miles with its back to the woods and its face to the sea. Worn shingled houses, trailer homes, tarpapered sheds, grassless yards, rusted derelicts of cars and trucks. A couple of service stations, a hardware store, a barbershop. A huge double-domed brownstone church in the French-Canadian style. In some of the yards fishing boats were pulled up on cradles alongside stacks of lobster traps.

Like a pair of old cripples Tommy and Vincie went into the liquor store and came out with a case of beer and a pint of rum each.

"Stop at Jeroar's on the way back," said Tommy once they were back in the cab. "I have to buy a few groceries. Have a beer, have a beer. Where's your opener?"

On the way up the road I got a beer open, with Vincie beside me vibrating like a tuning fork and trying to get the cap off his pint of rum. At Gerard Poirier's little general store I pulled over, and Tommy said, "Come in, come in, I'll only be a minute."

"I'll wait here, Tommy. I don't want to stand around in there."

"I'll just be a minute."

"No, I'll wait here. You'll be at that punch box again."

"No, no. I won't be long."

"I'll be in after a while. I'm thirsty."

Vincie at last got his bottle opened and with both hands raised it shakily and poured a drink into his mouth. When it went down he shuddered, then sat passively for a minute soaking it in. Suddenly he came to life and turned to me and said, "Have a drink of rum on me, sir."

I held my bottle up. "I've got a beer going."

"Oh yes, you're drinking beer. I like beer myself." He took a second small nip from the rum, and just like that, like a miracle, the shakes left him. He lost his woebegone aspect and was now quite cheerful.

"Beer's a pretty good drink." he said, becoming conversational. "Not like wahn." He had a drawling way of speaking, and that's how he pronounced wine. "I can't drink the wahn. It's not good for a man. D'you like wahn? I can't even look at a bottle of it now... I used to drink it all the time, but the doctor told me I had to stop. He said if I didn't stop it'd kill me. I mostly drink rum and brandy now, and some beer. A little brandy mixed with beer, I like to have that in the morning for a cure. Just one or two drinks, that's all I need. Then I don't have to look at it for the rest of the day." He took another taste of rum. I could see from the bottle that altogether he'd had about three ounces, no more. The first two drinks had magically erased his shakes and made him congenial, and this third drink just as quickly put him away. He began giggling and gesturing and babbling like an idiot. I couldn't make out a word he was saying. After a few minutes of this he dropped into a trance-like silence and with glazed-over eyes stared straight ahead at nothing, his body nodding slightly back and forth.

"Think I'll go and see what's keeping Tommy," I said.

I skirted a huge German shepherd standing by the door, his nose sniffing somewhere around my chest as I edged by, and went into the store. From the outside it didn't look much larger than a cabin, but Gerard had it packed to the rafters with just about anything you could think of – groceries, guns, appliances, wallets, watches, knives, axes, chain saws, fishing tackle, ice cream, harmonicas, camp stoves, pens, pennants, meats, rubber dolls, salt fish. In the midst of it all stood Gerard himself, a grizzle-haired barrel-chested little man, like a gnome in a treasure cave.

Tommy was bent over the punch box, trying to win another watch. With Gerard's sharp eyes fixed on him, totalling up the punches at a dollar a crack, Tommy's fingers traced from one square to the next before lighting on his choice. His big hand thrust in through the broken panel and extracted a brown paper bag. He ripped it open – three coloured balloons. He tossed them onto a heap of junk he'd already accumulated and pondered the box again.

He grinned at me, as though I'd caught him with his hand in the cookie jar. "One more, that's all I'm gonna do. The next one'll be the watch."

"You don't need another watch, Tommy."

"Oh, they're nice watches," he said.

"How many of them do you need?" He already had three or four, maybe more. They worked but they were only toys, worth a couple of dollars at the most.

"It must be the next one, Tommy," said Gerard. "It has to be the next one."

He came up with a pink comb this time, something you wouldn't pay ten cents for. He glanced over at Gerard. "I bet the watch is gone already. Someone's got it already. You said it was still there."

"No it's there, Tommy. Nobody won it yet. I'm pretty sure, now."

There were only five panels left unbroken. Another punch — a plastic ring worth two cents. He couldn't stop now, this near the end. He broke another panel and drew out the paper bag. He could tell by the feel of it that it wasn't the watch. He tossed it to me and I opened it. A half dozen plastic swizzle sticks. He didn't even look. "You keep that," he said. Another punch, then another, without checking the first.

"Hold on, Tommy, you might have it already."

"There's only the one left, might's well take that, too. There's no fucking watch here."

"Wait'll I look."

I pulled the two bags out of their holes and before I'd ripped either of them open he spotted it. "That's it — not that one, the other one — " The first bag held a card of hairpins. The second had the watch.

"There now, Tommy," said Gerard. "I told you it wasn't gone."

"Let me see, let me see."

I passed the watch to him.

"That's a nice little watch. Eh? That's a nice little watch."

"Yeah, it's quite the watch."

"I don't want it for myself, I got half a dozen of them up there, but it makes a nice gift for someone. Some little person might like to have it. It's no good to me. I'll give it away for a Christmas present. What do I owe you, Jeroar? I say, what do I owe you? Let's go, let's go. We can't stay in here all day."

"How many punches did you take, Tommy?"

"I don't know."

Gerard knows, but he goes through the motion of counting them anyway, as though he hadn't been keeping an eagle eye out all the time.

"Twelve punches, Tommy. Is that right?"

"I don't know, I don't know. What do I owe you?"

"Twelve punches, that's twelve dollars... and your groceries." He does some addition on one of the torn prize bags, checks it over, and says, "Twenty-six dollars and thirty-eight cents." And while Tommy digs the money from his wallet – "Do you have your lottery ticket yet, Tommy?"

"I got some, but I might get another one, I'll buy one from you now."

"I don't sell them. You have to go to the bank in town. I heard you won some money last time. You must be lucky."

"No, that was nothing. What's a hundred dollars? That's no fucking good. I was after the million. Nowadays a hundred dollars is no good."

"You wouldn't want a million, Tommy. You wouldn't know what to do with it."

256

"I wouldn't, eh?" His mouth spread in a wicked grin. "I'd know well enough. I'd buy me a nice young girl. I'd get a nice sixteen-year-old girl."

"Just the one? With a million dollars? You should get a dozen at least."

Tommy put the change away and stuffed his big trucker's wallet into his back pocket.

"One's enough for me. I say, one's enough for me. More than enough. I think I'd have to get outside help just to keep the one happy."

"That's true, Tommy. We're getting old, you and me. It don't stand up the way it used to!" He laughed loudly. "That's right, eh, Tommy?"

"Never mind that. I don't know about that. Where's my groceries. Let's go."

Back in the truck I said, "Gerard must love to see you coming. Twelve bucks on punches —

"I know, I know. I'm not gonna throw no more money away on that fucking thing. But I got the watch. I say, I got the watch, anyway. I always go to Jeroar's because he'll cash my cheques. The others won't do it. And I buy rum from him sometimes, if it's Sunday. He sells rum, he bootlegs."

Vincie was sitting catatonically between us, the pint between his legs, with no more gone from it. We were on our way before he took notice of us.

"Drink, Tommy?" he said.

"Open me a beer. Where's your opener?" he said to me.

"Drink... Drink rum." Vincie's face was gray and drawn. He was back to looking like a warmed-over corpse again.

"Just a minute. Wait'll I open a beer." Tommy found the opener sitting on the dash and uncapped a beer and passed it to me.

"I already have one," I said.

'Take a drink out of it. Take a good drink. I don't care much for that jeezly stuff. Take another good drink."

When I handed it back he opened his pint and poured enough rum into the beer bottle to raise the level again, so that his drink was half beer and half rum. "That'll do me. I don't drink much anymore, I've pretty well quit. It's too hard on the stomach. Where'd I put that watch? Strap it on for me, will you, I want to see how it looks."

"Wait'll I stop for a leak."

The road turns inland from Baie-Sainte-Lucille to Heathland, cutting off Waggoner's Point, and most of the way there's nothing but spruce and poplar forest. About a mile up the road I pulled over and when I got back in the truck I strapped the watch on for him. It just managed to fit around his wrist. It had a blue face with the numbers 3, 6, 9 and 12 in bold white lettering and a yellow plastic strap punched with round holes of different sizes. As we drove along Tommy repeatedly stole glances at it, pleased with the look of the thing, though it was an incongruous sight on that broad hairy wrist. After a while he fiddled with it and got it off and said it would make a nice gift for some little person at Christmas. "I never wear a watch, I got an old clock in the shanty, that's all I need... Did you know Jeroar's store was robbed?"

"No. When did that happen?"

"Oh, about six months are. A young Saulnier from Bass River did it."

"They caught him, did they?"

"Caught him? I guess they caught him. He's in the penitentiary now, in Dorchester. He walked in the store one afternoon and stood around till everyone was gone and there was just him and Jeroar there, and then he put on a mask and pulled out a gun and said he was robbing the store. Jeroar knew who he was, he'd been talking to the silly bastard, but when they were alone he put on a mask and told him to hand over the money. That big dog of Jeroar's started to growl and the Saulnier fellow fired two shots at it — but he missed, he's cross-eyed, and he didn't hit the dog. When Jeroar seen nothing happened to the dog he thought the guy was firing blanks, so he grabbed hold of him and threw him out the door. He wasn't scairt of the gun at all, he thought it was one of them guns that shoot blanks."

"A starter's pistol."

"When Saulnier got up off the ground he put a shot through the big store window and the bullet just missed Jeroar. There was glass all over the place. Then the Saulnier fellow got in his car and drove home. He lives just a couple of miles away in Bass River. Jeroar called the Mounties and they went and arrested him and he got five years in Dorchester. The man couldn't have been very smart. He must've figured from watching the movies that you have to wear a mask to pull a stick-up. But he didn't know why. Here's Vincie's place, pull over and let poor Vincie off."

I drove into the yard and stopped in front of the old house with its curlicue trim on the eaves and went around and helped Vincie out of the truck. He couldn't stand up by himself. I supported him into the house and lowered him onto a cot in the kitchen, which was the only room in the place he used.

"I'll go get your beer for you," I said.

"No, no, I don't want it... you keep it... That's for driving me..."

"No, I'll go get it."

"Don't want it... only make me sick. I got my rum here... don't want beer."

"Well, whatever you say."

Passing down the hall to the front door I noticed all the other rooms were bare, not a stick of furniture in any of them.

"He said to keep the beer," I said, climbing into the truck.

"Yes, yes, keep it, he'll die quick enough without it. He don't need any beer. He shouldn't have bought it in the first place, I told him not to when we were in the store."

Tommy explained that Vincie's sister and her husband had taken all the furniture, and had tried to take over the house, too.

"They were going to put poor Vincie in the asylum. They said he was crazy, but all they wanted was to get him put away so they could move into his house and sell their own. The only thing stopped them was they couldn't find a doctor who'd sign the papers. But they're still trying. Poor old Vincie used to be quite the carpenter. He's too blind now to work, he drank himself blind."

"He doesn't look long for this world."

260

"No, I don't think he'll make it through the winter. I had all his carpenter tools at my place, he left them with me one day, and they sat there for months. Real good tools, I thought he'd die before he took them back and I'd fall heir to them. But one day he showed up and took them and sold them. Poor Vincie, he'll never work again. There wasn't a better carpenter around."

Back at the shanty he said, "Come in, come in and have a beer. Have a drink of rum – "

But I had to get back to the boat. The starter was gone and the battery dead, and I'd had to pump it by hand the last week or so. Every day the water came up over the deck boards and every day it took me an hour and a half to bail it out. What I needed was a new starter. With a new starter I could recharge the battery and the electric pump would work; but I couldn't afford a new one.

In any case, it was getting late in the year and we'd soon have to move ashore and have the boat pulled up. After that, barring a lottery win, I'd have to try and sell it. Whoever bought it could get their own new starter.

§

Should he win the million, Tommy said, he'd give a hundred thousand to Clifford McCann, Carvossa's cousin, who lived down the road with his seventy-year-old mother. Last year Clifford's father died of a heart attack and his brother Mel was killed a few weeks later in a car accident. Then his wife walked out on him taking their two kids. Shortly after that he was laid off from his job at the pulp mill upriver. And then a month or two later it was discovered he had cirrhosis, though he wasn't a particularly heavy drinker, at least not by local standards. He and his old mother lived on her pension and his unemployment cheques, which were due to run out in a few months.

"I'll give something to everyone," Tommy said. "The ones that need it, all the poor people. I won't give a cent to those already have money. They can go fuck themselves. But I'll help all the poor people. I don't need all that money, long as I have enough to get by on I'll be happy. How much interest can I get on two hundred thousand?"

"Oh, about twenty thousand, I guess."

"That's plenty for me, more than I'll ever need. I say, it's more than *I'll* ever need. The only thing I'll be needing is six feet of ground, and what good'll a lot of money be to me then? I'll put enough away to get a nice living off the interest and give the rest to people that can use some help, and there's enough of those around here. My boy, there'll be new trailers around then – all kinds of shiny new trailers around then. I'll buy some land and get a nice little trailer for myself and move out of this place. I say, if I win the money you won't see me in this old shanty long. Ape Urquhart and the Fool won't have to worry about seeing my face around. And I'll buy that house they're in, too, and they can pay me rent to stay there. I'm sixty years old now. Men live to sixty-seven nowadays, don't they? That means I got seven more years to live. I worked all my life – I worked enough. If I win the lottery they can take their unemployment cheques and stick them in their arse."

He said he was supposed to go to the hospital for an operation to drain fluid from his stomach. "My stomach's all swollen, and it ain't because I eat too much, I hardly ever eat. I have a feed of platoes once a week and every few weeks I cook a few pounds of salt cod and that does me. Look at this belly, the size of it. You'd think I swallowed a punkin. It's why I have the gas, always having gas and farting, that's why I burp all the time – my stomach's all swollen."

§

One fall morning I saw Carvossa McCann poling his scow up the river to rake oysters. He was wearing a bright yellow rubber suit and hugging the pole and walking the scow under him with his back to the oyster bed, like on a treadmill. I could see his rake beyond him standing in the water where he'd left it the day before, the handle sticking up at an angle like a channel marker. Later in the afternoon I was still on the boat when he drifted down on the tide and came alongside and gave me a bucket of oysters. I offered to pay him something, but he said, "No, no, take them, for God's sake." And in a lower voice: "They're undersized!"

Carvossa was a thin, jug-eared little man who always seemed to have a week's growth of whiskers on his face. He was a sometimes fisherman who'd rake oysters for a week, at the most, then go off on a drunk and miss the rest of the season. He told me he'd be fishing smelts later in the fall and over the winter; but it would be the same story, a week or two of work and then back at the bottle.

I had a few beers on board and I gave him one and we sat and talked for a while. He told me that Tommy and Wild Bill Watt used to fish smelts on this very spot where I was anchored, when they were younger. "I remember one time I seen them, I was on the shore over there. It was a cold dirty day, raining like a son of a whore, and they was about ready to go home after setting the nets when Bill let a yell out of him and fell down in the bottom of the scow. He set up this awful moaning, I could hear him way over on the shore, and poor Tommy was scared he was going to die. He knew Bill had took some kind of attack before and they thought it might be his heart, though he didn't go to the doctor then. I don't know what it was. It could've been, because he had a few heart attacks in later years. Anyway, Tommy poled the scow to shore as fast as he could go, and he picked Bill up out of the boat and threw him on his back and went tearing up the road with him. Now Tommy's a big man but Bill wasn't too small then either, he must've weighed a good two hundred pounds. But Tommy hoisted him on his back and carried him all the way to Bill's brother's place which was about three miles back the road. And he wasn't just strolling along either, he was running most of the way with him, afraid he'd die before he got him there. I went along behind them, and I could hear Bill moaning like he was in terrible pain. When they got to his brother's place Bill suddenly jumped down off Tommy's back and run twice around the house and in the door. He just done it to pull a trick on poor Tommy.

"Anyway, that's what it looked like. Maybe he was suffering something and come to himself again and didn't want to look like he needed Tommy's help. I don't know, but he carried on like it was a joke.

"The funny thing was, he done the very same thing a couple of more times, and every time Tommy lugged him home on his back, anyway. You see, he couldn't tell if Bill was fooling or not, and he was afraid to take the chance. And Bill done the same as before, laughed at him and run in the house.

"Tommy was strong as an ox, but always good-hearted. He wouldn't hurt a fly if you didn't get him riled up. The only thing was, people wouldn't leave him alone. He used to get in some wicked fights at the dances. There was a lot of drinking went on and you'd get guys who'd start agitating him, but they soon found out it was the wrong thing to do. Tommy was always a big strong good-looking man and the girls all liked him, and that got some of the boys a little hostile. They'd make fun of him, the way he talked, he used to stutter some then and they'd mock him. I seen him take on half a dozen big hefty men at one time and beat the whole lot. Wild Bill thought he could handle Tommy once. He used to get pretty ugly when he had a few drinks in him. They called him Wild Bill, but he picked the wrong man when he tackled Tommy. One time he hauled off and hit him for all he was worth, but it didn't budge Tommy an inch. He picked Bill up and threw him against the dance hall wall and Bill never woke up till the next day. They had to take him to the hospital, he had a fractured skull and a broken shoulder. He never fooled with Tommy after that. They've always been good friends but Bill never tried to fight with him again, though he fought with plenty others."

§

Tommy wanted a ride downriver, but before he'd get into the truck I had to go into his shanty, he had something for me to do. "I got a letter today," he said. "Here, take a look at it. Who's this from? I can't see too good, my eyes aren't so good. No, to tell the truth I can't read, you know that, I never learned to read. I'm awful sorry I can't. Who's the letter from?"

It was from Karen, a niece in Moncton, the daughter of his divorced sister.

"I thought so, I thought that's who it was. Little Karen. Go on, go on, read it."

I read it to him. The niece wrote:

Dear Uncle Tommy,

Mama isn't feeling well lately and Jimmy has the cold and I am going to school as usual and finding it real hard especially the arithmetic. Are you going to come down for a visit at Christmas? I sure would love to have a nice pair of skates and little Jimmy sure would like to have a new toboggan. It sure would be nice to have these things for Christmas. Next summer we want to come up and visit you and we sure would like to have a tent so we could sleep out in it.

Your niece,
Karen.

"Poor little things," said Tommy. "How much do you suppose that stuff would cost?"

"I don't know."

"It don't matter, I'll buy it for them. I'll get old Merle to drive me there at Christmas, I'll hire Merle to drive me down for a day. They can pick out what they want and I'll buy it for them. That's what I did last year. I go see them every Christmas. Last year I spent close to five hundred dollars. Merle drove me down for twenty dollars and all he could eat and drink, and oh my, did he eat — I never seen a man eat like him. He could put away a barrel of codfish and still be hungry, he'd think nothing of it at all. We had a terrible time trying to find the place last year. Old Merle's not used to driving in the city, and he wouldn't turn his head to look at the street signs, and I could look at them but I couldn't read them. We must've drove around for two hours before I seen the place. I knew it to see it, I recognized the house, but I never bothered to learn how to get to it, I always had someone driving who could find it. But old Merle was too nervous, he was afraid he'd run into something and put a dent in his truck."

We picked up Carvossa, and on the way to Baie-Sainte-Lucille he told us one of his stories. He said he'd been out hunting with his cousin Clifford McCann and they heard a moose bellowing, and Clifford said, "Call him, Carvossa, call him!"

"Jesus! I don't know nothing about calling moose," said Carvossa.

"Make the sound he's making. That'll bring him here."

"Like hell it will. That's a *bull* moose. He'll think I'm a cocksucker."

"Stop here, stop here," said Tommy. "There's young Norman. Stop here. Call him over. Norman! Norman!"

A fellow of about twenty who was sitting on the front step of his house got up and strolled out the yard to the truck.

"How's she goin'," said Tommy,

"Not too bad, Tommy."

"Is your father around?"

"He's in the house. I'll go get him for you."

"No, no, don't bother. Tell him I'll be around another day, I don't have time now. I want to see him about getting some wood for the winter, just a few cord. Don't bother now. You're not working today?"

"It's Saturday."

"Oh, that's right. I forgot what day it was. Tell your father I'll be around to see him next week."

"Okay, Tommy, I'll tell him." He ambled back to his perch on the step.

When we drove off Tommy said, "Well, that's the end of that. Not a word out of him. I lent him twenty dollars two weeks ago and he was supposed to give it back in three days when he got his pay, and he never did. I won't see none of that money."

"You shouldn't lend that fellow money, Tommy," said Carvossa. "He's a thief."

"I didn't think he was."

"Oh, yes, he's the worst thief in the country. He'd steal the Lord's last supper."

"Well, that's the end of it. He'll never get another dime out of me."

"Why didn't you ask him for it?"

"No, I'll not ask him for it. He knows he owes me the money. If he's so small as to play a trick like that he can keep it. If that's all he's worth then it's a small price to find out."

"I'd ask the son of a whore for it," said Carvossa. "And he'd give it to me, let me tell you. He'd be shitting teeth for a week if he didn't."

"Never mind. I wouldn't be bothered about it." After a minute he said, with a sly grin on his face, "I see Rover's got hisself in trouble." Rover was Carvossa's dog who often wandered over to Tommy's place. "I hear O'Leary's little bitch is knocked up."

"Oh, I don't know that Rover done it," said Carvossa. "That big black bastard of Mervyn Appleby's was hanging round there, too."

"No. Rover chased him away. That big dog didn't hang around long. Rover put the run to him."

"Oh, he can get ugly. You gotta watch out if he don't know you, he'll eat the legs right off you."

On the other side of Heathland Tommy pointed out a woman hanging clothes in her back yard. "Look, there's poor Lucy MacLeod, see that woman there? A real fine teacher in her day, she used to teach school, poor soul, and never had a piece of tail in her life. But a fine woman all the same."

"Did she teach you?"

"No, she never taught me. I only went to school one day. It was a Saturday and there was no one there so I went home and never come back. No, to tell the truth, I did go for a couple of days, but the teacher give me some awful lickin's with the birch rod. I made up my mind not to go no more, and I didn't either, they couldn't get me to. I was too stubborn. But I'm sorry now I didn't stay long enough to learn to read and write. I'm awful sorry now that I didn't. I missed my chance, but it's my own fault. It's a terrible thing not to be able to read."

The summer before Eva had made a stab at teaching him to read, but her efforts soon petered out. If he wasn't drunk or hungover there were other obstacles. He enjoyed having company and didn't mind the lessons, but he was never able to put his mind very much to learning.

Eva would get him to recognize a small word, like "cat", and using that for a start she'd hold up a printed card and say, "Okay, now. What's this word again?"

"It's cat," he'd say, nodding his head solemnly.

"Good. Now... What's the first sound of the word? Say it, the first letter, what does it sound like?"

"Kuh-kuh-kuh-kuh..."

"That's it. Now, we'll take that letter away, I'll cover the first letter so the kuh-kuh-kuh sound is gone, and what word do we have?"

He studied the card, frowned, shook his head. She could see he was giving it his full concentration.

"It's not cat anymore," she said. "It's smaller than cat. What's like cat only smaller?"

His face brightened. "Oh, my dear, I know it now." He nodded his head. "Kitten," he said. "It's kitten."

Before going to the liquor store we stopped in at The Lighthouse, a new bar that had been opened in the spring, and the only one in Baie-Sainte-Lucille. Its walls were adorned with nets and lobster traps and wood carvings of fish and such things. After the waitress took our order Tommy said, "A nice little girl, a nice little girl." When she returned with our drinks he gave her a two dollar tip, instead of the usual dime or quarter.

"You have to give them a good tip," he said, "that's all the poor things make. They don't get paid any wages. I like to give them a nice tip." He looked at the double rum in front of him. "I don't know why I ordered this, I don't really want it, I don't drink much now. But you have to order something when you come in here, you can't just sit down and not order something."

"Tommy drank two pints of Beachcomber rum in two hours yesterday," said Carvossa. "And he wonders why he's got stomach troubles."

"You could've ordered a beer," I said.

"No, that fucking beer's bad for the stomach. It gives you gas, I think they're putting something in it these days. It's making everyone sick."

He had four double rums in quick succession, each time tipping the waitress two dollars. By the end she was feeling embarrassed. "That's too much, Tommy. You needn't give me so much," she said.

"Take it, take it, my dear. You can't work for nothing." When she went away he said, "Now you don't see that very often, someone saying their tip was too big. Usually they put their other hand out looking for more. A nice little girl."

"She ain't very little, Tommy. Jesus, she'd make two of me," said Carvossa.

"I was in here a couple of weeks ago with old Merle, just for the afternoon, and I spent seventy-five dollars." He grinned, shaking his head at himself. "I said I was never coming back after that. But I like to give a good tip. We had supper and a few rums once at the Fortress Restaurant in town, Merle and me, and I left a five dollar tip, and old Merle nearly fainted. He didn't leave a cent himself, he never tips. He said 'Don't give her that, Tommy, don't be foolish. Don't give her that,' he says. 'Give it to me. If you're going to give it away give it to me.'"

Two men in checkered lumber jackets came in the door and sat at our table. One of them had the rubbery face of a clown. He never stopped smiling and rolling his eyes and making expressions.

"How's she going, Tommy?" he said. "Doing much riding? Give us a couple of Moosehead," he called to the waitress.

"There's nothing to ride around here," said Tommy. "The women are too religious. They're always in church."

"My wife's religious, she goes to mass every Sunday, but that don't stop her. I never seen a woman like her before... Do you know my wife, Tommy?"

"No, I don't know her."

"Last night I come home from a week in the woods and she jumped on me soon as I walked in the door. She never let go till next morning – I had to ride her all night. I was riding her and thinking of you, Tommy."

"Eh?"

"I was wishing you was there to help me. We could've worked in shifts and I wouldn't be so jeezly tired today. I never got a minute's sleep."

"You're not fishing this fall," said Tommy. "I say, you're not – "

"That's some horny woman. We was going at it and she got so wild she started growling and farting and pissing all over me. It's true! I had to tell her, look, you start shitting on me forget it, out you go. A man can only take so much."

"I said, you're not fishing this fall, I see."

"Not this year. Did I tell you about my pig? I got a pig, Tommy, you know that? It's big and fat now, and I gotta kill it. But I hate to kill a pig, a pig or a chicken — it's like killing one of your kids. You raise it up from a little pink baby and then go and slaughter the damn thing. I hate it. It's not like a moose or a bear. I can kill those bastards with my teeth."

His friend, the man he'd come in with, was as stone-faced as he was expressive. He raised his head from his drink and said, "I'll come over and kill your pig."

"Yeah?"

"Sure. It's fun killing pigs."

"How'll you do it?"

"Cut its throat. You gotta cut its throat."

"Oh no, no. That's cruel. I won't let you."

"Okay, I'll kill it first."

"How?"

"Shoot the fucking thing."

§

As we drove off in the truck Tommy said, "I damn near died last night, and I didn't drink that much neither. I said I was going to quit today. I thought I was going to die, up all night puking. I say, I meant to quit drinking today, but it looks like I didn't. Watch out for that old follow."

I brought the truck to a stop while an old man hobbled slowly across the road.

"We're in no hurry," said Tommy.

"No, there's always time for everybody," said Carvossa. "If all hands look sharp and takes their time."

"Stop at the liquor store," said Tommy. "Since we're down here I better get a case of beer."

I went into the liquor store with him and he said to the clerk, "How much is codfish selling for?"

"Codfish? You got the wrong store, Tommy."

"No, no, I was just wondering, how much is codfish now?"

"I don't know. Fifty cents a pound, I think."

"Do you know what Jeroar wants? He told me two dollars. Two dollars for a pound of codfish! I'd rather eat snakes. I say, I'd eat snakes before I'd pay him that."

"Snakes are pretty scarce, too, these days."

"I know it. The Ape got them all, him and Agnes. They ate them all."

"The Ape? Who's that, Tommy?"

"You know the Ape, don't you?"

"No. I don't think so."

"The Tramp – Hazen Waggoner."

"Oh, Hazen."

"I call him the Ape. Give us a dozen of that good beer, the stuff from Quebec, I'll try some of that. And you might as well give me a pint of Beachcomber while you're at it."

§

"You wait here, Carvossa, we'll just be a minute. Bring a couple of beers in with you," Tommy said to me.

274

We were at another of the old houses still standing from the last century, shingles gray with age and weather. In this one lived a woman named Lena whose husband had gone off somewhere and never returned, leaving her with five kids... A raw-skinned woman with untidy hair and a toothless smile. She was sitting smoking at the kitchen table which was covered with dirty dishes and leftovers. "Would you like some dinner?" she said. "There's half a pot of codfish left."

"No, no. Have a beer. Have a beer."

"Well, I might now, Tommy."

"Give her a beer." Tommy bent over her, putting one arm around her shoulder, and said, "You're getting better looking every day, my dear." He thrust a big hand up her dress and she laughed giddily, as though she'd been tickled. "Don't, Tommy! Go away, now."

"I just wanted to see if it was still there."

One of the daughters, Jane, a fourteen-year-old, came into the kitchen, and Lena said, "Jane's not feeling well. She has to go to the doctor's Monday."

"That's too bad," said Tommy. "What's the trouble?"

"I don't know, Tommy," said the girl. Then pertly, "I must be knocked up."

"Oh, oh."

"It's her kidneys," said Lena.

"And where's little Donna?" Donna was the oldest, a girl of sixteen.

"She's with Aunt Katherine in town. She's going to have her baby pretty soon."

"Now who's the father of that?"

"Mom don't like him," said Jane. "She don't like niggers." Giving us a cute little grin. "One of them *French* guys from the Bay."

"Where is he? When are they getting married?"

Lena shrugged. "Christ knows. He's gone to Saint John."

"He don't want to come back," said Jane.

"Oh, oh. I'd make him come back," said Tommy. "I say, I'd make him come back. You should drag him back and cut his cock off, doing a thing like that to a young girl."

We stayed long enough to have a couple of beers, and for Tommy to get Lena to promise she'd come visit him before long.

Now that he'd had a bit to drink Carvossa was in a travelling mood. He was bent on going to town to borrow some money from his brother there and then make for the taverns. But Tommy didn't want to, and neither did I. We let him off where he could thumb a ride and then turned down the shore road towards the shanty.

"Did you ever think of getting married, Tommy?" I said.

"I'm too old for that now. I almost got married once, but I'm glad I didn't, not to the one I was going to. She was knocked up and I was going to marry her, but I knew I wasn't the father. Everyone was riding her, not just me. I told her I changed my mind and she settled for Everett MacGougan instead. The two of them were always drunk and fighting. He finally killed her last year, he punched her in the mouth and she fell down and banged her head against the stove. They give him six months for it. He was always beating her up, every time you seen her she had bruises all over her face. The drunken jackass was bound to kill her sooner or later. And they only give him six months for manslaughter... I wouldn't mind getting married and having kids, though. But I wouldn't let my wife have them. It's too painful for a woman to go through, having kids. I'd adopt some."

We got onto the subject of what we'd do if we won the lottery, which was only a few days off. The draw was going to be on television, and I said I'd drive to town that night and watch it in one of the taverns. Tommy didn't like taverns and said he wouldn't bother coming along. He had too many memories of tavern brawls and he was too old and crippled for that now. With his size and his reputation from former days there was always the chance some drunken fools would start annoying him.

"I'd like to travel," he said.

"Where'd you like to go?"

"Newfoundland. I'd like to see Newfoundland."

"That's not going very far."

"No, but I never been there and I'd like to see it. I heard a lot of good things about it."

"What about Europe?"

"I already been there. I was there during the war. I was in the Merchant Marine sailing on them convoys to England and Scotland. I wouldn't mind going to England again. All I seen of it the other times was some bars on the waterfront and I got so drunk I hardly remember that. Oh, I got drunk then, them big glasses of gin, and I must've drank barrels of that English beer. I had some awful hangovers. I still can't drink gin or English beer today, I get sick at the sight or smell of it. We used to sail at night with not a light on and German submarines all around us. I seen ships sunk right beside me. I don't think I been the same since. After a couple of trips me and another fellow walked off the ship at Three Rivers in Quebec, and kept going right on up the street and never come back. We went to work in the woods instead. We asked a man on the street if he knew where we could get work, and he said, where're you men from? We told him New Brunswick and he said, well, if you're from New Brunswick then you must be good in the woods. I'll hire you myself. So we worked all that winter cutting pulp. Then later I joined the Army, but by that time the war was about over, so I never had to go overseas and fight, I only got as far as the camp in Sussex."

"If we win the money we can take a trip to England and Scotland and all over Europe. What do you say?"

"We'll do it. I'd like to go. It wouldn't cost too much, now would it?"

"Not if we win the big one."

"How'll we get there? I don't want to fly. I never been in an airplane and to tell you the truth I never want to be."

"We can take a boat."

"Okay, we'll take a boat."

"First we'll have to go to Montreal to cash in the ticket. We can go up by train."

"And drive home in a big new car. There'll be a lot of happy people around here when we get back. Oh, new trailers, and money for everyone."

"But don't give it all away."

"No, no, I'll hold onto enough for myself. But it don't take much to keep me. All I want is a place to live, to get out of that goddamn old shanty, I been there too long. Even if I don't win I think I'm going to move. Let the Fool have her way, it won't be for long. When Bill's dead she'll have nothing to gloat over. He's already cut her out of his will, house and all. His sister told me. I got no good reason to stay... I'll get a little piece of land across the river and an old trailer. If we win the million — I say, if we win all that money we won't be worrying about old shanties and old trailers and old boats no more. I been saying my prayers. Someone's got to win and it could be us as soon as the next guy."

§

The night of the draw, in mid-September, I rowed ashore and drove to Tommy's shack to get his ticket numbers to take with me to the tavern, but I found him fast asleep on his bunk. Two empty Beachcomber pints stood on the table, and a case of Molson's was on the floor, with only three full ones left. I didn't try to rouse him. I had my own three tickets with me and all I had to do was write down the winners from the TV and then check them later with his numbers. I was familiar with his habits. Having passed out from the afternoon's drinking he'd likely sleep until ten or eleven and then come to and be up most of the night. I could stop in on my way back.

§

A fellow named Barrieau joined me at my table just as the lottery show came on. He set sucking his beer through a huge walrus mustache, staring at me.

"I saw you smoking a pipe," he said by way of introducing himself. "I love the smell of pipe smoke. I used to smoke a pipe myself but I had to quit 'cause it made me cough. I sure miss it... I used to make my own pipes."

"Yeah? How'd you do that?"

"I made dozens of pipes. It was my hobby. I gave them all away... I could light one of my pipes and go for a walk round town and be gone an hour, and when I got home my pipe would still be burning."

"No kidding. What'd you make them out of?"

I had my eyes glued to the TV screen. There was a song and dance act going on before the draw, to keep everyone biting their nails in suspense. My three tickets were on the table in front of me, and I had a pen and paper out to write down the winning numbers.

"Oh, any kind of wood at all. Maple, birch... I see you got some tickets on the lottery. I didn't buy none. I'm not lucky... I don't think I ever won a thing in my life. Some people are born lucky. They're just born that way – "

"Hold on a minute, eh? They're starting the draw now."

There were eight revolving spherical cages on the stage, each with a pretty girl standing beside it to hold up the numbered ball that popped out, with the result then appearing in typed characters across the screen.

"A million dollars," said Barrieau. "I don't know what I'd do if I won a million dollars. I still wouldn't be able to smoke a pipe 'cause of my cough."

There were fifteen sets of numbers to be drawn, with five prizes of a million and five of half a million and another five of a quarter million – along with a raft of lesser sums, if you were off by a digit or two. By the time the sixth or seventh winner came up and my tickets were nowhere close I knew it wasn't my night. It was like playing poker – sometimes you're hot and sometimes you're not; you either can't lose or you can't win. And I had the can't win feeling.

It made no difference, though. Like Barrieau I wasn't the lucky type, and I'd never expected anything different. It wasn't myself I was counting on, it was Tommy.

By my calculations he was long overdue for a change of luck. He had such a simple belief in his chances it made winning seem possible – an innocence that the gods of luck surely had to look kindly on.

The fact he'd won a hundred dollars on the last draw seemed to indicate his fortunes were on the upswing. And then, of course, he held seven tickets to my three ...

The numbers marched across the screen, as if punched out by an invisible typewriter, and I got them all down on my pad. My three tickets were a wash-out, I didn't make it within a mile of even the minimum hundred dollar prizes. I put the list of winners in my pocket and ordered a few more beers.

§

It was close to midnight when I reached the bridge crossing the Rum River, and turning left at the crossroads I followed the river towards its mouth. Tommy's shanty was near the end of the road, four miles down, where the river emptied into the Bay. There were no lights along the way and the narrow gravel road dipped and wound as it followed the contours of the shoreline. I was driving with an open beer between my legs and half a case on the seat beside me. About a quarter of a mile from Tommy's there was a sweeping bend, where the road turned to come face onto the river, and as I swung round this I suddenly saw him in my headlights, his legs stiff and spread for balance, flagging me down. I had to veer hard to miss him. I put the brakes on and backed the truck to where he stood.

"What's going on?" I said, rolling the window down.

"I'm glad you come along." He was out of breath, coughing asthmatically. "I need a drive. I thought I'd have to walk all the way."

He moved heavily across the headlights and climbed in the passenger side. In the cab light I saw that he was in his sock feet.

"I thought I'd have to walk all the way to Carvossa's," he said. "You better give me a beer." He didn't appear to be drunk, not by the sound of him or the way he moved.

"I had an awful close call," he said. "Open me a beer, will you."

"What happened?"

My shanty burnt. It burnt right to the ground."

"*What?*"

"I woke up and the whole place was on fire. I almost burnt to death. If I hadn't woke up I'd be dead." He took the bottle out of my hand and tipped it back. I could hear the beer bubbling down his throat.

"You better give me a drive to Carvossa's," he said. "I can put up there for the night."

"But what happened? How'd it start?"

"I can't tell you. I was asleep."

I had the truck moving, driving the remaining distance to the end of the road.

"I don't smoke, you know I quit on account of my asthma, so it couldn't have been a cigarette. I was up around eight-thirty and had a pint of beer and then lay down again. That's all I know. I can't say how it started, unless somebody put a match to it. I don't want to say they did, but it sure didn't start by itself. The smoke must've woke me up. The bed tick was on fire and there was flames coming up from the floor and I couldn't breathe. My little man, I got out of there some fast, I never moved so fast in years. I left my boots by the bunk, and I thought I'd have to walk all the way to Carvossa's in my sock feet."

I turned into the field by the shore where his shanty had stood. Most of it was collapsed by now, with just a corner of the frame still standing, a heap of charred wood smoldering away like a bonfire. In the headlights a plume of smoke rose skyward.

I looked across the field but the lights were out at Agnes and Hazen's place.

"They never came over?" I said.

"If they come over it was earlier. All I know is I never seen them."

"You think it was them? With you in there and everything?"

"I don't know. I know it was afire when I woke up and I never lit it myself. I wouldn't burn my own shanty down. I don't think I would. If they didn't do it I can't think how it happened. Unless I knocked the lamp over in my sleep... I don't know if I blew it out or not, or if I ever lit it."

"What'll you do?"

"Not a damn thing. It's the trouble with being drunk, you don't know whether you done something or not, and you can't start blaming other people if you don't know."

I turned the truck and pointed its nose up the road. It was only then that I remembered the lottery; it had completely slipped my mind.

"The tickets," I said.

A rational person might have thought it was no time to be mentioning pipe dreams, in the face of a man's house burning down around him; but we'd been going on about our million for so long I'd virtually come to believe in it – especially after a full evening in the tavern. In my mind it was suddenly more important than ever.

"Did you save your lottery tickets?"

"No, they're gone," he said, "just like everything else. All I come away with is my pants and the shirt I got on. The tickets was in my coat pocket on the top bunk. I didn't have time to think of them. I'd no time to –" He broke off. "I didn't go and win, now, did I?"

The change in his voice expressed the horrible possibility. If he'd won a million and the ticket had gone up in smoke...

"No. At least, I don't know, I don't have your numbers. You were asleep when I came by."

He said nothing for a minute. Then, "It's just as well. It's better we don't know. I hope I didn't win. It'd be an awful thing if I did."

"You're sure they're not in your wallet or some place?"

"It wouldn't matter if they were, I lost my wallet, too. I had forty dollars in it. I might've cost you a lot of money. Maybe we did win something."

"I doubt it. Anyhow, it can't be helped." We were silent for a moment. "What're you going to do for a place to live?"

"Oh, don't worry about me. I'll find something. There's lots of old shanties around."

"I hope it's in another spot."

"I was going to move anyway. I was going to get out of there anyway. But now I don't know."

"You could probably afford a little piece of land, with your salmon money."

"Sure I could. I could get a few acres from Mervyn Appleby for fifty dollars. He told me so."

"Well, you should take him up on it."

"If I was sure I lit the fire myself I would. But what if I didn't? What if it was them? I can find another shanty somewhere, there's lots of old smelt shanties around, nobody fishes in the winter now, not like they used to. I can get one hauled right next to where the other one was, and stay there a while longer — just in case. Just in case they done it."

Carvossa lived in a tar-papered cabin near the bridge. He was in bed when we walked in, and Tommy shook him awake. He sat up with a start and fumbling

285

around got a kerosene lamp burning. He was fully dressed except for his boots. His yellow oilskins hung from a nail beside his bunk.

When he heard about the fire he said, "Oh, it was her, Tommy, no doubt about it, it was her all right. It's not the first time she pulled a trick like that, you know that as well as me. You want to get the Mounties after her. She waited till her probation was up and then she acted. I'd get the Mounties if I was you."

"No, no. Have a beer. Give him a beer."

"You want a beer, Carvossa?"

"I don't mind if I do. If it's no trouble." I went out to the truck to get a couple, and when I came back Carvossa was saying, "It ain't safe to have that woman around. I'd have her thrown in jail. They should lock her up and lose the key."

"I don't have proof. How can I get her arrested? I never seen her, and there was no one else around that time of night. I fell asleep and never seen or heard a thing till I woke up and everything was burning. I could've upset the lamp in my sleep... Maybe I left it on the chair by the bunk and hit it with my arm. If it was my own fault I can't lay the blame on someone else. But to tell you the truth, I don't think it was my fault. Only I can't prove it. I don't know *how* it happened."

Later, when I was leaving to drive back to the boat, Carvossa came out the door after me. In an undertone he said, "That's tough for poor old Tommy, the poor bastard. But it could've been worse. He could've been killed. There was nothing in that shack of his worth nothing anyhow, just a lot of old rags and a couple of pots and pans. We'll find him another one as good or better. We won't see a man go without shelter around here. No goddamn people gonna be out in the cold in our end. All hands sticks together around here."

§

The unsettling thing about it was, there were a couple of winning tickets never turned in for that draw – one for a million dollars and one for a quarter million. It had never happened in earlier draws, and the Lottery officials had no explanation, other than to say the tickets must have been lost by the holders. As they said, people sometimes just lose things.

EPILOGUE

Tommy Waggoner had his last drink in the year 1979, on the day he died. He was 67 at the time, the very age that seven years earlier he predicted he would live to.

I personally had my last guzzle three years later, in 1982, when I was 41.

The title of the first part of this book, "What It Was Like", is taken from a sentence that speakers at meetings of Alcoholics Anonymous sometimes begin their talk with:

"Well, I guess we're supposed to say something about what it was like, what happened, and what it's like now . . ."

I think I've given a glimpse into the first. In a general sort of way I'm probably always doing that in my writings, recounting what it was like to have been here.

February, 2016
Fredericton, NB